Adaptively
Radiant

JOSEPH E. HENNING

ISBN 13: 978-1-7330617-2-8

1

THE NINE STONES

Justin and Kaito patiently wait at the loading dock to board a high-speed hydrofoil for the thirty-seven-mile boat ride from Kyushu to Yakushima. Kaito's grandparents invited them for the weekend, along with family members and friends, to celebrate Kaito's twenty-first birthday. The distant relatives recently connected on social media, exchanging photographs in anticipation of today's reunion. In every picture, Kaito wears either an outlandish hat, a peculiar facial expression, or some variation of mismatched socks. Today seems to follow suit, with his attire consisting of a red bucket hat, green jeans, and a black T-shirt displaying an old man's long gray beard.

Justin grew up in Hawaii but lives in California where he just finished his second year of college at UC Santa Cruz. He flew into Japan yesterday for a two-week stay with plans to do a lot of sightseeing during his trip abroad during summer break. After his time in Japan is up, he intends to catch a flight to Hawaii before eventually returning to California for the fall semester. Justin is a very independent, optimistic person with a shy, rational side.

The hydrofoil pulls away from the dock into the clear blue water of the harbor. At first, the vessel creeps along ever so slowly through the no-wake zone. Various seabirds dip and dive among the commotion, looking for a quick snack. The boat, bursting at near capacity for today's voyage, gradually increases speed until finally reaching the optimum cruising rate of forty knots.

Yakushima is one of the seven inhabited islands found in the Osumi Islands. Geographically speaking, the island is shaped like a disk, 16 miles in diameter and 195 square miles in area. The circumference is completely encircled by a road, but the only way to access the steeply mountainous, forest-covered interior involves a hike on one of the numerous trails. The dense forest extends to the shoreline, and its mountainous inland region is officially the wettest place in Japan.

The boat slows down upon entering Miyanoura Port on the northeast side of the island. They wander over to the rental car facility and find a group of six waiting patiently for their arrival: Kaito's three friends, his aunt, and two younger cousins.

Ten years ago, Kaito's parents passed away in a tragic automobile accident while returning home late one evening from a company function. Shortly afterward, his aunt Ami and uncle Shin legally adopted him. They also have two children of their own, a ten-year-old girl named Amaya and a seven-year-old boy named Yoshi.

Kaito pulls the two girls in for a group hug and smacks the guy's hand in a loud high five before he conducts the introductions. He acts a bit childish at times with his humorous nature, but he is easygoing, generous, and enjoyable to be around. "I would like everyone to meet my cousin, Justin Toshi Blackwood, who is visiting from California. Justin, this is Kat, Miya, and her boyfriend, Jeikobu."

After Justin shakes their hands, he turns to Aunt Ami, Yoshi, and Amaya. "Hi. Nice to meet you three. I'm looking forward to getting to know each of you."

After the introductions, they hop into a campervan Kaito's friends have rented for the weekend. The vehicle has two bucket seats in the front and a three-person bench seat in the back that flattens down to create a sleeping area for three. Jeikobu, Miya, and Kat have elected to sleep in the van, not wanting to over-stay their welcome. Justin and Kaito ride along with them but will sleep inside the family home.

Aunt Ami and the two kids lead the way in their car with the others following closely behind. They pull out onto the main highway and settle in for a brief drive. Up ahead, Jus-tin sees Yoshi turn around in the car, vigorously chewing gum. The young boy unleashes an enormous pink bubble that bursts all over his face, covering his nose and chin. Yoshi puts the gum back into his mouth to repeat the process, only this time Amaya reaches around and pops the bubble with her finger. The two begin wrestling and drop out of sight in the back seat of the car.

Justin sends his sister, Melia, a text, letting her know he has arrived on the island. "Hey, sis! Made it to Yaku. Looking forward to a great weekend exploring."

They veer off the main highway onto a private road that trav-els away from the ocean. A thin row of tall bamboo lines both sides of the narrow roadway that continues for 150 feet before dead-ending at a lavish, single-story, traditional Japanese-style home. The entire property is surrounded by an eight-foot-high maroon wooden fence with three separate entrance gates, one in front, next to the house, and two others in opposite corners of the triangular-shaped backyard.

The vehicles come to a stop under the large, covered park-ing area, where a roofline connects to the three-car garage on the right and the front door on the left.

Kat speaks up. "This place is beautiful!"

"Wait until you see the tree house out back," says Kaito. "My grandfather built it many years ago for Aunt Ami and my dad when they were kids. He named the tree house Origami in honor of my grandmother, who spent countless hours watching them play while honing her paper-folding skills. He also built this crazy, elaborate koi pond garden and a huge greenhouse, where Grandma grows exotic flowers."

Grandfather Yoshiaki speaks English in a very calculated and deliberate manner, using minimal words. He is a highly intelligent, quiet man who enjoys tending to the garden and working on small carpentry projects. On the other hand, Grandmother Mana speaks not a word of English but brings nothing but love everywhere she goes. An avid floriculturist, she cultivates several varieties of flowers and plants.

Justin is introduced to his great-aunt and great-uncle. Mana greets him with a smiling face as she places her warm hands on his stubbly cheeks and gives him a much-appreciated hug. Afterward, Yoshiaki firmly shakes his hand. "It's very noble of you to travel such a great distance. May you find that which you seek here in Nippon. We have much to discuss later."

At the conclusion of the introductions, Kaito and his friends go for an afternoon drive, with Justin choosing to stay behind. The moment they pull out of sight, Yoshiaki walks down the pathway to the garage and enters through the side door.

Aunt Ami escorts Justin to his sleeping quarters inside the tidy home. They walk down a dim hallway of partitioned rooms made from wood and paper, stopping at the third door on the left. Mana slides open the shoji to reveal a twelve-by-twelve-foot living space containing a twin bed accompanied by an end table with a lamp. A small, round wooden dining table and a single chair occupy the center of the room. On top of the table rests a glass container of water and a matching cup, a dwarf bonsai tree badly in need of some pruning, a pair of garden snips, and a handwritten note. The only other objects in the room are an old black footlocker and a woven rubbish bin.

Mana arrives with fresh sheets, a blanket, and a pillow. She waits at the door with her arms extended, and Justin reaches out to accept the linens. *"Arigato."*

"We'll leave you to your privacy," says Ami. "The toilet, sink, and bath can be found at the end of the hall." The shoji slowly closes, and their two silhouettes can be seen walking away.

Justin drops his backpack into the empty footlocker. After making the bed, he lies down with his eyes closed and takes several deep breaths, in through the nose and out through the mouth. Sometime later, he wakes up extremely thirsty, pours a glass of water, and reads the note. "Enjoy this slow-growing dwarf cryptomeria bonsai tree. Carefully consider all options before selecting a branch to prune. Yoshiaki and Mana."

Justin whispers under his breath, "This looks more like a bush than a tree." He sets the note on the table, picks up the garden shears, and grabs hold of the top branch to snip it away. But he reconsiders at the last moment and instead inspects the entire tree before singling out an awkwardly growing lower branch. After gently securing the tip with his fingers, he snips away the branch in one clean cut. "Looking better already."

He guzzles down a second glass of water, slides open the shoji and walks down to the three doors located at the end of the hallway. In the first room he can see a toilet, the next a sink and mirror, and in the last a shower with neatly folded towels on a shelf. He turns around and walks back down the hall past his sleeping quarters to the living area at the front of the house. The back wall has two sliding doors that open in opposite directions with a window on either side.

Justin walks up to one of the windows that looks out into the backyard. It's late afternoon, and the sun has already slipped behind the mountains. He slides open one of the doors and steps out onto a stone-paved patio with three walkways that meander off in different directions. One wanders left along the house, leading out to the garden and koi ponds. Another swerves in an S pattern off to the right, fading its way into Mana's green house. And the third moves straight back into the yard a solid thirty paces before reaching a grove surrounding the family tree house.

Children's laughter can be heard coming from the tree house, and he takes the center path straight ahead. Large, sprawling lawns grow along either side of the stone pathway that leads out to the tree line. The grass extends all the way over to the gardens on the left and the greenhouse on the right.

Long ago, Yoshiaki symmetrically planted twenty-seven saplings of Japanese red pine in six rows spaced twenty feet apart. Starting with two trees in the first row, each additional row increases by one to where the sixth row contains seven trees. Nowadays, the red pines tower at nearly fifty feet tall with most of the foliage occurring at the top. The leaves are long, slender, and needlelike, accompanied by two-inch cones.

The tree house design has four separate sections. The lower area resembles a patio gazebo sitting four feet off the ground on rock pillars. Then two wooden planked-rope bridges connect the deck to platforms on adjacent trees. Finally, the rope bridges connect back together at the tree house another ten feet up, resembling a mountainous log cabin with a wraparound deck.

Justin calls out from below, "Hello. Can anyone hear me?"

Aunt Ami looks down on him and waves. "Hi. Come on up."

He walks up the stone steps of the gazebo and selects the rope suspension bridge to his right. Tension fasteners hold the walkway firmly in place, giving it very little play underneath. He weaves around the platform and enters the second rope bridge that leads to the top. Yoshi and Amaya come outside to greet him but quickly scamper back inside to resume working on some basic origami paper folds.

"Did you have a nice nap?" asks Aunt Ami.

"Very much so," replies Justin. "Refreshed and ready to go."

"Good, glad to hear it. Come meet Uncle Shin. He arrived while you were resting."

Justin steps inside the tree house, where eight pieces of framed art are displayed depicting a lotus, a folding fan, a cherry blossom, a Daruma doll, a butterfly, a crane, a gourd, and a plum.

A spiral staircase is centered in the room and wraps around the tree to the loft. The entry level consists of a love seat, two reclining chairs, a dinette set, a basic kitchen, and a small toilet room. Plumbing and electricity were connected to the tree house several years ago but were not part of the original design. The interior walls and flooring have been finished in a deep, maple-colored stain that is accented by windows with beige drawstring curtains.

Shin hollers from the loft, "Aloha!" and walks down from the spiral staircase to greet Justin with a firm handshake.

They sit in the reclining chairs and discuss Justin's childhood growing up on Maui. The kids soon lose interest, and everyone starts funneling down the suspension bridges to the main house where Mana has prepared dinner consisting of thick udon noodles in a mildly flavored, deep brown broth, vegetable tempura, fish cakes, tofu, and a side dish of thinly sliced cucumbers tossed in marinade. A plate of assorted homemade butter cookies sits in the corner, waiting to provide a sweet finish.

When dinner is over, Uncle Shin, Aunt Ami, and the kids say good night and retire to their sleeping quarters. Moments later, Mana meanders down the opposite hall to her bedroom, leaving only Justin and Yoshiaki awake. After a brief chat, Justin thanks him for the hospitality and makes his way down the hall to his sleeping area. He quietly enters the room and gently slides the door closed behind him. He looks over the bonsai tree in deep thought and handpicks a single branch to snip off. "From now on, you will go by the name Dragonfly."

When morning rolls around, a commotion fills the household with a buzz of excitement. Yoshiaki has gone all out for Kaito's twenty-first birthday party this afternoon. He has arranged a setup crew and catering company to lend a hand with the preparations. The sound of hammering can be heard from the backyard as metal stakes are pounded into the ground. Dishes rattle in the kitchen, and a mild breeze blows through, bringing whiffs of deliciousness along for the ride.

The festivities this evening will take place centered around the gazebo in the backyard, where two white tents have been propped up in the grass. One contains several round dinner tables and some buffet tables, while the other has a stage, a dance floor, and lounge seating in the back. Both the gazebo and the tents have lights strung all along their exteriors.

Yoshiaki also hired some practicing geishas to perform a synchronized dance to begin the birthday party, followed by an instrumental performance to end the evening. In between the geishas, an up-and-coming young cover band will entertain the guests.

Yoshiaki has requested that Kaito and Justin join him for a tea ceremony that afternoon. The cultural event known as *chado*, or way of tea, involves the ceremonial preparation and presentation of powdered matcha green tea. *Chado* is considered one of the three classical Japanese arts of refinement, along with *kado* for flower arrangement and *kodo* for incense appreciation.

Dressed in a striking red kimono with her hair held back in an intricate bun, Mana gathers the boys. They follow her along a covered exterior corridor that leads to a separate detached building surrounded by koi ponds scattered amid a pristine garden. She opens the door to reveal a purpose-built tearoom with a low ceiling, tatami flooring, and a hanging scroll featuring calligraphy in kanji. The men walk inside, closely followed by Mana, who closes the door behind them. Sitting on the floor is a bamboo vase containing a single summer blossom facing outward to the center of the room. The building materials and decorations are deliberately simple and rustic.

Kaito translates the symbols found on the scroll. "Harmony, respect, purity, and tranquility. The four key principles of *chado*."

Yoshiaki has been patiently waiting for their arrival and signals for them to come closer. "Thank you for joining me today. Please, make yourselves comfortable."

Mana pours each of them a cup of tea from an elaborate porcelain teapot. She gracefully approaches Yoshiaki and whispers something in his ear, leaving a tiny smudge of bright red lipstick on his lobe. After performing an elegant curtsy, she slips through the shoji and fades out of sight.

Yoshiaki sips his tea and takes a long look at Justin. "Did your grandfather present you with a gift last month on your twenty-first birthday?"

"As a matter of fact, he did. An old pocket watch, supposedly from Great-Grandfather Saito."

"Good. And did my brother mention anything else to you about the watch?"

"Not much, other than to keep it in a safe place."

Yoshiaki frowns. "Did he mention for you to bring it to Japan?"

"Yes. It's back in my room. Shall I go get it?"

Three weeks ago, Justin turned twenty-one, and his grandfather, Hayato, Yoshiaki's brother, flew from Hawaii to California and presented him with the family heirloom. The pocket watch is a two-time-zone, silver captain's watch and chain from Japan, made in the 1860s. The cover pops open to reveal the two separate time zones and a temperature gauge. An unusual-looking circular symbol has been etched into the open interior cover that flips down.

Justin retrieves the watch from his sleeping area and tries to hand it over, but Yoshiaki refuses to accept it. He motions for him to sit. "Hold on to that for now."

He begins to tell them an elaborate story from his childhood, growing up alongside Hayato in Hawaii. The brothers were notoriously competitive in all aspects of life and could hardly agree on anything. One summer in their young adult lives, a special girl moved into the neighborhood, and they were smitten. Each tried his best to win her over, but ultimately, their competitive nature scared her off. She went on to marry another man, and the two brothers drifted apart. The following year, Hayato turned twenty-one, and their father presented him with the pocket watch.

Two years later, Yoshiaki reached his twenty-first birthday and also received a family heirloom passed down from their father. Shortly thereafter, he moved to Japan for a fresh start and never saw his brother, Hayato, again.

Yoshiaki removes a cloth from his pocket, unwraps a folding pocket knife, and turns to address Kaito. "Please accept this gift that has been in our family for several generations." A brief electrical shock jolts their fingertips during the exchange. He stands to finish addressing them. "Your great-grandfather Saito proudly looks upon you both today. Cherish these heirlooms he obtained long ago. I must go now. The guests will be arriving shortly." He exits through the back door, and his footsteps can be heard fading into the distance.

Kaito inspects the folding knife that has been etched with the same symbol found on the pocket watch. He carefully opens the slip-joint knife to reveal a razor-sharp blade with an unusual serrated tip. Justin hands him the pocket watch to compare the two side by side, and their striking resemblance confirms these two pieces belong together. Kaito's heart starts beating rapidly, and a warming sensation pulsates through his hands when he sees a tiny keyhole in the temperature gauge.

Contemplating his options, Kaito decides to delicately insert the knife tip a mere eighth of an inch into the keyhole and hears a distinct clicking noise. He locks eyes with Justin for a split second, looks back down at the watch, and attempts a gentle counterclockwise turn to no avail. So, he lets go of the knife, re-grips his fingertips, and effortlessly makes a clockwise quarter turn. The blade comes to a natural stopping point and the temperature gauge separates from the watch face, revealing a tiny piece of folded paper no larger than a pinky nail.

He gently removes the paper from the watch and slowly opens it up. One, two, three, four. Finally, the fifth open fold reveals a three-by-four-inch piece of paper with a rudimentary drawing of Yakushima island. The flipside contains a map of the valley on which the family property sits, easily recognizable by the distinct triangular boundary lines. The left corner of the textless map depicts a stone pathway leading to a tree.

Kaito hands the delicate document to Justin for a look. "The map indicates somewhere behind the property. I recall visiting a lot of dense forest back there as a child, but not any paths." He pauses for a moment, then continues. "Wait. I do vaguely recall an old riverbed. Do you think that could be what is shown on the map?"

Justin excitedly replies, "That has to be it! How long does it take to get there?"

"I don't know. Maybe twenty minutes."

Justin walks toward the doors. "What are you waiting for? Let's go."

"Wait a minute. You want to run out into the woods an hour before my birthday party in search of what exactly?"

"Come on. Where's your sense of adventure? Let's go have a quick look around. We'll turn back in time to make the festivities."

Kaito folds the map back together and replaces it within the pocket watch. He closes up the folding knife, wraps them together in the cloth, and hands it over to Justin. "Would you mind holding on to these? You're more trustworthy than I am. Let's go check it out."

Justin reaches out to accept his offer and places the cloth in his pocket. They walk past the garden and koi ponds on the way over to the back gate, which spills out into a natural grass pasture behind the property.

Kaito points left. "If I remember correctly, the old riverbed is that way."

They walk another hundred yards before hearing the sound of trickling water and cut through an opening in the foliage to reveal a lightly flowing creek that weaves along a rocky stream bottom.

Justin scoops up a handful of water for a tiny drink and washes his face. "Let's walk downstream for a few, and if nothing comes of it, we'll head back and maybe give it another try tomorrow."

They trudge along the swerving riverbed that butts up against the forested mountain base, eventually stumbling upon a fresh-water pond equivalent in size to an average backyard swimming pool. A well-preserved fallen tree quietly rests on one end of the shore.

Justin recognizes several dwarf cryptomeria bonsai trees growing wild in the area and develops an armful of goose bumps. "This could be the place. Look around."

Kaito climbs a large boulder overlooking the water hole for a better view of the surrounding area. A ring of rippling water suddenly appears in the center of the pond, and he sees a large blue-and-white koi swimming figure eights. The koi plunges underwater and disappears into a car tire–size hole where a thick handle of rope partially pokes out from the opening. He calls over to Justin. "There's something strange at the bottom of the pond."

Justin hops up onto the rock next to him, looks down into the water, and estimates the rope at a depth of eight feet. "Stand back. I'm gonna swim down and grab it." Without hesitation, he strips down to his boxers and slides off the rock into the clear, cool, fresh water.

Kaito speaks up in a somber voice. "Be careful. Koi bite." He cracks a smile and bursts out in laughter. "Just messing with you."

Justin takes several deep breaths and slips underwater with his eyes wide open. He swims down to a small cave and notices the rope is attached to a dark-red, circular object inside the otherwise empty cavern. He slowly pulls on the rope to reveal an old sunken fishing float. He clutches the rope in one hand, cradles the glass float in the other, and frog kicks to the shoreline.

Kaito races over to help him out of the water, and they sit down in a patch of wild grass to inspect the object. A pea-size hole is visible on top of the float and instantly becomes the culprit for sinking the object. However, upon closer inspection, it appears to have been drilled rather than accidental. When Kaito tilts the float to its side, water starts draining out, and several objects shift within the glass during the process.

With all the water now drained out, Kaito looks over the glass, trying to locate an opening, and slowly begins to twist off the top as if it were a pickle jar. Sure enough, after three complete revolutions, the glass lid detaches from the main body, and he reaches inside to remove nine small stones. The grayish-blue river rocks are flat, smooth, and roughly two inches across. Each one has an animal engraved on one side and kanji etched on the other.

Another glass float suddenly bubbles up to the pond's surface and bobs in the water. Justin hops up to see the blue-and-white koi swim a figure eight around the object and dash back down into the underwater cave. He reaches out to grab the float and brings it back over to the grass. Justin twists off the airtight lid and removes two delicate pieces of paper written in kanji, so he hands it to Kaito for translation.

"'Many years ago, a savage storm ripped through our homeland, bringing high winds, torrential rain, and mass devastation. Family, friends, and neighbors alike suffered through the catastrophe, managing to survive on sheer will alone. Thousands fell ill to incurable disease and famine, perishing in the aftermath of the storm. When the weather finally subsided, the cleanup and rebuilding process began. A strong, energetic young man at the time, I felt up for the challenge of getting involved and volunteered to help reconstruct the local infrastructure.

"'One day while working on a second-story rooftop, a strong gust of wind knocked me off balance. I fell to the ground, became unconscious, and slipped into a coma for five days. On the sixth day, I awoke, recalling visions of nine locations and nine animal species, one found from each. Fearing the images would fade over time, I created these stones to preserve my memories.

"'The following year, I was offered an opportunity to visit the faraway land of Hawaii and agreed to the relocation in search of vast, untold fortunes. Rather than bring the nine stones along for fear of misplacement or theft, I thought it best to hide them in a safe location in Japan, with hopes of returning one day to pursue my visions. The pocket watch and folding knife were my only possessions of value at the time, having won them fair and square in a game of chance. Their previous owner custom-built the watch to hold precious jewels in the small hidden compartment. Figuring this to be as good a place as any, I decided to store the map of the stones' location within the watch.

"'Life in Hawaii gave me newfound hope, and I made the decision to stay permanently. The following year I met a lovely lady named Manami and we married within three months. She soon gave birth to our two boys, who we named Hayato and Yoshiaki. Oahu Island treated us well for many years, enabling times of prosperity that helped in raising our children.

"'As time went on, the boys grew into men and became responsible members of society. On each of their twenty-first birthdays, I gifted them one of the heirlooms, with the pocket watch going to Hayato and the folding knife to Yoshiaki. Although I originally believed my sons would one day attempt these challenging quests, a spontaneous premonition suddenly clarified it would actually be my grandchildren.

"'Please accept these nine etched stones as a token of belief in the visions brought forth to me from our ancestors. I feel confident the two of you will unlock their true meaning one day soon. Your great-granddad, Kuro Saito.

"'PS This quest will begin in the forest of Jomon Sugi, here on the island. Look for an oddly behaving Yaku monkey to help you solve this riddle of the forest. Destiny awaits both of you. Now go!'"

Kaito sets down the note and tries to absorb the information it contains. Unexpectedly, a gust of wind scoops it high up in the air and releases the two sheets of papers onto the pond's surface. He lunges to grab them but is beaten to the punch by the blue koi, who secures the papers in its mouth and leisurely swims them back underwater, never to be seen again.

Justin lies down in the grass, frozen in a state of perplexity and stares up at the sky. Realizing the party will begin soon, he quickly gets dressed in preparation for the return walk.

Kaito stands at the water's edge, pleading with his hands clasped for the koi to reemerge. A small flock of little green Japanese white-eye birds rapidly buzz overhead, squawking up a storm. One of them drops a turd square on his shoulder during the flyby, and the two cousins burst out in laughter. "Gather up the stones and keep everything together in your bag when we get back to the house. Let's keep this between us for now, and we will talk more about it tomorrow."

They return to the property and slip past the arriving guests unnoticed. Kaito quickly washes up and makes a dramatic entrance to the party, instantly garnering the center of attention. Meanwhile, Justin changes into some dry clothes and stashes everything away in his backpack.

By the time he arrives at the party, the geisha dance has just concluded, and the guests are talking about the impressive performance. He sits at the table with Kaito and his friends.

Jeikobu looks over at him, jiggling one of his eyebrows up and down. "Where have you been? You missed the geisha dancers."

Miya notices the gesture and stomps on his foot under the table.

"Oh, you know, just relaxing and getting better acquainted with this spectacular property. Great party, by the way."

The group wanders over to the buffet line, where servers assist in plating the assortment of local delicacies. Instrumental music begins to play as the band warms up, and after a minute or two they break out in a jazz melody sung in Japanese. The band members are dressed in black suits, white dress shirts, crimson bow ties, sunglasses, and matching crimson fedoras.

The guests enjoy a delicious meal while listening to the live music, with laughter and conversation making their rounds. At the conclusion of dinner, three children bravely wander on stage and begin dancing. An elderly couple joins them, and soon enough, the dance floor is congested with people letting loose.

The band lives up to expectations, putting on an entertaining show. Afterward, the geisha girls bring around tea, coffee, and a variety of sweets before performing some classic Japanese music as the evening winds down. One holds a hand-plucked, three-stringed instrument resembling a banjo; another musician blows into a bamboo flute; and the third plays a drum hung over her right shoulder.

Their performance concludes the evening with sophistication and grace. Yoshiaki grabs the microphone to wish Kaito one last happy birthday and safe travels to the departing guests.

2

THE FOREST

As morning shines the first rays of warmth, Justin awakens with a renewed sense of energy and purpose. Batches of rainfall arrived in waves all night long, pounding the rooftops, but the foul weather seems to have blown over. He sips some hot tea in his room as he prunes the bonsai tree. "Dragonfly, you are complete!" He sets down the garden shears to admire the ornate shape of the miniature tree. After a brief moment of reflection, he slips out of the room and wanders out back to further explore the grounds.

Mana sees him down in the yard and waves Justin over to the greenhouse. He follows her inside, where the air radiates with the scent of fresh flowers. Ami is busy transplanting a deep-purple morning glory, and the kids are planting seeds in small containers next to her.

The greenhouse is filled with rows of plants and flowers that are sectioned off by variety and growth stages. Mana grows quite the assortment of flora in the facility, including Q-tip plants, orchids, evening primrose, moonflowers, jasmine, hydrangea, and irises. She once cultivated more than thirty types of flowers alone, but that number has dwindled over the years. These days she takes pride in growing fewer specimens of superior quality.

After a brief tour of the greenhouse, Justin goes back outside and sees Kaito strolling barefoot to the gazebo, still dressed in last night's clothes. They exchange a quick wave, and he walks over to join him. "Sleep well, cousin?"

Kaito sips a cup of coffee. "Why don't you grab the stones and meet me in the tree house?"

Justin fetches the mysterious river rocks from his backpack, and they gather around a hand-carved cedar dining table to examine the nine stones. Kaito inspects each of them one at a time and translates the kanji first, then reads off the animal image.

"Jomon Sugi and a monkey. Iriomote island and a cat. Mount Oyama and a deer. Maui and a curve-billed bird. Big Island and a beetle. Kauai and a lizard. Morro Bay and an osprey. Mono Lake and a coyote. And Death Valley and an octopus?"

Kaito groups the river rocks into three piles. "These stones refer to locations in Japan. These three mention locations in Hawaii. I'm not sure about these others."

"California!" exclaims Justin.

After thinking it through, Kaito continues. "OK, here's the plan. We're supposed to visit some waterfalls today before catching the late ferry back home. Let me talk to Jeikobu and the girls to see if they would be willing to hike into the forest for a look at the ancient tree Jomon Sugi, and we'll go from there. What do you think?"

Justin gathers up the stones. "I'm definitely in. After all, I was hoping this trip was something to remember for a lifetime, and it's off to a solid start."

Kaito pitches the alternative day trip to his friends out front by the campervan. The girls prefer to visit Senpiro-no-taki, a magnificent, one-hundred-foot waterfall but, in the end, agree to make the hike. After all, it's not often you get a chance to see the oldest tree in all of Japan. They agree to depart shortly and start saying their goodbyes to the family.

Meanwhile, Justin has ventured out to the garden in search of his great-uncle. He spots Yoshiaki scattering pellets of food across the koi pond into the open mouths of waiting fish and strolls toward him, passing by a waist-high stone Buddha statue along the way. A bold aroma of rosemary and thyme scents the air, and the sound of running water trickles throughout the garden.

Yoshiaki holds out the bag of fish pellets for Justin, and he reaches down deep to scoop up a large handful. They begin tossing food to the fish as Yoshiaki shares one final story.

"Have you heard the legendary koi fish story of Japan?"

Justin shakes his head.

"After one hundred years of struggling, a single koi finally crested the top of a special waterfall, making it into the river above. Gods witnessing this mammoth achievement rewarded the spirited fish for its perseverance, transforming the koi into a golden dragon. Supposedly, the dragonfish now negotiates the skies above that river, constantly seeking pearls of wisdom. The waterfall became known as the Dragon Gate, and any koi that summons the strength, courage, and determination to swim against the tide and through the gate is bestowed the same honor as the original fish that overcame adversity long ago.

"This story exemplifies principles of perseverance, strength, and courage, reminding us to never give up, no matter the odds. To have trust in yourself and believe. Do you understand?"

"Yes, sir, and I promise not to let you down." Justin goes on to express his gratitude for the open-armed acceptance he has received, especially considering the circumstances of their distant family dynamics.

Back out front, the others wait for Justin with the camper-van running. He gives Aunt Ami and Mana one last hug each, climbs aboard, and waves goodbye to Amaya and Yoshi, who come running after them. They slowly drive along the bamboo-lined road to the sound of pebbles crushing under the tires and pull out onto the main highway.

They stop off at the nearby Yakusugi Museum and purchase tickets for the lift to the Arakawa or A1 trailhead, the main hiking route to visit Jomon Sugi. The area has restricted access to lessen the environmental impact of tourism and can be visited only by bus or a prearranged taxi. The plan is to catch a bus to the A1, trek up to Jomon Sugi, and double back by late afternoon. Kaito and Jeikobu have previously made the hike, and their experience should benefit the group.

During the short bus ride, Justin and Kaito sit together, discussing the upcoming hike. Kaito quietly goes into detail regarding the Jomon Sugi stone he holds in his hand. "Undoubtedly this image is that of a Yaku monkey. The small aggressive primates are unafraid of people and have been known to bite. There are something like seven thousand of them living on the island, and we're bound to see a few along the way. Keep your eyes open."

They reach the A1 trailhead, and the busload of excited hikers start preparing for the long trek. Several groups of guided tours depart ahead of them, varying in size from four to eight adventure seekers. Fortunately, there are six large huts scattered in the mountains, all of which offer a dry place to sleep and basic restrooms. The huts can be used free of charge and function on a first come, first served basis.

The trail starts off along an old set of train tracks where a rustic wagon rests just off the road. Kaito leads them at a moderate pace, hoping to lessen the chance of slip-and-fall accidents. They soon come upon a twenty-five-foot-high bridge that crosses over the rapidly flowing Arakawa River and snap a few memorable group photographs. After the short break, they resume hiking and eventually stop for lunch at an abandoned logging village beside the river.

Kat hops up for a walk along an old crumbling stone wall that weaves across an open pasture. High clouds blanket the sun on an otherwise pleasant summer day. She sits down on top of the three-foot-high wall to guzzle water from a purple stainless steel flask. "Hey, Kaito! Are those rain clouds forming in the distance?"

"Nah, that's nothing to worry about. We might get some light showers, but the weather checked out good on the report. Even the bus driver mentioned we should expect uncommonly dry, pleasant conditions today."

Kat removes one of two granola bars from their wrapper and sets one beside her. After quickly finishing the first bar, she reaches down to grab the other one, but something snatches it away a split second prior. She turns around to see three Yaku monkeys: two juveniles standing on opposite sides of their mother, who clutches the confiscated granola bar.

Miya walks over to see what all the commotion is about and calls out in excitement, "Look, look, look. Monkeys!"

The others scramble over for a better view. It's their first opportunity to see Yakus today.

Also known as the Japanese macaque, Yakushima monkeys weigh up to thirty pounds and stand nearly two feet tall. They have a distinctive feature called a *momoware*, or split peach, which parts their hair in the middle from right to left. The semiterrestrial mammals travel in large groups of up to fifty, with females spending more time in the trees, while males spend most of their time on the ground.

Several screeching monkeys rustle in the background, well camouflaged within the thick foliage. A large male suddenly appears and starts making a deep, grunting noise that echoes off the walls. The two juveniles scamper off into the brush, leaving the adult female alone in the pasture. The mother Yaku releases several loud vocals, drops the granola bar, and hustles off into trees.

"What was that all about?" asks Kaito.

Kat nervously replies, "The mama monkey grabbed my snack, and then some other monkeys were yelling from the trees. So, this big mean one showed up, and I'm not exactly sure what happened from there." She smiles and perks up. "But I'm fine now."

Justin and Kaito glance at each other and start walking in the direction in which the Yakus disappeared in the tree line.

"Where are you two going?" asks Jeikobu.

Kaito quickly answers him. "We're gonna check it out real fast. Chill here with the ladies."

They come to a stop forty yards away, where the pasture ends, and the forest begins. Kaito listens closely, cupping his ear in an exaggerated stance, but all is quiet. "Should we run in there and chase them down?"

Justin casually looks around. "Fumbling out into that forest, off course and unsure of what we are even looking for, sounds like a recipe for disaster. Let's not get lost out here. Why don't we stick to the plan and push on? If no other monkeys appear, we'll search farther from this location on the way back. After all, the river rock has both a monkey and Jomon Sugi etchings. We should at least make it to the old tree, right?"

"That's exactly why I love you, cousin, genius!" Kaito looks at his wristwatch. "We still have another two-hour trek to reach Jomon Sugi. Let's get going."

The hike resumes along an incredibly monotonous yet pristine stretch. They eventually come to a fork in the road and veer onto a steep trail that leads them away from the train tracks, with several roots, rocks, and staircases to maneuver. They come across a calm stream with a sign warning hikers the stream can become uncrossable in heavy rains. Several chestnut-colored birds flutter about, skipping from tree to tree, swooping down along the water's edge.

The group takes a quick break to observe the flock of foraging birds and refill their water bottles. After crossing over the stream, they hike to Wilson's Stump, one of the trees felled in 1586 as ordered by Hidoyoshi Toyotomi, a great Daimyo lord known historically as the unifier of Japan.

A mild rain begins to fall as the group enters Wilson's Stump. Justin gathers everyone close for a photo, wanting to capture the heart-shaped skyline seen through the stump opening. Standing in the middle, Kat and Kaito on his left, Miya and Jeikobu on his right, Justin flashes the pic. Once finished admiring the tree and paying respects to the shrine, the group sets off on their final stretch to Jomon Sugi.

They push on from the landmark tree in a sudden, steady rainfall, passing several groups of hikers hustling back out. Kaito stops a party of four and speaks to the guide. "What's the big rush?"

"Everyone's pulling out! An unexpected storm blew in from the north, packing some heavy moisture. I spoke to the police station on two-way, and they confirmed it's here to stay. You guys should turn back, and we can all hike out in a larger group. You know, safety in numbers."

The others watch from several feet away, unaware of what they are discussing.

Kaito looks over at his friends and back at the guide. "Do you know if the hut ahead has any room?"

"I believe so. Most people left when word spread about an hour ago." The guide glances over at his three fellow hikers and back at Kaito. "Listen, we need to get moving. You should seriously consider leaving now. Safe travels to you." He flips on his headlamp and disappears down the trail.

Jeikobu walks over. "What did he say?"

"He said an unexpected storm blew in, and we should hike out now to avoid the worst of it, which has yet to come. If this rain holds up for any length of time, those streams will swell, and we'll never be able to get across."

Kat and Miya are huddled together, holding hands, and shivering in the pouring rain.

Kaito considers their options. "The guide is fairly certain the hut ahead has some availability, or we could follow them back out now. Why don't we vote on it? With a count of hands, who votes for the hut?"

All five of them raise a hand, making the unanimous decision an easy one.

"OK, that's settled," says Kaito. "It's not much farther. Let's go."

Miya takes three steps, slips on a wet rock, and mildly twists her ankle trying to avoid a fall. "This sucks!"

They bypass one final goliath tree with a sign reading Jomon Sugi, and Kaito loudly calls out, "There's the hut."

Jeikobu holds the door open for the others, who slip inside one at a time after removing their wet shoes. A group of six occupy the entry level, and one of the men greets them. "Welcome to our humble abode. Try the second floor or loft."

They walk up the wooden staircase to a crowded second story and one of their group members speaks up. "*Konichiwa*. The loft is wide open."

Kaito scales up a wooden ladder and looks around. "Come on up. It'll be cozy but sure beats the alternative."

They climb up the ladder one at a time and settle into the empty loft. Jeikobu and Miya spread out a compact tarp in the far-left corner and set up their makeshift bed with a couple of light blankets from their backpacks. She lies down, cold and tired, with her eyes closed, and quickly falls asleep. Jeikobu leans against the wall, munching on a handful of crackers.

The others fan out in the loft to relax and dry out. Very little conversation occurs, as everyone seems content on resting. Rain continues falling for several hours at a maddening pace. Roaring gusts of wind rip through the forest, rustling leaves and snapping twigs. Mild thunder groans in the distance, looming and warning those who will listen as the afternoon turns into evening. Justin and Kaito begin to quietly discuss the famous Jomon Sugi tree they have come to see.

The large evergreen tree species, cryptomeria japonica, goes by the name of Japanese sugi pine and Japanese red-cedar. Endemic to Japan, the tree species have reddish-brown bark that peels in perpendicular strips, long, needlelike leaves, and small seed cones. A relative to the giant sequoia, the sugi pine grows best in forests with deep, well-drained soil subject to warm, moist conditions. They are the national tree of Japan, with some, more than one thousand years old, granted the title of yakusugi.

Jomon Sugi is considered the oldest and largest among the old-growth cryptomeria trees on the island and ranks as one of the oldest trees in the world. Experts disagree on its actual age, but the range varies from two thousand to seven thousand years old, leading to all kinds of speculation. But given the range of estimations, one could reasonably assume somewhere around four to five thousand years old.

Jeikobu removes a battery-operated lantern from his backpack and turns on the light. The group huddles to devise a plan for the next day. "At first light, Kaito and I will walk back down the trail to examine the stream, assuming the weather improves. If it looks passable, we'll come back for you three and make the trek out. Otherwise, we will wait out the storm."

Miya massages her stiff ankle. "Let's make some tea."

Jeikobu retrieves a small camping stove from his pack to boil the water.

"Seriously, I thought you were kidding. Hot tea sounds amazing right now. How's your foot feeling, Miya?" asks Kat.

"A little sore, but I'll be fine."

They enjoy some tea and a snack while trying to make the best of the situation. Not long after, the entire hut quiets down, and the lights shut off one by one.

Justin removes a blanket from his pack, blows up an air pillow, and settles in for what he hopes will be a good night's sleep. He dozes off overhearing Kaito and Kat talking quietly between themselves. Even though he can't distinguish the exact words, their affection toward each other finally becomes apparent to him. The two have always shared a special bond and attraction, yet they have never admitted it. To this day, things have been strictly on a platonic level, but that seems about to change.

Justin opens his eyes one last time and sees the two sharing a delicate kiss. Embarrassed, he turns over, trying not to make a sound.

Kat whispers to Kaito with a slight giggle in her voice, "I think your cousin saw us."

Kaito looks over to see Justin lying quietly on his side, facing the wall. He gives Kat one additional soft kiss and flips off the lantern to get some sleep.

Rain comes and goes all night, tapping on the rooftop of the otherwise quiet mountain hut. Justin is suddenly awoken by a deep, mysterious sound resembling that of a pull-cord lawn mower unable to start. He remains motionless, attentively listening to each and every sound coming from outside but doesn't hear the noise again. So, figuring he dreamed the clamor, he covers his head and tries to go back to sleep.

Seconds later, his eyes pop open again after hearing two rapid pulses of the same mysterious sound. He looks around at the others sleeping and peers down at his cell phone, revealing the time to be 3:33 a.m. The grunting noise suddenly comes again, concurrently changing the time on his cell to 3:36 a.m., and again to 3:39 a.m. A lightning flash illuminates the loft.

Justin's heart starts beating rapidly as he quietly walks over to the window for a look outside at the dark forest. Lightning flashes to reveal a large monkey strutting near the hut, and a faint clunking noise can be heard at the front door. Seconds later, lightning strikes again, showing the primate walking away from the hut with what appears to be one of his hiking boots.

"That little thief," he says ever so quietly.

Lightning flashes again. The monkey is now standing on the trail staring directly up at him, dangling his shoe by the laces in a taunting manner. Seconds later, another flash shows the animal walking away dragging the boot.

Something unexpectedly grabs Justin on the shoulder, startling him immensely and causing a chilled sensation to the bone. He slowly turns around to see a shadowy figure immerge in his peripheral vision. Justin is terrified and remains still until a flashlight is turned on to reveal Kaito's sleepy face.

"What are you doing?"

"You shouldn't sneak up on people like that. Seriously, that's not funny. I almost had a heart attack."

"Sorry, sorry, my bad." Kaito starts rotating the flashlight back and forth between them, depending on who's speaking at the time.

"No worries; forget about it. Listen, an odd noise woke me up, so I came over here to have a look outside, and you'll never guess what I saw. That crazy male monkey from earlier?"

Kaito shrugs his shoulders, unsure what he is talking about.

"You know, the big one from lunchtime that came grunting out of the forest?"

"OK, right, right, right. I'm with you. Go on."

Justin lets out a brief exhalation of frustration and continues. "Yeah, so that big old monkey appeared suddenly, walked right up to the front door, grabbed my boot, and took off down the trail. But more than that, he looked up and started teasing me with the stupid thing." He starts demonstration a wagging motion with his hands, making a funny face. "That little jerk was purposely shaking it back and forth."

"Do that again with your face."

Justin makes the same hand motion and facial expression, causing Kaito to laugh quietly.

"Let's go after that ornery little son of a monkey."

A chilly blast of mountain air rushes across their face when they crack open the front door to slip outside. The rain has stopped, but water continues to drip down from the pitched rooftop above. Kaito locates his size tens in the pile and laces up his shoes. Justin, on the other hand, puts on his only boot and borrows one belonging to Jeikobu. They flip on their headlamps to scan the area for any sign of the troublemaker but see nothing at first.

"There. Right there!" exclaims Kaito.

His flashlight shines on the monkey walking down the trail thirty feet ahead. The primate pauses in midstride, turns his head around to glance back at them, and takes off running down the dark, muddy path with Justin's boot dragging behind.

The cousins scurry down the slippery stairs after the thieving monkey. They begin to hear a faint humming echo in the distance, repeating a rhythmic, four-note pattern on a decreasing scale pitch, followed by the same four-note pattern on an ascending scale. The guys slow down and listen closely. *Hummmm hummm humm hum, hum humm hummm hummmm.* After a brief pause, it starts again. *Hummmm hummm humm hum, hum humm hummm hummmm.*

They continue stumbling along, listening to the sound that increases in volume and clarity, becoming distinctly feminine and rather alluring. Just up ahead, they can barely make out the monkey dropping Justin's boot near a sign. Within a matter of seconds, their flashlights automatically shut off and the animal scatters out of sight.

Thousands of tiny fluorescent green lights suddenly appear in a miniature tornado of swirling illumination. The spinning whirlwind of light consciously moves alongside them, serving as the cousins' guide in the otherwise pitch-black forest. When Justin hobbles over to retrieve his boot, the humming melody starts up again, this time coming directly from the large tree right in front of them, the Jomon Sugi.

Hummmm hummm humm hum, hum humm hummm hummmm.

It repeats once again after a pause.

Hummmm hummm humm hum, hum humm hummm hummmm.

The fireflies break formation into three groups of rapidly twisting balls of light hovering ten feet above the ground in a triangular pattern. The illuminated spheres remain in place for several seconds and then bolt at the tree, impacting and covering the lower trunk like an artist throwing a bucket of paint on canvas. Majestic facial features appear in the fluorescent backdrop of the glowing bark, creating a detailed mouth, nose, and eyes that come alive with movement. The fireflies swirl about, shifting in unison to form gestures as a woman's voice speaks to them.

"Eons ago, as a spirit, I came across and permanently entered this triumphant tree, eternally dedicating myself to its guardianship. The one and only goal, survival at all costs. Over the next several millennia, natural disasters claimed many of the neighboring trees by way of tsunami, wildfire, and heart rot. But the most damage of all occurred just over four hundred years ago, only this time by way of human hands. On a quest for building materials, man irrevocably devastated substantial portions of woodland on the island, even toppling down my dear old friend, now referred to as Wilson's Stump. After surviving it all, I proudly stand before you today with an important message to deliver.

"The two of you have embarked on a journey of great proportions. If you stay true to the course, follow your instincts, and rely on each other's assistance, you can accomplish immeasurable achievements moving forward. Accept this special gift and guard it with your lives. For one day its contents will come to your assistance in ways you can't yet imagine. For now, keep this close to your heart and hold on to it tightly, for it contains valuable information on every species of the flora that ever existed on Earth.

"Throughout the long quest ahead, you will need to collect eight additional objects, each containing something unique. However, to unlock their full potential, you will need all nine items together."

The woman's voice stops, and the humming sound begins.

Hummmm hummm humm hum, hum humm hummm hummmm.

It pauses for a moment, then starts again.

Hummmm hummm humm hum, hum humm hummm hummmm.

Several fireflies separate from the main group to form a small tornado of brightly spinning lights. The neon twister steadily moves up the tree trunk, stopping at a large branch that deposits something into the light. The fireflies gradually lower down, cradling the object, and Justin instinctively reaches out to accept the gift. A red, golf ball–size piece of hardened, bubbly tree sap drops into his palms.

The fluorescent green twister soars up to the main group of flying neon daredevils that now hover in midair. After whizzing about, the group of fireflies disperses back into the forest and fades out of sight. The moment they disappear, the flashlights start working again. Kaito shines his at Jomon Sugi, and the tree's special facial features can no longer be seen.

Japanese people have long believed that certain trees possess special characteristics for a variety of reasons, including old age, interestingly shaped trunks, or a series of knots resembling a human face. These exceptional specimens were believed to house protective spirits referred to by many names but most commonly called a Kodama. These spirits supposedly preserve the knowledge of those trees that gets passed down by the elderly of that area over successive generations. The mythological belief states that cutting down an old tree containing a

Kodama would draw blood from the bark and bring misfortune to those involved.

Justin looks down at the red, cloudy mass of hardened tree sap. "That was incredible."

Kaito gives him a colossal bear hug. "Can you believe it? How cool were those fireflies?"

They walk back to the hut, quietly entering through the front door to see everyone is still sound asleep. Kaito leads the way upstairs to the loft and they calmly retake their sleeping spots.

Kat rolls over and whispers to Kaito, "Where did you go?"

"To the bathroom, Katsumi. Go back to sleep. We still have a few hours until daylight." He puts his arm around her, and she inches closer for warmth.

Justin opens his eyes to see Kaito and Kat still sleeping. He sits up and stretches out his arms, looking over at Miya and Jeikobu preparing hot tea. It's morning and the sun's first rays of warmth are penetrating through the windows. A small amount of commotion can be heard downstairs. After a magnificent yawn, Justin says groggily, "Good morning."

"Morning," replies Jeikobu.

"Hello, good morning," says Miya. "Hand me your cup if you would like some tea."

Justin finds the cup near his inflatable pillow and hands it over. He looks out the window and sees clear skies peeking through the canopy.

Jeikobu fills Justin in on the news. "The guide from downstairs just relayed a weather report; everything looks good today. Most of the hikers have decided to trek out together if we want to join them."

Miya finishes pouring the tea and hands Justin his cup. He sits back down to sip the hot beverage and warms up his chilly hands. Kaito and Kat begin to toss and turn, waking up. "I say we pack up and venture out of here as one big, happy family. What do you think?"

Kaito abruptly jumps into the conversation. "Sounds good to me."

Kat joins the soirée. "Good morning, everyone. Could I please have some tea?"

Miya pours both Kat and Kaito cups, and the group discusses today's plan. They agree to walk out with the others and start to pack up.

A short while later, the converged band of fourteen hikers begin the soggy trek back to the trailhead. Most of the hike goes as expected, with only a few showers and relatively calm conditions. They end up having to cross over a swelled stream or two, but nothing significantly dangerous. Three quarters of the way along, Miya's sore ankle buckles and twists as she stumbles on a loose railroad tie. Already slightly weakened from the day before, the severity of her injury increases with the unfortunate misstep, and she falls to the ground in agony. Kaito suggests they stop for a break, and the large group concurs. Thankfully, Miya doesn't sustain any additional injuries in the spill other than the now badly sprained ankle.

Jeikobu removes a stretchy bandage and some oral pain medicine from his first aid kit. After giving Miya some ibuprofen, he proceeds to tightly wrap her ankle for support. With the bandage securely in place, he scavenges a fallen branch suitable for her to use as a walking stick. Sore ankle and all, Miya toughens up, signaling her readiness to proceed. Kaito carries her pack, and Jeikobu assists her on the rest of the walk out. They end up falling behind the main group but stay within eyesight of the hikers, eventually making it back to the trailhead.

A bus soon arrives and drops them off at their campervan. For the first time since yesterday, cell phone service returns, and Jeikobu instantly books Miya and himself a hydrofoil ride home to properly care for her ankle. Kaito, Kat, and Justin decide to continue on, and make the necessary travel arrangements to visit nearby Iriomote the next morning. This island is mentioned on one of the stones and is the closest to where they are now. Rather than trouble Yoshiaki and Mana this evening, they rent a hotel room within walking distance to the airport.

After being dropped off, Kaito checks them in to the seaside hotel, and they settle into their room. The quaint accommodations are decorated in tropical decor consisting of palm tree linens and bamboo furnishings. The living area on the left has sliding glass doors that open to a small patio overlooking the harbor, and on the right, a simple kitchen leads into a hallway with a toilet, sink room, shower, and bedroom.

Justin sets his backpack on the floor and stretches out on the couch. "I just wanna chill here for a minute and do nothing. My feet are killing me. That was a long couple of days in the wilderness."

"See you boys later; shower time," says Kat.

Kaito sits down in a chair next to Justin. "She heard us return this morning."

Justin looks over and whispers, "What did you tell her?"

"Not much. I played it off as nothing."

"OK, cool. I think we need to keep this between us for now."

"Agreed. Let's get cleaned up and grab something to eat. I'm starving."

They walk down the street to a nearby restaurant for a much-needed hot meal. After dinner, they stop off at a general store to purchase additional hiking equipment for the trip to

Iriomote, and then make their way back to the hotel. Justin sends his sister a text message, mentioning he might be out of touch for a few days while traveling to an inner island.

Melia eventually calls him back. "Hey, Justin! How did the hiking go?"

Justin is excited to speak with her. "Melia, what's up, girl? The hike was amazing although difficult and lengthy."

"I'm good—missing you as always—but good. So, you and Kaito have decided to continue backpacking and are planning to island-hop another week? Awesome. I wish I was there with you."

Justin looks over at Kaito and Kat in the kitchen. She is sitting on the countertop, and he is standing closely in front of her. Her arms are wrapped around his neck, and they are embracing in a long hug. Justin grabs his backpack and walks out on the deck to finish his conversation. He retrieves the stone etched with a cat on one side, recalling that the kanji on its flipside reads Iriomote.

"I wish you were here too, but I'm really glad you called. Will you do me a favor and research cats on Iriomote Island? Send me whatever you can dig up."

Melia spells out the word to make sure she heard him correctly. "I-r-i-o-m-o-t-e?"

"Yes, that's right."

"What kind of cats? Domestic? Wild?"

"Whatever you can find out, I suppose."

"No worries, I've got you covered. Is everything all right?"

He contemplates explaining what transpired at Jomon Sugi but decides against his first instinct. Quickly becoming lost in his own thoughts, he slowly zones back in, hearing Melia call out, "Hello? Justin? Justin? Did we get disconnected?"

"No, sorry, I'm still here. There's something I need to tell you, but now's not the time. Look, I gotta go. Let me know what you come up with on the cats."

Melia answers with suspicion in her voice. "Sure, but why?"

He tries to play it off. "It's nothing, it's nothing. Send me what you can find, and I'll call you in a few days. Love ya."

"Love you too. Please take care of yourself."

3

EIGHTFOLD MOUNTAINS

Tuesday morning's flight takes the travelers to Yaeyama Islands, Japan's southern and westernmost populated islands. The word *yaeyama* means "eightfold mountains" and refers to their peaks, visible from far away at sea. The city of Ishigaki serves as the region's transportation hub, boasting the only major airport, in addition to a busy seaport with frequent ferries to most of the surrounding islands. From here, they board a ferry for the ride to Iriomote.

Sitting comfortably on a high-backed, oversize, cushioned seat, Justin powers on his cell phone to check for messages. The mailbox icon appears onscreen, indicating newly received messages await in the in-box. He thumbs through the list, swiping away an online bank statement, duplicate fall registration forms, yesterday's general store receipt, and a credit card preapproval. He stops at an email from Melia with the subject line, "Appointment confirmed with a tour guide today at three p.m."

He opens the message.

"Hey, Justin. I spent a couple of hours last night researching information on the Iriomote-ama-necko, as the Japanese say. Apparently, the cats are an endangered species endemic to the island, with an estimated population of only one hundred remaining.

"I called and spoke to a hotel concierge and a museum curator, each of whom recommended the same tour guide. He is an American living in Japan the past twenty years and specializes in extreme adventure seeking. This guy does it all: hiking, kayaking, mountain climbing, and scuba diving. Supposedly, if anyone can find a wild Iriomote cat, he's the man. After finally getting hold of him, I have arranged for you to meet him today at three p.m. to discuss a plan. His name is Cole Gleason, and he'll be waiting for you at a popular fried-fish cart located adjacent to the ferry terminal. Good luck, and let me know if you need anything else. Melia"

Justin thanks her in a reply email and powers off his phone to conserve energy. Moments later, the high-speed ferry pulls out of Ishigaki on the twenty-mile run to Iriomote's Ohara port. Along the way, Justin relays the meeting information to Kaito and Kat as the three companions anxiously await the next step of their voyage into the unknown.

Within the blink of an eye, the ferry arrives at Ohara, following a relatively calm, event-free boat ride. As the passengers begin exiting one by one, Kaito politely asks a female attendant for directions to the famous fish-fry food cart, and she simply points down the wharf. Sure enough, several people can be seen waiting in a long line with many others sitting at picnic tables under umbrellas, enjoying the local cuisine.

They stroll down an old dock to the crowded eatery and spot a tall Caucasian man leaning against a concrete wall, reading an outdoor-themed magazine while puffing on a wooden-tipped cigar. He is wearing an army-green bucket hat, black sunglasses, a white long-sleeve T-shirt, camo cargo pants, and sandals. Clearly not a tourist, they figure him to be their guy, and Justin bravely walks up to him.

"Would you happen to be Cole Gleason?"

"The one and only."

"My name is Justin Blackwood, and I believe you spoke to my sister, Melia, on the phone yesterday regarding a guide for hire."

"Oh yeah, I talked to her; nice girl. She said you folks are visiting the island for a few days, hoping to catch a glimpse of the elusive Iriomote wildcat."

* * *

Kaito chimes in. "Supposedly, you are the man who can help us find one."

"First and foremost, there's certainly no guarantee of locating one of those creatures, no matter what anyone tells you. This island spans an area of two hundred ninety square kilometers and features countless mangrove trees, a few mountain ranges, and some extremely dense forest. Navigating through this diverse ecosystem tends to be a major pain in the butt, and there is only one main road that parallels nearly two-thirds of the coastline. The island's rugged interior has virtually no access other than kayaking upstream or hiking in on foot. In other words, finding one of these cats can be a rather daunting task."

Justin replies, "We understand the difficulty of the task at hand and really do appreciate your candor. But the three of us have traveled a great distance getting here today with every intention of seeing a wildcat."

"Your sister mentioned the three of you are college students completing a summer research project. I totally respect that, which is why I agreed to help out. Look, here's what I told her. You guys are welcome to join me tonight on a camping trip to Haemida Beach, just down the road. It's a favorite spot of mine to have a bonfire and do some shore fishing. My truck is loaded with gear and ready to go. There have been several confirmed sightings of the cats there throughout the years, so it's as good a place as any to start."

Kaito whispers to Justin, who replies to the guide, "OK, that sounds good to us."

"My schedule is free the next couple of days if you want to further explore the island. We can discuss additional locations and options, plus the accompanying fees if you want to continue tomorrow. Five hundred dollars cash should cover tonight. That includes refreshments and dinner, a chance to do some fishing, all the necessary camping gear, and my beautiful mug to keep you company. Any questions?"

Kaito places his arm around Kat. "Done. When do we leave?"

"Right now, if you are ready."

They shake hands to seal the verbal agreement. Cole outweighs him by a good thirty pounds of muscle that becomes evident to Kaito by his crushing grip. Kaito lets out a slight whistle, shaking his hand back and forth to dispel the mild pain. He reaches for his wallet and hands Cole the money. He received a considerable sum in monetary gifts at the birthday party and has been feeling flush with this wad of cash.

They follow Cole to the parking lot and pile into his white, four-wheel-drive SUV, which has been completely outfitted to better handle the various terrains on the island. A cargo roof rack basket has been installed to carry additional gear and luggage on the top, after-market wheels and tires to enhance the vehicle's traction and stability, and a tow winch up front, mainly to assist stranded vehicles.

They travel southwest for three miles until Route 215 officially ends. A narrow paved road continues from this point for another couple of miles, eventually dead-ending at the rarely used campground. They park in front of an old, rickety wooden fence and make camp next to a ringed firepit several steps into the sand.

Justin assists Cole with constructing a pop-up canopy, setting up a hammock, and helps pitch a couple of tents.

Kaito decides to go for swim. He grabs Kat's hand, and they start walking down the sand. "We're gonna splash around in the shore break. See you guys in a few."

After the camp has been set up, the men begin to rig up fishing poles in a variety of ways. They attach top water poppers on two of the poles, intended for spin casting across the waterline in search of large game fish. A third pole with a lighter line gets a two-inch shrimp lure designed to catch smaller bait fish in the shallows. The last two are rigged up with large hooks and weights on a three-way swivel that will be thrown out once they have caught some live bait.

Kaito returns to camp, visibly refreshed and energized from the brief swim. "What an amazing place!" He grabs a water bottle from the ice chest, twists off the lid, and takes two big gulps.

Justin looks up from tying the last nonslip loop knot. "Where did Kat wander off to?"

"She went for a walk down the beach. Can I help out with anything?"

Cole quickly answers, "Yeah. Let's go get some firewood."

All along Haemida Beach, a natural bluff partially covered in vegetation separates the ocean and sand from the forest and mountains. Dead branches from fallen trees and driftwood are scattered all about, providing an abundant supply of fuel to collect and burn. After making three or four trips apiece, they accumulate what appears to be enough timber for tonight's fire.

Cole explains the available options for tomorrow to give the group ample time to decide. "All right, listen up. After racking my brain, I've come up with three different day trips to choose from. We'll only have enough time to try one, so choose wisely."

He lies in the hammock, lights a cigar, and continues. "One, we investigate the low mountains. Two, we kayak upriver to the waterfalls on the north shore. Three, we stick to the coastline and slowly cruise the entire island. There are a lot of potential stops along the way, including Cape Nakama and Cape Kaza, some hot springs, and the old port town of Funaura."

A moment of awkward silence falls over the campsite until Kat sarcastically speaks up. "Ah, hello? Waterfalls!"

Kaito verbally expresses his own opinion. "Mountain climbing sounds incredible to me."

Justin tosses his thoughts into the mix. "The Capes would be killer to see, plus I would imagine the cliffs offer a great vantage point for viewing."

The three go back and forth for several minutes, whispering among themselves at one point. They ultimately decide on Kat's preference of kayaking to the waterfalls, agreeing it would be much easier on their legs after all their recent hiking. Plus, her argument of being named Kat and their search for the Iriomote wildcat made too much sense to Kaito and swayed his vote in her favor, breaking the tie.

Cole claps his hands together. "Great choice. We should be able to cover a lot of ground tomorrow paddling to the waterfalls. Locals have seen wildcats on the embankments many times over the years." He blows out three consecutive smoke rings and continues. "It really is a crapshoot, trying to locate one of these furry little critters. Even for someone like myself with a certain set of outdoor skills and knowledge of the area. In other words, we need some luck."

43

With the decision made, they conclude the discussion and walk down to the shoreline for some sunset fishing. Justin and Cole each have a pole in hand, continually casting and reeling in the multicolored poppers. Several yards down the beach, Kaito attempts to catch smaller fish with the shrimp lure, while Kat sits next to him in the sand.

Suddenly, a Steller's sea eagle swoops down to pluck a healthy-size fish from the surface and ignites a frenzy of activity. Justin feels tension on the line and calls out "*Hanapa'a!*"

Shortly thereafter, Cole feels a strike on his line and yells, "Hook up!"

They each have hooked into giant trevally, one of the fiercest predators in the sea. A highly prized species for both food and sport, the trevally is a large marine fish in the jack family reaching lengths of 60 inches and weighing up to 150 pounds.

* * *

Kaito watches them in admiration and suddenly feels tugging on his line. He quickly pulls back on the pole to set the hook. After reeling for a couple of seconds to ensure the fish is on, he ecstatically calls out, "Triple hook up," and all three anglers simultaneously share in the experience of catching a fish.

Incredibly excited for the boys, Kat fumbles trying to stand and falls face-first into the sand. She brushes the particles off her face, sprints into camp for her camera, and runs back to photograph the electrifying event.

Kaito goes ballistic when he quickly lands a two-pound snapper called a spangled emperor. The golden-bronze fish has distinguishing blue lines, pale-blue spots, and blue pectoral fins.

After several minutes entangled in a contest of will, Cole lands a ten-pound giant trevally when the fish finally succumbs to exhaustion. He grabs the fish by the gills, hoists it high in the air, and lets out an emotional roar of excitement, knowing full well this won't be another story of "the one that got away."

Farther down the beach, Justin also has reeled in his similar-size trevally. He puts one hand on the pole, another on the leader line, and walks away from the water dragging the flopping fish across the sand. He manages to subdue the trevally and walks back to camp along the water's edge to reunite with the others, who congratulate one another on their amazing catch.

Cole turns on his headlamp. "Holy crap! How lucky are we? And it all happened so fast. Would anyone like to volunteer to get the fire started? I'll deal with the fish."

"I'm on it," says Kaito. "Guts tend to make me a little squeamish."

* * *

Kat starts preparing for dinner while Kaito lights the fire. She unpacks plates and utensils from a plastic bin and removes some previously prepared food from the ice chest, including pickled vegetables, freshly cut coconut, and assorted melons.

Meanwhile, Justin and Cole have hauled their catch up to camp and begin processing the fish for consumption. They gut the spangled emperor and two trevallies prior to taking the fish back down to the water for a final rinse. The cleaned fish are then coated in oil and rubbed in seasoning. Metal cooking skewers are slid through the larger, whole trevallies, and the smaller emperor is wrapped in foil.

Cole lights up a wooden-tipped cigar. "I'm going to have a quick look around and set out some gut piles on the perimeter. Scavenging animals, including cats, find the smell of rotting flesh irresistible. Keep an eye on dinner."

Just before Cole returns, Justin grabs some long, metal cooking tongs to partially open the foiled fish. He notices the eyes have turned opaque and removes the fish from the camp-fire grill. "Let's eat!"

Kaito bows his head in Kat's direction and waves an arm at the food table. "Ladies first."

She walks directly past him, smiling, winks, and proceeds to help herself.

Afterward, the three men plate themselves a healthy amount of food and join Kat around the campfire. While they are enjoying the freshly prepared meal, a white pickup truck slowly loops around the campground, crunching an occasional rock or two and pulls up beside them. The window rolls down and a man speaks. "*Konbanwa.*"

Cole handles the situation. "Don't worry, I know the park ranger. Sit tight." He walks over to the truck, waving and loudly calling out, "*Konbanwa.*"

Justin closely watches the two men engage in a short conversation just out of earshot, and the park ranger pulls away to continue patrolling the grounds.

Cole returns to the campsite. "The beach concludes his rounds for the evening, and he won't return until the same time tomorrow."

After dinner, Justin puts on his UCSC hoodie and joins Cole around the fire, while Kaito and Kat crawl inside their tent.

Cole lays in a hammock, puffing on his cigar, but soon retires for the evening in anticipation of an early start in the morning. "That's all for me. Good times landing those fish today. See you in the morning."

Justin stretches out on a camping cot while his thoughts stray to tomorrow and what lies ahead. He stares up into the night sky at an unusually bright, flickering star. His mind begins to stray, and he eventually dozes off.

The campers pack everything up in the morning while discussing their epic evening of fishing. Unfortunately, not a single wildcat has made an appearance, but the group remains hopeful. They drive back to Highway 215 and soon come upon a sign reading Iriomote Wildlife Center. Cole pulls into the parking lot and turns off the ignition. "The museum doesn't open for a couple of hours, but the caretaker, Mr. Nakamura, has agreed to let us in early. He lives a double life as the park ranger we saw last night."

The museum door swings open, and Mr. Nakamura welcomes everyone inside. "The Iriomote Wildlife Conservation Center was established as a base for conservation activities regarding the Iriomote yameneko wildcat. This small natural history center has exhibits on the critically endangered feline, including a stuffed cat and a documentary video. The museum also contains information on additional wildlife found throughout the island, including the Ryukyu boar, various birds of prey, and the highly venomous Habu snake, a species of pit viper whose bite has a fatality rate of three percent and a permanent disability rate of seven percent."

* * *

Mr. Nakamura mentions that several wildcats wear tracking collars, but he is under a confidentiality order not to divulge the animals' locations. He subtly approves of their intention of searching the north shore waterfalls, hinting at recent sightings by local fishermen on the rivers. They thank him for his time, deposit a modest donation in a jar on their way out, and proceed several miles down the road to Uehara Port. Upon arrival, they locate a small hotel with availability and check into a pair of one-bedroom, adjoining rooms.

4

LOOKS LIKE WHITE BEARD

Referred to by locals as Little Amazon, the Urachi River sprawls through twenty-four miles of subtropical jungle along rocky shorelines littered with luxuriant mangrove trees. Cole, Justin, Kaito, and Kat arrange two tandem kayaks, load up, and embark on a pleasant paddle through naturally carved valleys exploding with an immense diversity of fauna and flora. Endemic Yaeyama palms wave their majestic fronds high above the lush green fern- and mangrove-lined shores teeming with abundant wildlife. Various waterbirds, schools of fish, and plenty of insects can be seen along the sandy riverbank. Justin even gets a look at a sounder of swine: Japanese boar also known as the white-mustached pig.

The paddlers eventually reach an upstream, makeshift dock called Battleship Rock, where they tie off the kayaks and trek out on the cross-island trail. They travel along a well-trodden path for three-quarters of a mile, ultimately coming to a view platform overlooking Mariyudo Falls. The impressive fifty-foot, cascading, two-part waterfall tumbles over the rocks, dropping into a large pond surrounded by jungle. Mariyudo, meaning round pool, is often enjoyed by swimmers looking to cool off from the hike. A warning sign reminds visitors that all fresh water found on the island contains certain species of relatively harmless leeches.

After a quick look around, they trek on to a second waterfall known locally as the Seat of the God. Much like Mariyudo, the Kanpire Falls offer hikers an ideal opportunity to relax, have some lunch, and take photographs. Not much of a waterfall, the Kanpire Falls more so constitute a section of the river that flows into a wide, shallow stream with a multitude of naturally occurring swimming pools.

* * *

Cole suggests they stop for a break. He sits down next to Justin on a large flat boulder that partially overhangs the river. "Look at all these people."

Kaito and Kat remove their shoes to cool off in the water.

Cole guzzles from his canteen. "There are way too many tourists here today for skittish wildcats. At least we still have plenty of daylight to check out Pinaisara Falls. We'll paddle back out, hop in the car, and try again at another location."

Justin slings his backpack over one shoulder and jumps down onto the sandy shore. The others take notice of his actions, realizing their visit to Kanpire Falls has concluded. They gear up and hike back out to Battleship Rock where Kaito hops aboard their kayak and reaches out to assist Kat. She grabs hold of his hand and takes a long stride to reach the watercraft. In doing so, her sock slips down, revealing two small, slender, dark spots on her lower calf.

Cole recognizes the leeches from countless firsthand experiences. "Hold on a second, you two." He points down at Kat's leg.

Kat looks down at her leg and totally freaks out, unaware the bloodsucking creatures had attached themselves. She lets out a squeamish cry and frantically swats her leg to knock one of them off. Kaito calms her down and assists in properly removing the other with a fingernail. Small red dots appear where the worms were once attached to her leg, but there is no bleeding because the leeches secrete an anticoagulant into the host's bloodstream.

Kat finally calms down, giving Cole a chance to provide her with some concrete advice. "It's important to keep wounds clean in tropical climates, or they can quickly become infected. Do you have a first aid kit? Otherwise there's one in my pack."

"Nope," replies Kaito.

"OK, here you go. Clean the bites with an alcohol pad and apply a couple of Band-Aids. You should be fine; just keep an eye on it."

Kaito bandages Kat's leg prior to the push off from Battleship Rock. They paddle downriver, watching anything that moves within the foliage. A black-eared kite sits perched high above in a tree limb, eyeballing the kayaks slipping past, and Justin captures a terrific photograph of the raptor by maximizing the zoom on his phone's camera. He grew up watching animal documentaries on television with his grandfather and finds immense pleasure in the great outdoors.

The four kayakers complete their morning paddle without further incident and return to the hotel for a break. Kat enters the room she's sharing with Kaito and drops her belongings on the floor. "I'm going to take a shower and get rid of this jungle funk."

Justin and Kaito relax in the living area to enjoy a cold beverage and discuss this morning's outing. They hope for better luck this afternoon, kayaking Pinaisara Falls. Justin decides to sneak in a power nap and asks Kaito to wake him up when it's time to go.

Kat emerges from the washroom wearing a bathing suit covered by a sarong, clearly not typical hiking attire.

Kaito looks over at her. "We're going to leave fairly soon. Shouldn't you put on something more appropriate?"

"I'm really tired and don't have enough energy for another outing. Would you mind if I stay here to rest and maybe go to the beach? The long morning wore me out, plus these leech bites have started to itch, and I don't want them to get worse."

"Of course, that's completely understandable. Thanks again for coming along. I'm happy you're here with us."

She gives him a warm hug, followed by a soft kiss, and walks out the door with a beach bag in her hand.

Cole shows up at the room, and they wake Justin for operation kayak part two. The three companions load up and make a short drive to Funaura, a quaint little village that formerly served as one of the island's main ferry ports. These days, only local fishermen use the once-prominent ferry harbor, although it still acts as the starting point for excursions to Pinaisara Falls.

They stop by the local concierge desk to rent three single kayaks and paddle off into the bay. Halfway to their targeted destination, Justin spots movement in the mangrove trees and Cole veers off to shore, telling them to stay put in the slow-moving current. He beaches his kayak and walks over to a patch of mangroves overhanging the river. A small, red-coated mammal with black feet is curled up in a ball on a limb. Unfortunately, the animal is too high up for him to recognize the species, and he starts climbing the tree for a better look. When he reaches the second limb, the critter scurries up farther, and he gets a good glimpse of it. It's not a wildcat but rather a Japanese marten, an omnivorous mammal resembling a large ferret.

Cole is very disappointed the animal wasn't a wildcat and starts shaking the tree branch violently to vent his frustration. The frantic outburst stirs up a clan of sleeping monsters, and several two-inch-long Japanese giant hornets funnel out of a tiny hole in the tree. He scrambles down frantically and takes off running for the kayak, yelling out to the men floating offshore. "Go, go, go!" He quickly gets back on the water and rapidly paddles away from shore.

Justin and Kaito watch from their kayaks on the river, trying to figure out what the heck is going on. They see Cole swatting at the air above his head, and again at the back of his neck. When he makes it halfway to them, they can hear him call out. "We need to put some distance between us and the hornets. Hurry! Get going!"

Justin looks over at Kaito. "Did he say hornets? Oh no, let's get out of here!" He grabs his paddle and takes off upstream.

Kaito follows directly behind him calling out. "Faster. Go faster, Justin. I don't want to get stung!"

They paddle quite a way upriver, gradually slowing down to wait for Cole at what seems like a safe distance from "hornet beach." He trails behind them several lengths but eventually catches up.

"What happened back there?" asks Justin.

Cole scratches the back of his neck. "So stupid of me. I thought I saw a wildcat in the tree, but it was too high up, and I wasn't one hundred percent sure. I should have grabbed my binoculars for a closer look, but instead, I stirred up a hornets' nest of all things."

"All you all right?" asks Kaito.

"Yeah, I'm fine."

"Could you tell if it was a cat?"

"It looked like one, but it was a marten. Let's get a move on."

They continue kayaking upriver until eventually reaching the designated landing spot. Cole closes one eye to focus and fires an invisible bullet at the shoreline, splitting dead center on the crosshairs. Justin catches his drift and taps Kaito on the shoulder with his paddle, interrupting him from the monotony of paddling.

Cole makes three consecutive right-side strokes, causing his kayak to rotate forty-five degrees and resumes alternating side-to-side strokes straight at the beach. He lands onshore and waves the other two in behind him. Kaito comes in next and beaches his kayak. Justin comes ashore last to the sound of sand scratching and pebbles displacing beneath the kayak as the vessel comes to a grinding halt. He steps into the shallows, feeling the cool water trickle down into his boot, and ties off to the low-hanging limb of a sturdy mangrove tree.

With the watercrafts secured, they sit down on some dry rocks for a break. The weather has remained quite pleasant all day, but the first sizable downpour occurs now, only to quickly pass overhead. Kaito pulls out a couple of energy bars and tosses one to Justin as they refuel for the hike to the falls.

At a height of 180 feet, Pinaisara Falls checks in as the tallest waterfall in the Okinawa Prefecture. In local dialect, *pinai* means beard and *sara* means waterfall, hence the translated name, meaning "looks like white beard." The idea being, the waterfalls appear like the long white beard of an old man at a distance. From the pool plunge below, one can see an overwhelming view of the falls high above, and in olden times, the scenic location was a place where islanders offered prayers for rain. Reaching the top requires an additional hike, where a magnificent, panoramic view of the island awaits.

"You guys ready? We're running out of daylight and need to keep moving," says Cole.

Kaito scrambles to his feet and walks over to the trail entrance. Justin slowly rises, feeling somewhat fatigued, and joins them. They make the hike up to the falls where the pool plunges by late afternoon. An intense sound of water crashing down echoes throughout the moss-lined, rocky gorge. Mist and spray explode everywhere, spritzing into the air. Water runoff has formed a large, naturally made swimming pool that funnels into a stream.

A group of five sit around a large boulder overhanging the pool, drying out their shoes and socks. Kaito yells out a greeting from a distance and waves. A man standing on the rock waves back at him, and the two carry on a conversation. The hiker explains that they just trekked back down from the waterfall and advises him not to make the climb up, considering how dangerous some of the sections were at this time of day.

Meanwhile, Justin is busy exploring, carefully stepping from rock to rock. He feels a slight cramp in his right calf and sits down to massage his leg. Kaito walks over next to him, looking up at the waterfall, enjoying the sensation of mist touching his face.

"I'm not walking up there today."

"My thoughts exactly," replies Justin.

Cole rejoins the cousins, and the three men unanimously agree not to hike the falls. Instead, they opt for a turnaround trip and immediately start trekking back out. Dusk arrives on cue, toting a five-mile-per-hour breeze that gently rustles through the vegetation. Scattered gray clouds brushed in warm pink punctuate the skyline as the sun slips farther behind the Earth's ever-so-slight rotation.

Justin suddenly realizes he forgot his hat back on the rocks. "Oh man, I left my hat back at the falls. Wait here for me and I'll jog back to get it."

Kaito offers to go with him, and the two double back up the trail.

Justin spots his hat on the rocks from far away. "Cool, I can already see it from here."

By the time they finally make it to the pool plunge, his hat has somehow disappeared. Justin looks around in disbelief, wondering where it could have gone. Something catches his attention out of the corner of his eye, and he looks right to see an elusive Iriomote wildcat sniffing his baseball hat.

Kaito bumps Justin on the elbow. "I guess she likes your hat."

The cat hears him speak and stands frozen in time, staring directly at them.

* * *

"Shh. Hold still," says Justin. "We don't want to scare her away."

After a brief stare off, the agile feline makes three stealthy leaps to double the distance between them.

Kaito lowers his hand. "Here, kitty, kitty, kitty."

The cat turns to look in their direction and takes another extraordinarily far leap onto an embankment, then slowly struts in the direction of the jungle. They grab Justin's hat on the rocks and watch the wildcat brush up against a tree limb disappearing into the thick foliage. They continue in hot pursuit, carefully stepping across to the area where she slipped away.

Kaito looks around and investigates a fallen tree nearby, kneeling down at one point to have a peek inside the dinner plate–size hole. He sees a slender, brownish-olive scaled snake curled up several feet in and carefully steps back after recognizing the species. "There's a super poisonous pit viper inside. Getting bit by one of those would be a nightmare, especially this far out in the middle of nowheresville."

Justin cautiously moves next to him, and they simultaneously kneel to look for the snake from a distance. Much to their dismay, the reptile has vanished, leaving them perplexed at the snake's whereabouts.

Kaito stands up and sees the pit viper is now resting on top of the fallen tree. He notices the snake is clutching something in its tail and slowly pulls Justin up by the back of his shirt. "Do you believe in karma?"

Justin rises up and sees the serpent. "I believe in destiny if that's what you mean."

The surrounding foliage seemingly vibrates with energy, and the canopy above closes tightly together. The snake gracefully stretches out to reveal a total body length of eight feet with yellow, pulsating stripes across its scales. Next to the serpent lies a tiny, brown, drawstring pouch slightly larger than an acorn.

The pit viper violently wraps its tail around the pouch, coils back together, and springs forward, flipping itself onto a nearby tree branch. The snake begins to speak to them in a raspy voice. "I sense the adrenaline running through your veins."

An overwhelming sensation of curiosity and fear complicates the men's minds as they motionlessly observe the snake's every move. The pit viper drops down from the branch and performs several somersaults in their direction, all the while keeping a tight grip on the pouch. Frozen and unable to move, they continue watching helplessly as the snake approaches, partially uncurls, and flips the pouch in the air. The serpent quickly slithers between them, leaps up to snatch the pouch, and scales back up the fallen tree.

The snake lisps and hisses its words. "You humans are an infant species that relies on traditional methods of perception."

The viper crawls to the edge of the tree stump and pulls itself upright, revealing its white underbelly while still holding on to the pouch with its tail. "Sight, sound, touch, taste, and smell are all ordinary senses possessed by most life-forms."

After pausing to flick its tongue back and forth several times, the snake continues in a raspy voice that now sounds feminine. "But no other animal is blessed with extrasensory perception, ESP, a sixth sense, or second sight. You must learn to develop those skills and trust your instincts."

Kaito flashes back to a childhood memory. He is seven years old and with his parents at an outdoor celebration. His mother is wearing a white summer dress dotted with cherry blossoms, and his father has on a gray business suit. They are peacefully strolling hand in hand, smiling, laughing, in love. Young Kaito runs ahead and stops to admire a stone water well.

His mother calls out to him in a soft, lovely voice, encouraging him to return. "Kaito, Kaito."

Always curious by nature, Kaito runs over to a nearby shrine just a few steps ahead, where several people are gathered in worship of a water kami. He visualizes the kanji written on the stone well, and the name Suijin runs through his mind.

The pit viper rolls backward, curls into a ball, and begins speaking in a masculine voice, seeming to have read Kaito's mind. "Am I Suijin? No, I am not Suijin. We are all Suijin." A variety of snakes, eels, turtles, and flopping fish appear from the forest, surrounding them.

Suijin, meaning water people or water deity, refers to heavenly and earthly manifestations of the benevolent Shinto god of water. Also referred to as Suiten by Buddhists, the water kami is widely revered in Japan as a guardian of fishing folk and a preserver of pure, unpolluted water for human consumption, as well as for other uses, like agriculture and sanitation. Suijin is celebrated at many festivals and typically enshrined near rice patties, irrigation canals, mountain streams, rivers, agricultural waterways, and wells.

Still curled up in a stationary position, the snake continuously fiddles with the pouch, constantly clinging to it in varying ways, twisting and curling around the object. The viper speaks to them again, but this time the voice is feminine. "From now on, you shall call me Habu." The animals start backing up and disappearing into the jungle.

The viper puffs its head and neck to resemble a king cobra hood and methodically weaves from side to side. Now Habu speaks in the masculine voice. "I have a riddle for you today. If you can solve it, the pouch is yours. Choose incorrectly and it stays with me." The snake inches close to Kaito's face. "To even the odds, only you will be allowed to participate." In the blink of an eye, Habu strikes Justin on the left forearm, injecting a dose of high-toxicity venom containing cytotoxin. The serpent coils back to a crouched position and looks over at Kaito. "Guess incorrectly three times and your friend here will suffer the consequences."

A burning sensation electrifies Justin's arm, and two marks made by the snake's fangs begin glowing a deep red, resembling droplets of volcanic lava. He stands motionless, unable to speak, locked in a trance.

Habu proceeds to speak a riddle in the feminine voice. "Through winds of time, hope blows, spreading change. A unified, elemental grandmaster that forms tangible realities. Shape-shifting, tide-altering, resilient mechanisms that platform life. What am I?"

Looking over to see Justin suffering in pain, Kaito closes his eyes, channels his thoughts, and takes a first guess. "Dreams!"

Justin groans loudly, crying out in agony from the burning sensation within. His forearm instantly swells from the snakebite as blood pulsates through his enlarged artery, causing a spiderweb of veins to appear running up to his shoulder and down to his fingertips.

Habu replies in an agitated, masculine voice, spitting venom on Kaito's shoe. "Wrong answer, mortal." The snake's eyes double in size. "Two more guesses; choose wisely."

Kaito hears an elderly man's voice inside his head. "We are lost without focus." He channels his thoughts and begins envisioning triangular patterns that occur in nature. The images rapidly fire off in his mind. Mount Fiji, an orca fin, the geometry of spiderwebs, crystals, shark teeth, and a cat's ears. One final image appears of his great-grandfather Saito and his long, gray beard shaped in an upside-down triangle.

Kaito visualizes a brilliant gem and takes his second guess. "Diamonds."

Justin cries out in excruciating pain. The bright-red snakebite puffs up a quarter inch and shape-shifts into an ominous, triangular-patterned face.

Kaito has a final flashback, remembering a lovely morning spent with his parents at the beach. The three of them are sitting on the shore, using plastic shovels and buckets to build a sandcastle. The image flashes to Kaito and his mother burying his father in the sand, leaving only his head and toes aboveground. Suddenly, the incoming high tide delivers a sizeable wave that comes crashing down and topples over them. They help uncover his father and frolic in the ocean to rinse off. After exiting the water, they wrap up in dry towels and sit down on a beach blanket. Kaito recalls the gentle stroke of his mother's hand clearing sand from his cheek, remembering her unconditional love and support.

The image fades, and he suddenly feels an electrifying sensation radiate down from his neck into both arms and out through his fingertips. "Sand. My answer is sand!"

Justin is abruptly released from the trance, and the intense pain from the venom subsides. The swelling on his arm goes down, and an overall sense of relief sets in. However, the triangular-shaped face remains on his forearm, scarred into his skin.

"Wise beyond your years," hisses Habu in the masculine voice. The viper whips his tail, flinging the pouch at Kaito, who reaches out and snatches the object.

The snake returns to the feminine voice and proceeds to explain the contents found within the pouch. "The bag contains a handful of star sand dusted with magic." Habu flicks her tongue a few times in Justin's direction before continuing. "Much like that sap he possesses, this sand contains immense power that must be learned. In your hand lies a gateway to every single species of water life on Earth. Learn to wield this great ability through practice, for one day you might be called upon to demonstrate what you have acquired."

Star sand is found on several southern Ryukyu islands. The tiny grains are the shells of microscopic, single-celled organisms called hole bearers who produce a calcium carbonate shell with either one or multiple chambers. Live hole bearers are primarily marine creatures, although some live in brackish waters, feeding on small organisms such as bacteria.

Habu concludes, "Remember these words closely, for this is the last you will hear of me. Respect your ancestors, embrace the future, and fuse them together in the present."

The pit viper shakes violently, losing her animated appearance and transforming back into a regular snake. The pulsating, bright-yellow stripes stop moving, her eyes shrink, and the serpent's size returns to normal. The snake crawls through a patch of leaves and disappears into a field.

Kaito opens the pouch for a quick look at the glistening star sand and runs over to assist his cousin. "Are you all right? Can you speak?"

Justin bends and twists his arm a few times to test it for pain. "It's tender, but I'll live. Let's keep this between us." He removes a long-sleeve flannel shirt from his backpack and puts it on to cover up his forearm.

They reunite with Cole for the return paddle downriver in relative darkness but eventually see a glimmer of hope when the first port city lights appear. When they reach the landing spot, two men guide them to shore and assist with offloading. They hop back into the SUV and make a short drive to the hotel in silence. Cole turns off the ignition. "Sorry we couldn't find any wildcats today. Shall we meet for breakfast tomorrow? The restaurant on the corner has really tasty food."

Kaito grabs his bag and steps out of the vehicle. "Don't worry about it. We had a blast regardless. See you in the morning."

* * *

Meanwhile, Kat is sketching butterflies at the kitchen table when they enter the hotel room and is happy to see they have returned. "Yay, you're back. There's food in the fridge if you guys are hungry. A nice lady at the front desk suggested the restaurant on the corner."

Justin makes his way to the bathroom and carefully unwraps the bandage. He strips down and takes a long shower, enjoying the simple pleasure of warm water running over his body. Dirt, grime, sweat, and a bit of blood funnel down the drain near his feet.

Back in the kitchen, Kaito enjoys a fish and noodle dish while listening to Kat share a story about her afternoon at the beach. Justin wanders in to make a plate and sits down next to them at the table. After Kat finishes her story, he opens up a new conversation. "What do you think about extending the trip tomorrow and inviting Cole to join us to Mount Oyama?"

Kaito slurps in a noodle with an exaggerated noise. "I like the guy. He's quite the knowledgeable outdoorsman. If Cole is available and willing, my answer is yes. We can use his experience along the way, especially in unfamiliar territory. Right now I'm beat and could really use a good night's sleep to clear my thoughts."

"Great, we agree, then. Let's pitch him the offer tomorrow at breakfast."

Perplexed at their intentions moving forward, Kat glances at each of them. "You guys are planning a trip tomorrow to Mount Oyama? Wow, that's a lot of traveling!"

Kaito looks up at Justin from his noodle bowl, sets down the chopsticks, and turns his full attention to Kat. "Justin intends to visit as many locations as possible during his time in Japan. Mount Oyama came up in conversation and we settled on visiting the island next. Do you want to join us?"

Kat reaches down to massage her sore leg. "Let me sleep on it. My leg needs to rest, and I'm just not sure how well it will hold up."

Justin wakes in the morning to find Kaito and Kat sitting outside, dressed, and ready for the day. He joins them for a bit of fresh air before taking off for breakfast. Once across the street, they enter a small restaurant and sit next to Cole at a back-corner table. The waitress pours them each a glass of water and takes their order.

Kaito waits for her to walk out of earshot and slides Cole an envelope containing their agreed-upon amount for his services. Cole reaches out for the envelope, thumbs through the bills, and places the money inside his coat pocket. The waitress drops off their breakfast, and they eagerly dig in, while Kaito pitches Cole the idea of joining them for a couple more days.

Although he is unfamiliar with the island, their offer piques his interest. "I have a prior commitment tomorrow for an all-day hike. But if I can find the party an alternative guide, maybe, just maybe, I'll go. For the right price, of course." He winks at Kaito.

5

DEVIL'S SEA

Kat wakes in the middle of the night with a fever. Mild swelling and redness have formed on her leg surrounding the leech bites, and she takes three ibuprofen in hopes of reducing her temperature and to help subdue the pain caused from the infection. After cleaning the area with a rubbing alcohol pad, she gathers ice into a ziplock bag and lies back down, placing the pack on top of her head. She eventually falls back to sleep only to rise at daybreak dripping in a pool of sweat. She informs Kaito of her condition, and they agree it's best for her to go home to seek medical attention. She takes a cool shower and packs up, giving Kaito just enough time to change her travel itinerary. Fortunately, a jetfoil to Kyushu departs shortly with an available seat.

Kaito escorts her outside to wait for a taxi, and they embrace in a long hug before she gets into the car. "Are you sure you will be all right getting home alone? I feel bad not coming with you."

"I'll be fine. Take care of your cousin, and I will see you in a few days." She closes the door and waves goodbye as the cab slowly pulls away.

Cole shows up, and the men depart for Miyakejima, where Kaito has booked them a three-night stay at a bed-and-breakfast with modest accommodations.

Miyakejima is located 110 miles off the coast of Honshu near Tokyo and is within the northern tip of the Dragon's Triangle, aka the Devil's Sea. The invisible lines of this mysterious area are shaped in a floating triangular pattern stretching from the base of Japan to Guam and finally Luzon in the Philippine Sea. This area is one of the twelve vile vortices in the world, where the pull of the planet's electromagnetic waves is the strongest. Several boats and planes have mysteriously disappeared here over the years, with many people even claiming to have seen ghostships at sea there.

At the center of the island stands Mount Oyama, an active volcano measuring more than 2,500 feet high. Thirteen eruptions have occurred over the past five hundred years, most recently in the summer of 2000. Since that time there has been a constant flow of sulfur dioxide gas coming from the volcano.

After the plane touches down, they secure a rental car and stop by a recently opened hot springs en route to the hotel. An attractive twenty-year-old woman stands behind a desk dressed in khaki shorts and a white golf shirt. She greets them with a warm welcome, collects a moderate fee, and shows them to the men's facilities.

Kaito and Cole sit down inside a ninety-nine-degree Fahrenheit pool, but Justin has his mind set on the hot one. He enjoys a brief foot massage from the smooth stone floor on his way to the window-front bath, where a sign warns patrons of the intensely hot water. He grabs hold of the metal handrail for support, cautiously steps into the ankle-deep blistering water, and quickly steps out. An old man with long gray hair tied into a ponytail looks over at him, grinning from within the pool, and rests his head back down on a rolled towel.

Another guest speaks up in a British accent. "It takes some getting used to."

"I'll say. How hot is the water?"

"I'm guessing one hundred eight degrees Fahrenheit. With the temperature this high, most people only stay in for a minute or two, including me." He steps out of the water, picks up his towel, and walks off.

Justin takes a deep breath and makes two bold steps down into the hot water. He walks around to an empty spot in the corner and sits on the ledge of the pool to allow his body some time to adjust. After dangling his feet momentarily, he musters up some courage and submerges shoulder high in the intensely hot spring water. "This feels like torture. I can't believe people enjoy water so hot."

Two men exit the bath, leaving only Justin and the old man on opposite ends of the pool. Four others approach casually talking among themselves and begin getting accustomed to the water. Justin decides he has had enough and makes his way over to the enclosed pool and sitting area outdoors. The old man eyeballs him on the way by, then rests his head back down on the towel.

Once outside, Justin stretches out on a woven lounge chair, and the steady onshore breeze quickly helps cool down his overheated body. He takes a mental photograph of the exquisite tropical landscape and remains outdoors to observe the sunset. Shortly thereafter, a warning is issued over the loudspeaker, informing guests the hot springs will be closing momentarily. He reunites with the others in the locker room, and they wander out front to check out.

The same young woman from earlier engages Kaito and Cole in a discussion about their visit. Their brief conversation in Japanese ends with a couple of laughs, and she turns to Justin, speaking English with a twinkle in her eye. "So, how was your experience today here at the hot springs?"

He finds her especially attractive and replies in a shy manner. "Good. Thanks for asking. I'm glad we decided to give this place a try."

"I'm happy to hear you enjoyed it. How long are you here on the island?"

"Three days. My cousin and I flew over from Kyushu with a friend for some sightseeing."

Kaito nudges Cole on the shoulder and addresses the young lady. "Thanks again for everything. Have a good evening!" They walk out the front door to the car, leaving Justin inside.

She waves goodbye to them. "What else do you have planned on your vacation?"

Justin glances at her name tag. "Well, Yori, tomorrow morning we are going to have a look at Tairo Pond, maybe do a bit of hiking, and, if time allows, pay the lighthouse a visit."

"Tairo Pond is fantastic! A great place to explore nature and go for a swim. I grew up on the island and know the area quite well. If you have any questions on the rest of your stay, don't hesitate to call me." She grabs a business card from the desk and writes down her cell number on the back. "I'm off the next couple of days, but you can try to get hold of me here if anything comes up."

Justin reaches out to receive the card, and a static electricity charge zaps their fingertips. "I appreciate the offer. That's very kind of you." He stares down at the business card, then looks back up. "Well, I had better get going. My friends are waiting in the car. We still have to check into our hotel. Thanks again for the kind gesture."

She smiles brightly with flushed cheeks. "You are more than welcome."

Justin nervously taps the card in his hand a couple of times, programs her number into his cell, and tests out the line of communication by texting her a smiley face emoji. "It's been nice meeting you. Have a good evening." He exits out the front and glances back over his shoulder for one last look at Yori just as the door closes.

Kaito shifts the car into drive and slowly pulls back onto the main highway. "So, what's up with the girl from the hot springs?"

"You mean Yori? She's supercool. Grew up around here, apparently. Anyway, I told her we are vacationing here for a few days and she gave me her number to call if I have any questions during the trip."

"She gave you her number?" replies Kaito. "Brave girl to trust a troublemaker like yourself."

"Yeah, it seems she's off the next couple of days and—"

Kaito interrupts him in midsentence. "Let me get this straight. She gave you her personal number, mentioned being off work the next couple of days, and left you with an open-ended invitation to call if you need anything?"

"That's basically how it went down."

Kaito laughs out loud and playfully smacks Justin on the shoulder. "Cousin, cousin, cousin. Do I have to teach you everything in life? She clearly was flirting with you and hinting at the possibility of hanging out together."

Thinking it through, Justin realizes Kaito is probably right. For whatever reason, he feels strongly drawn to Yori and has every intention of giving her a call at one point or another.

Upon reaching the hotel, an elderly woman dressed in blue jeans and a black sweatshirt escorts them upstairs to their room. She unlocks the door and flips on the lights to reveal a ten-by-thirty, rectangular-shaped studio. The room lacks any traditional beds, with guests expected to sleep on the tatami mat flooring. After informing them of some vending machines downstairs, the pleasant woman wishes them a good evening and closes the door. Justin walks over to the farthest pile of linens and sets down his luggage next to a sliding glass door that opens to a small balcony. The other guys place their belongings on opposite ends of the room and sit on the floor, exhausted from the long day. Within half an hour, everyone has dozed off.

The loud thud of a car door slamming wakes Justin from a deep sleep. He stands up, yawns, and opens the sliding glass door for some fresh air. The sun is shining brightly in a cloudless sky that is painted in shades of morning blues. He steps out onto the tiny balcony overlooking the ocean to see Kaito and Cole eating breakfast downstairs.

Kaito looks up. "Come join us. There's food in the lobby."

"OK, I'll be right there."

Justin wanders downstairs full of energy from a good night's sleep. Much to his surprise, Yori is standing behind the front desk, speaking to the woman who checked them in the night before. He quietly approaches, trying not to interrupt, and waits for the right moment to greet the two ladies. "Good morning."

They both look straight up at him, and the older woman responds. "Hello, sir. How may I help you?"

Yori mentions something to the woman in Japanese that Justin doesn't understand and then turns to speak with him. She is a very charismatic, polite, friendly person who works well with the public. "Hi, Justin. Nice to see you again." She radiates a glow of happiness.

"Did you stay here last night as well?" he asks.

"No, no. My grandparents own this hotel, and I live with them in the back house. Would you like something to eat?"

Justin glances over at the lady and back to Yori. "Sure. That would be great."

"OK. Follow me and I will show you."

She walks around from behind the front desk wearing a black tank top with a green sarong wrapped around her waist. She has a mesh beach bag slung over one shoulder, and sunglasses hold back her long black hair. "Right this way."

Justin looks over at the lady behind the desk, who has begun to nervously shuffle through some pieces of paper. He follows Yori across the room to a buffet table spread with fresh-cut fruit, toast, egg rolls, and assorted beverages.

"All the fruit is grown here, and my grandmother squeezes the orange juice each and every morning for her guests. Please help yourself."

Justin pours a cup of tea and gestures to Yori, offering her one.

"Oh no, thank you. My friend will be here any moment. We're going to the beach today."

A moped pulls into the parking lot on cue, stops in front of the building, and honks the squeaky horn twice.

"That's my ride. Gotta go."

"Have fun at the beach," replies Justin.

Yori walks over to the front door and stops with her foot halfway outside. "Maybe we will bump into each other this afternoon, and you can tell me all about your day." She slips outside, slides onto the moped behind the driver, and speeds off down the highway.

Justin walks out back to the grass courtyard carrying a plate of food and coincidentally passes by the same old man from the hot springs who wore his hair in a ponytail. They both recall

Justin's embarrassing moment of toe-tapping the hot water yesterday, and the old man once again rolls his eyes at him.

Justin sits at the table and listens to Kaito and Cole discussing today's trip to the pond. Apparently, Kaito has done some research online early this morning and has been sharing some of the information. "I was just explaining to Cole how Tairo Pond is a large pool of fresh water formed in a crater that was created by an eruption nearly two thousand years ago. The pond is ninety feet deep and surrounded by a primeval forest that is home to more than two hundred species of wild birds." He wipes his face with a napkin and tosses it onto the plate.

Cole gets up from the table. "I'm headed upstairs to finish preparing for today's expedition. See you in a bit."

Kaito turns his full intention to Justin. "According to the stone etchings, we are supposed to be searching for a deer up at Mount Oyama, but that seems unrealistic for a couple of reasons. One, we can't get up there because of the poisonous gas leaking out of the volcano, and two, according to what I read, no deer live on this island."

"None of what's happening makes a whole lot of sense right now. But I have a feeling if we continue to trust ourselves and stay focused, life will bring us what we seek."

"That sounds like a fortune cookie."

Justin tries to remain positive. "Mount Oyama makes up most of the island, so technically, we are already here, right?"

They finish breakfast and gear up for a long day of adventure seeking. Once inside the car, Kaito leans his head against the window and quickly dozes off with Kat on his mind. She made the trip home safely and went to the medical clinic. A doctor inspected the leech bites, cleansed the area properly, and prescribed antibiotics to counter the minor infection.

Cole breaks a long silence in the car ride. "The pond is supposed to have some nice sandy beaches with easy water access. What do you say we first venture out on a hike along the Kazan Taiken Walking Trail and then stop for a swim on our way back?"

The Kazan Taiken, meaning volcanic eruption, is a walking trail built on top of a thousand-square-acre lava field Mother Nature created during a sizable volcanic eruption that buried four hundred residences. The trail offers a close-up view of the buried village, including ruins from the elementary and junior high schools. A stark reminder to visitors of the true devastation caused by such a powerfully eruptive force.

They enter the boardwalk and set off on a two-hour, round-trip hike along the barren trail. Lava flow decimated all plant life during the eruption many years ago, but a select few species have somehow found a way to adapt and thrive within the hardened black rock.

Kaito reads from a handout picked up back at the trailhead. "In a couple of hundred yards, we will start to see the remains from the Ako district. This pamphlet recommends stopping at the lookout point."

The trail takes them up and over rolling mounds of lava rock en route. They come across a small flock of frolicking finches in a nearby shrub, and Justin stops momentarily to admire the birds as the other two continue walking. The open terrain is very straightforward, making it practically impossible to get lost.

A single olive-green finch flies out from the group and lands on a thin, leafless tree branch right beside him. The bold little creature lets out a loud screech to silence the entire flock and initiates a lovely birdsong. Justin listens in delight to the complex sounds produced from the friendly songbird and wonders what it might be trying to say.

A buzzing sound alerts him to an incoming text, and he wrestles out his cell phone from a zippered pocket of his backpack. He notices the unusual phone number and is pleasantly surprised to find a message from Yori.

"My grandparents are preparing a sunset dinner for the guests back at the hotel. Would you like to meet up with me for a bite to eat?"

He sends her back a quick reply. "Thanks for the invite, and I'll most definitely see you then."

Justin snaps a quick photo of the finch to capture the moment and gets back on the trail. Far off in the distance, a siren starts blaring, and he wonders what is going on. The sound reminds him of the tsunami-warning sirens back home in Hawaii, but that's not a tsunami warning; it's a gas leak alert.

6

THE RUINS

Several years before, equipment was installed to monitor the levels of hazardous gas Mount Oyama constantly leaks out. When the toxic fumes reach a certain level of endangerment, the sirens blow a warning to immediately seek shelter. In fact, not long ago, island residents were required to carry gas masks with them at all times.

Justin looks across the lava field to see approximately twenty people scrambling in panic mode for the trailhead. A man and his two teenage boys jog by, and one of them yells out, "Run!"

Up at the lookout point, among the chaos, Kaito catches a glimpse of what appears to be three small wolves crouched down in a stalking manner and slowly moving in the direction of the junior high school ruins. He watches the pack slip out of sight behind an old, crumbling block wall. Kaito is perplexed by what he sees, considering wolves have been extinct in Japan for more than one hundred years. He bravely decides to duck under the handrail and make the short walk down instead of following behind Cole and the scrambling hikers.

Back on the trail, Justin decides to take the advice of the father and sons and starts hustling out. The black lava rock is extremely sharp and falling could result in a significant injury. Having grown up in Hawaii, Justin learned to maneuver on the rocks barefoot as a child, and he methodically weaves down the trail in no time.

A few hundred yards back, Cole leads the group of frightened hikers down the trail at a steady clip. He notices a young mother struggling to carry her crying toddler and quickly drops back, offering to help. She accepts his kind gesture, allowing him to hoist up the child in his arms, and they resume running down the trail together until they reach the parking lot. Justin is standing by their rental car, holding a shirt over his nose and mouth to avoid breathing any harmful fumes.

Suddenly, the sirens shut off, and a man steps out from one of the nearby parked cars waving his hands and yelling, "It's a false alarm! It's a false alarm! The radio says it's a false alarm." In disbelief, most people continue racing to their vehicles and drive off down the highway. But word spreads quickly that, indeed, it was just a false alarm after a federal agency issues an official statement of apology, blaming the siren blasts on a system malfunction.

Cole unlocks the car door and sits in the front seat. He turns on the radio and listens to the broadcast station repeating a false alarm statement. "Incredible. What a gigantic mistake by the monitoring system. People are going to be furious, and someone will surely get canned for this one."

Justin sits down in the car, trying to absorb what just happened, and realizes Kaito is nowhere to be found. "When was the last time you saw Kaito?"

Cole looks around the parking lot but doesn't see him anywhere. "Last I recall, we were standing side by side back at the viewpoint, and the sirens went off. We must have been separated in the confusion."

"Do you think we should go look for him or wait here at the car?"

"Why don't we give it another few minutes and if he doesn't show up, we'll go find him."

Over by the lookout, Kaito stands still, listening closely for any unusual sounds. He scans the perimeter, searching for any signs of movement, and when the warning siren is turned off, a grunting noise from animals panting nearby is revealed. An eerie sensation jolts through his spine, causing goose bumps to spread across his shoulders and arms. Kaito reaches into his pocket and removes the small bag of star sand. He gives the pouch a light toss from one hand to the other, then replaces it in his pocket. The exercise reduces his anxiety level, and he focuses his attention back to finding the wolflike creatures. Unbeknownst to him, each piece of star sand within the pouch has begun to glisten brightly, resembling sunlight reflecting off a diamond.

Kaito senses movement coming from behind him, and he turns around to see that a white crane has just landed. The large bird sits perched on a boulder and stares down at him. He hears rustling in the bushes and spins around to witness a lumbering tortoise appear from the shrub. Then, in unison, the three gray wolves lurk out from different directions and begin circling him in a twenty-foot radius. Their eyes are glowing fluorescent green, and purple drool oozes out from the corners of their snarling mouths. The old saying hungry wolves make better hunters seems all too real, and Kaito starts to feel like the prey.

"Get back!" Kaito flinches at them like a street fighter taunting his opponent prior to a scuffle.

One of the wolves loudly snaps back, clasping her jaws together in a fierce grimace, and a few drops of purple saliva fly into some shrub, disintegrating the leaves and branches. Kaito roars loudly at the beasts, flapping his arms, trying to scare them off. He quickly analyzes his predicament and comes up with two options: fight or flight. Biding his time, he studies the pack's movement and notices a sizable gap between two wolves. At just the right moment, he dashes past them and cuts around the corner of a crumbling brick wall. He then takes a quick right, followed by two lefts, and winds up inside the remnants of an old classroom. The roof, doors, and interior contents all had been burned away in a fire caused by the lava flow; only the walls remain.

With his back against the wall, Kaito listens closely and can hear the pack's footsteps and snarls fading away in the opposite direction. He remains still and peers around the doorway to see the coast is clear. Kaito exhales a sigh of relief, leans his head back against the wall, and slides down to sit on the ground. His phone suddenly rings, and he quickly reaches down to silence the incoming call after just the first ring. He remains still, listening attentively for any unusual sounds. Thankfully, the wolf pack must be too far away to hear the ring tone.

He stands back up and sees all three wolves lurking on top of the eight-foot walls. A large male calmly sits between two females with drawn canines. After making eye contact with Kaito, the agile male impressively leaps across to an adjacent wall and casually drops to the ground. The two females jump down and flank him on either side.

Back at the trailhead, Justin and Cole have begun to worry and decide to move forward with plan B. Justin attempts to call Kaito, but he gets sent to voicemail after the first ring. "He didn't answer my call, and I don't see him anywhere on the trail. I'm starting to get worried."

Cole steps out of the car and looks around. "Here's what we're going to do. You stay here at the car and wait to see if he turns up, and I'll work my way back to the lookout."

Meanwhile, Kaito prepares to defend himself against the wolf pack. He notices a pair of loose rocks about the size of a grapefruit, picks one up in each hand, and hurls them one at a time. The first rock misses high and left, skimming past the male's head. Kaito's second attempt appears dead on target at the female, but she rolls over on her side to dodge the incoming rock.

Now less than ten feet away, the canines are certainly within lunging distance, and Kaito fears the worst is yet to come. He calls out loudly, trying to scare them off. "Go away. What do you want from me?" Trying to outrun them seems pointless, so he calls out again. "I guess it's now or never."

Kaito grabs another rock and runs straight at the big male, hoping to crack him first and deal with the other two afterward. He swings hard with all his might and completely misses as a man's voice loudly calls out in a thunderous, echoing tone, "Vanish," and the wolves disappear, leaving behind miniature whirlwinds of vapor where they once stood.

Half a mile from the lookout point, Cole continues pressing forward at a steady rate, constantly scanning the perimeter for any signs of Kaito. He passes a group of five tourists and asks them if they have seen anyone fitting his description, but they have not. He eventually reaches the same railing they leaned against and faintly hears Kaito call out, far off in the distance. Recognizing the sound came from the ruins, Cole slips under the railing and scurries his way down.

Back inside the ruined school, Kaito wakes up facedown in a small pool of blood. To combat the wolves, he swung so hard that he lost his footing and fell to the ground, striking his forehead. The impact opened a small gash across his left eyebrow and left him temporarily unconscious.

Kaito slowly sits up, dazed and confused and with a staggering headache. He reaches up to feel his eye, looks back at his hand to see his fingers partially covered in blood, and removes his shirt to hold it against the wound. He starts to hear a clickity-clack, clickity-clack sound resembling that of a horse's hooves and turns to his right just in time to witness an albino deer toe-tapping along the lava rocks. The oversize buck displays a magnificent set of antlers paired with an extraordinarily muscular body. Kaito stares at the animal in a cloud of admiration, noticing Mount Oyama standing proudly in the backdrop, and visualizes the kanji etched on the river rock.

Cole eventually makes his way down to the ruins but ends up walking to the elementary school instead of the junior high. The two share an adjoining piece of property that was once separated by a ballfield and a playground. He suddenly hears Kaito call out from the opposite direction and runs to the junior high, shouting, "Kaito. Kaito, can you hear me?"

Unfortunately, Kaito is still out of earshot. He remains seated on the old classroom floor, trying to recuperate from his fall while watching the albino buck graze on a patch of dry grass. When he finally attempts to stand, his knees buckle, and he sits right back down.

In the blink of an eye, an old man no more than three feet tall comes staggering into the classroom assisted by a knobby, wooden staff that dangles a rolled-up scroll tied with twine. He has a long, white beard that flows down his chest coming to a pointy tip and wears an extravagant gold robe accompanied by a matching scholar's headdress, a rope belt, and brown leather sandals. An intricately detailed folding fan is sticking out of his front pocket.

The large buck looks up from grazing and takes several purposeful strides to place himself between them. The old man speaks to the deer in a calm, positive tone as he twists the tip of his beard. "Now, now. It's all right. He doesn't want to hurt us."

He makes a clucking noise with his tongue and cheek, calling the deer to his side, and turns to speak politely with Kaito. "Shall we begin our conversation with the two most burning questions on your mind? Come on, don't be shy. Speak up."

Kaito straightens his posture. "All right, who are you?"

"Yes, good. See how easy that was? My name is Jurojin, and today is your lucky day! I see you have already met some of my closest companions." He pats the deer gently on top of his head.

Jurojin, a deity from China's Taoist pantheon, originated long ago as the "Old Man of the South Pole," or the personification of the Southern Polar Star. The Taoist god of longevity is often depicted carrying a scroll tied to his staff on which is written the lifespan of all living things. This scroll is also said to have a record of all good and bad deeds committed by all living beings. Essentially, the ancient document contains all the world's wisdom.

"And for your next question, you want to know if I am real. Correct?"

Kaito checks the balled-up shirt a few times to confirm his wound has stopped bleeding, then sets it on the ground beside him. "Yes, that's right."

Jurojin strokes the deer's head. "What I can tell you is this: those wolves you just saw were simply figments of your imagination, not real. The last of their kind roamed these lands nearly a century ago. Now, that cut over your eye...well, as you can feel, it's most definitely real. Intangible versus tangible, if you will." After a quick pause, he continues. "Would you mind if I ask you a question?"

"Yes, of course."

"When you were being harassed and chased by the ghostly beasts, did it move you emotionally?"

Kaito thinks about his question before answering. "Yes, most definitely."

"Then in some sense they were real to you, even if only in the moment. Reality is perception, what you want to believe. But remember, things are not always what they seem. So, back to your question. Am I real? It all depends on who you ask."

Jurojin pounds his staff into the lava rock, cracking a small section in two. Obeying his command, the crane takes flight and glides past him, snagging the scroll. The large white bird soars over Kaito and releases it to him on the flyby. Kaito instinctively reaches out with impeccable timing and grasps the rolled paper.

The old man waves his folding fan several times over the deer's antlers. The buck glances over at Kaito and struts off behind the brick wall, out of sight.

Cole can be heard calling out nearby. "Kaito. Kaito, can you hear me?"

Jurojin begins to speak. "Your friend will arrive here shortly, asking what just happened. Tell him you made a mistake by coming down here after the false alarm was issued. He'll ask you about your head injury, and you will reply that you tripped and fell jumping from rock to rock."

The old man starts a slow-paced walk in the direction where the deer disappeared. He stops just before turning the corner. "Take care of yourself. You have a mild concussion, and that cut will require stitching to properly heal. Oh yes, I almost forgot. Remember, in life we all must adapt to thrive and survive." He turns the corner but can still be heard one last time. "Don't misplace that scroll. You may need it someday."

Now that the old man has left, Kaito contemplates whether he should hike out alone or call for help. His mind remains rattled due to the headache from the fall and the mystery surrounding his brief encounter with Jurojin. Fortunately, Cole has located his whereabouts, and he can be heard calling out, "Kaito! Kaito, can you hear me? Holler back."

Relieved to hear Cole's voice, Kaito musters the strength to yell back, "This way! I'm over here."

Cole comes hustling through the doorway and sees Kaito in a bloody mess. He quickly removes his backpack, unzips the top pocket, and takes out a first aid kit. "Are you all right? What happened?"

"I stupidly decided to explore the ruins after the false alarm statement was issued. In the process, I slipped jumping from the rocks and hit my head. When I woke up, there was blood everywhere."

"All right, try to remain still and let me have a closer look at your head. You were probably knocked unconscious, and I think you have a concussion. I learned advanced first aid during my time in the military."

"The cut on my eyebrow just stopped bleeding. Do you have any water?"

Cole saturates some gauze pads in water and hands over his canteen. He then clears the dried blood from Kaito's forehead until he can clearly see the sizable gash. "Oh, you're gonna need stitches to close that up. I'll attach a makeshift butterfly bandage that should hold until we can get you to a hospital." He fetches two small bandages and applies them across Kaito's eyebrow to hold the wound closed. "All right, that should do it. Do you want to try to stand?"

"Yeah, I'm ready to give it a try. Help me up."

Cole grabs Kaito under the armpits and hoists him to his feet. "Are you all right?"

"I think so."

"Take a few steps to test your footing."

Kaito gingerly takes ten paces and turns around, then asks for some painkillers. Cole locates some ibuprofen in the first aid kit and hands it to him.

"OK. I think I'm ready to go. Let's get out of here," says Kaito.

Cole lends him an extra T-shirt from his backpack, sends Justin a quick text, and they begin to walk back out.

At the parking lot, Justin receives the message from Cole and grabs his binoculars to search the trail. He can see them lumbering along a quarter mile away, with their arms inter-locked at the elbow. They eventually return to the car and proceed directly to the local hospital. A doctor diagnoses Kaito with a midgrade concussion, sews up his eyebrow, and recommends he visit his primary care physician immediately upon returning home.

A nurse wheels Kaito out to the lobby with a small bandage concealing his newly stitched eyebrow. Justin looks up from a magazine and taps Cole, who has dozed off, on the elbow. "Doc said I should call it a day and get some rest. Would you mind taking me back to the hotel?"

Cole hustles outside to pull the car around, while Justin stays with his cousin.

Kaito waits for the nurse to leave. "I was fortunate enough to locate what we came for. We can discuss the details later, in private."

A surprised look appears on Justin's face, but he refrains from commenting and instead helps Kaito out to the car. On the drive back to the hotel, Kaito apologizes for having to cut the trip short to fly home tomorrow morning. The injuries are not severe enough to warrant arranging a flight this afternoon, nor does he have the energy to attempt it anyhow. During the conversation, Cole volunteers to accompany him the entire way back to Kyushu, and he gladly accepts.

Kaito looks over at Justin. "We booked the hotel room for two more nights if you want to stay. Maybe you can do some additional sightseeing."

"Yeah, I will probably do that. It may take a couple of days to update my travel arrangements back to Hawaii."

They return to the hotel at the same time Yori is getting dropped off. Justin watches her climb off the scooter, give the driver a big hug, and enter the back house. When the scooter drives past, he is pleasantly surprised to see a female driver.

The men carry Kaito's luggage upstairs for him. "Thanks again for everything. I truly appreciate what you guys did for me today. I'm going to take a shower, put on a fresh set of clothes, and relax."

Justin pats him on the shoulder. "Rumor has it the hotel owners are cooking up a sunset feast tonight. Maybe you can join us out back if you're feeling better. Otherwise, I can bring you up a plate later."

"I'll take a rain check on joining you for dinner, but the food sounds delicious if you want to bring me some." Kaito wanders off to shower.

"Poor guy. Hope he feels better soon. I'm going to check out Tairo Pond and have a swim. You wanna go?" Cole asks.

Although a swim sounds tempting, Justin can't stop thinking about Yori. "I'm gonna chill here. Maybe I'll see you later at dinner."

Cole turns around grinning and starts walking back downstairs. "Tell that girl I said hello."

"What girl? Wait. What?"

After Cole takes off, Justin decides to give Yori a call.

She answers on the second ring. "Hello, Justin."

"Hi, Yori. Sorry to bother you, but our day trip was cut short and, uh, I saw you returned. Are you doing anything right now? Do you want to maybe hang out for a while?" Justin can't believe how nervous he feels.

"Yeah, sure. I'm about to run an errand for my grandparents. Would you like to join me?"

"OK, that sounds great!"

"Come over to the back house, and we'll get going."

Justin makes his way over and bangs on the metal door knocker three times. Yori answers wearing a baggy pink T-shirt, low-cut white jean shorts, and a black baseball hat picturing a crescent moon on the front. She has a set of keys in one hand and her wallet in the other. Her cheeks are slightly pink from a mild sunburn, but her face glows with exuberance. "Hi, there! Shall we get going?"

They hop into her car and drive south on the main highway.

"So, where are we headed?" asks Justin.

"Friends of my grandparents own a fishing boat. The vessel just returned from an overnight trip loaded with kinmedai, and the crew has saved us a few for tonight's dinner."

"What are kinmedai?"

"A type of, how do you say, red snapper. My grandparents' favorite fish. Very good to eat!"

"I love snapper; it's so tasty. Especially pink snapper, which we call opakapaka in Hawaii."

"My grandparents typically prepare the fish three ways for dinner. First, they thinly slice some strips to place on top of a fingerling of rice, sashimi style. Then the heads are thrown into a large pot of water along with onions, garlic, bok choy, and spices to make a hearty soup. And last but not least, my favorite. They like to cook a few kinmedai whole by pouring boiling water over the fish to tenderizes the skin, which is eaten along with the delicious white meat."

"That sounds really good. You're making my mouth water. I can't wait for dinner tonight."

Justin proceeds to share a story about his father being an executive chef at a resort in Maui. He talks about life growing up with a parent possessing a unique set of kitchen skills and how incredibly well they ate on a daily basis. Not necessarily big, extravagant, seven-course meals but consistent, quality food made with fresh, local ingredients.

They arrive at the port and park in front of the small processing plant. Various fishing boats are tied up to the concrete pier where deckhands offload the catch in small baskets.

"Come on. You can carry the fish," says Yori.

They enter the building through a side door, which reveals several people engaged in various processing activities. Yori points to a back office, indicating their direction. Justin is looking around, trying to absorb his surroundings, and nearly collides with a forklift that buzzes past him carrying baskets of fish to a weigh station in the corner. They walk by a row of bins containing fish on ice and eventually reach the back office, where Yori tells Justin to wait outside the door.

He sits down on a metal bench and continues to observe the commotion on what seems to have been a good day of fishing for the small fleet. Yori appears from the office with a man in his late sixties. The two exchange a hug, and he returns to work. "My uncle is the general manager and good friends with most of the boat owners. He said one of the employees will bring the fish around."

She sits on the bench next to Justin, and they share a few laughs about how fishy it smells inside the plant. A stocky teenage boy comes walking around the corner wearing orange fisherman's overalls. He is carrying a cardboard box with both hands, and it appears quite heavy, considering how much his muscular biceps are flexing. Yori jumps up to say hello when the guy approaches and sets down the box. He peels back the thick, plastic lining inside to reveal several quality snappers on ice and then closes everything up, gives them a quick peace sign, and takes off.

"That's my cousin," says Yori. "Would you mind carrying the box? Be careful, it's kind of heavy."

"Sure, no problem." He bends over and picks up the fifty-pound box. "Lead the way."

Yori guides him through the processing plant and back outside the door through which they entered. She pops open the trunk for Justin to set down the box of fish, and they walk across the street to a farmers market to pick up a sack of produce. By the time they return to the hotel, it's nearly three o'clock in the afternoon, and her grandparents are eagerly standing out front waiting for them. Yori asks Justin to carry the box inside. "You can set it down right here on the countertop."

Justin carefully sets down the fish on a granite slab center island. "Beautiful kitchen." "Thanks. My grandparents remodeled last year and spent a small fortune on it."

Yori's grandmother walks into the kitchen, immediately unwraps the box of fish, and removes three of the smaller snappers. She washes the fish and sets them down on a large wooden cutting board to chop off their heads with a cleaver. Afterward, she tosses the heads into a large pot of simmering water and sets the fish bodies aside.

Yori starts to help her grandmother with the preparations. "Have a seat over there in the living area, and I'll be with you shortly. Please make yourself at home."

Justin sits down on a brown leather couch and watches the action taking place in the kitchen. Yori fetches a knife from a wooden block and dices up some onions, garlic, carrots, and bok choy for the soup. She lifts the cutting board and slides the pile of veggies into the soup pot, using the knife. Her grandmother then takes over, sprinkles various spices into the soup, and places a lid on the simmering pot.

Her grandfather enters the kitchen to fillet the beheaded fish on a separate cutting board. He slices small strips of the delicate fish, covers the glass bowl in plastic wrap, and sets it inside the refrigerator for later.

Still sitting on the couch, Justin picks up an old hardcover book from the coffee table for a closer look. The cover has a red shrine across it, and he starts flipping through the pages.

Yori sees what he is looking at, finishes up in the kitchen, and sits down next to him on the couch. She mentions how the book is about the history of Shinto, which is deeply woven into the fabric of Japanese spirituality and mythology. They talk about how, under the ideal of Shinto, the emperor governs through rituals offered to deities. These rituals are practiced in shrines all over Japan, and it is thought the human, natural, and supernatural will align and prosper.

"Shinto or *kami-no-michi* means the way of the gods," says Yori. "Shintoism emphasizes themes such as family, community, tradition, nature, purity, cleanliness, harmony, sincerity, shrines, the sacredness of Mount Fuji, rituals, and festivals.

"It began in its earliest form twenty-three hundred years ago and continues to have a considerable influence on Japanese culture and society. From it springs the origin of many customs, including removing your shoes before entering a house and taking a daily bath. A few examples of Shinto sayings and teachings include respect your ancestors, do not be sluggish in your work, and sincerity is a witness to truth and the mother of knowledge.

"Shinto is based on the belief of various kami that animate everything in the world. What do you think about all this?" asks Yori.

"I think it's fascinating to learn about ancient cultures and the incredible diversity of people all over the world. It's a large part of why I traveled to Japan this summer and learning more about Buddhism and Shintoism has been interesting."

She replies with a smile. "Good answer. We're done in the kitchen. Would you like to go for a walk?"

Justin waves goodbye to her grandparents and follows Yori through the front door. They walk down a natural dirt trail that twists and turns under the canopy of a lush, green forest for a quarter of a mile. The dense vegetation suddenly lightens up, and sunlight pours down to the forest floor through a large opening in the tree branches high above. Because of this, the area has supported life it might not otherwise have been capable of, and Justin catches a glimpse of why Yori brought him out here. A variety of flowering bushes and plants scatter the grounds, blooming in an array of shades of purple, yellow, white, and orange. Through the cascading rays of sunlight shining down on the flora, hundreds of butterflies can be seen hovering, fluttering, flying, and gliding every which way.

In Japanese culture, butterflies carry several meanings but are most closely associated with metamorphosis and transformation, and they are a symbol of good luck, health, and prosperity. There is also a widespread belief that butterflies, or *choho*, are the soul of the living and dead. It is said that spirits of the dead take the form of butterflies when on their journey to the other world and eternal life.

Yori tells Justin a story. "I can remember the first time my grandmother brought me out here as a small child. It was a pleasant spring morning, and she held my hand as we walked along the trail. My grandmother had—well, she still has, but I remember her having these wonderfully soft, warm hands that really made me feel safe. She pointed out various birds while telling me a little something about each one of them. Eventually, we arrived at this very spot, and I felt something purely magical in the stillness of nature, even among the hundreds if not thousands of butterflies that surrounded us." She takes a deep breath and continues. "I will cherish that feeling of sheer joy she brought me for the rest of my life. To this day, this is still one of my favorite places, and I wanted to share it with you today."

Justin feels immensely flattered by her kind words and gesture. He reaches down to gently brush his hand across hers, and she reciprocates by folding her fingers around his as they make a connection. For the next several moments, the two stand motionless, enjoying the serene experience. Eventually, they say goodbye to the butterflies and stroll back down the path with an electrical buzz flowing between them.

Justin receives a phone call from Kaito on the return walk, stating he has changed his mind about leaving tomorrow morning and instead has made the necessary arrangements to leave this evening. Apparently, he found a couple of seats on the 6:45 p.m. flight to Tokyo, closely followed by a connecting flight to Kyushu. Cole will escort him for precautionary reasons and then make his way home.

Justin and Yori return to the house and agree to meet up at dinner. He cuts across the yard to the hotel lobby and makes his way upstairs to the room. Kaito is lying on the bed, phone in hand, swiping and typing away, while Cole is sitting on the floor, organizing his luggage for departure.

"So, you guys are leaving tonight?" says Justin.

Cole looks up. "Yeah, your cousin over there said he preferred to leave this evening, and he was able to make the travel arrangements work. In fact, we need to leave in a few minutes to make our flight. Do you want to drop us off at the airport, or shall we return the rental car?"

"Go ahead and return the car. I'll be fine."

The guys finish packing up, sharing a few laughs about the last couple of wild days. Justin thanks Cole for being a helpful adventure guide and gives him a manly hug. After they step apart, Cole grabs his bags and walks downstairs to the car. Justin can't help but wonder if this is the last time they will ever see each other.

Kaito sits up in the bed, unzips his backpack, and removes the scroll presented to him earlier in the day. He tells Justin the entire story of his encounter with Jurojin, including all the juicy details. "I just want to make sure you understand what happened while everything is still fresh in my mind."

He then removes the sack of star sand gifted to him on Iriomote Island. "I called Grandfather Yoshiaki this afternoon to inform him of our progress. After a lengthy conversation about each of the three encounters, he concluded that the gifts and stones would be best kept together. Please take good care of them on your journey to Hawaii, and I will reunite with you there when I can."

"Are you sure about this?"

"Yes, we talked it through, Yoshiaki ruled in your favor, and I have accepted his judgment. Before I go, can you show me the nine stones one last time?"

Justin removes the bag of river rocks and spreads them out on the bed. The monkey, cat, and deer etchings now have a slight golden glow, but the rocks themselves remain their natural colors. The other six stone etchings of the bird, beetle, lizard, owl, coyote, and octopus do not have the mysterious glowing effect.

The cousins exchange a heartfelt goodbye and walk down to the car. Kaito slides into the passenger seat and rolls down the window. "It's been a heck of a ride, Justin. Take care of yourself."

"Thanks, Kaito. Hope you feel better soon."

Justin watches them drive off, then walks back upstairs to the room. He locks the door and closes the curtains to further examine the lump of sap, the pouch of star sand, and the scroll, wondering about their true meaning. Although he is tempted to experiment with the gifts, Justin decides now would not be the right time. Instead, he secures the three items inside his backpack with the nine stones, keeping them for another day.

He checks his phone to see the time is creeping up on six and jumps into the shower. Feeling refreshed and ready for the evening, he slides into some blue jeans, wrestles on a clean T-shirt, and opens the curtain to see several people eating dinner on the patio below. He spots the snapper prepared three-ways on a buffet table against the wall and wanders downstairs to get something to eat.

Once there, Justin sees Yori in a red sundress and sandals. She is speaking with a middle-aged couple who are vacationing at the hotel, and she is politely explaining the various dishes found on the buffet table. Justin stands off to the side, allowing them to finish the conversation before he walks over to say hello.

Yori smiles, happy to see him, "Hi, glad you made it down. Would you like to have something to eat?"

"Indeed, I would. The food looks and smells terrific!"

"Please help yourself and have a seat over there in the back." She points to a wrought-iron table where four people have just sat down to eat dinner. "That's my sister, her boyfriend, and a couple of their friends. I will join you in a few minutes." She walks back inside to grab some additional utensils for the guests.

Justin goes through the buffet line and makes up a plate. He lays down a bed of rice, two pieces of flaky white fish, and some steamed vegetables. He places three pieces of sashimi next to the main course and fills a cup with soup from a decorative porcelain serving bowl. *This is going to be fantastic!*

Justin carries his food over to the table, sits down on an empty chair, and introduces himself. The group kindly says hello in English, then continues their conversation in Japanese. Yori soon arrives with a large bowl of soup and whispers something in her sister's ear. They share a giggly laugh and she sits down next to Justin.

"How do you like the food?"

"It's really good. My favorite has to be the sashimi."

"Good to hear. And, how's the soup? I've been looking forward to some all week."

Justin blows on a spoonful of the broth. "Really tasty. Hot, but tasty."

Yori tries it. "So good. I love this soup. By the way, my sister and her friends are going to the lighthouse after dinner, and they invited us to come along. The sky is very clear this evening, so we should see lots of stars. Would you like to go?"

"Yes, that sounds like fun. My cousin just left for the airport, and I have nothing planned for a couple of days."

"Ah. Sorry to hear he had to leave, but I'm glad you stayed."

Over the rest of dinner, Justin and Yori discuss the best options for spending his remaining time on the island. She really likes visiting Tairo Pond, and they devise a plan to make a day of it tomorrow. They finish the meal over a few plum cookies and some flirtatious small talk.

"Meet me out front by the car," says Yori. "I need to say goodbye to my grandparents and see if they need my help with anything before we go. It shouldn't take long."

Justin grabs his sweatshirt from the room and waits for Yori in the parking lot. She shows up as expected, and they jump into the car. Along the way, they talk about the unusually square-shaped lighthouse. "It's one of the oldest in Japan, and on a clear day, you can even see Mount Fuji from it."

They arrive at a small, dimly lit parking lot and walk up to the lighthouse. Yori looks around for the others but doesn't see them anywhere. She suggests they walk down to the coast and check a set of benches that overlook the sea where they eventually locate the crew. The group picks Justin's brain, asking him numerous questions about life growing up in Hawaii.

Eventually, Justin and Yori say goodbye to the others and go for a beach walk. They kick off their shoes to the side and stroll along barefoot in the cool sand, holding hands. Yori begins to get chilly and Justin removes his sweatshirt to lend her.

"Thanks for bringing me out here tonight." He wraps his arm around her shoulders, and she leans in, enjoying his warmth. Feeling the moment is right, Justin places his hand on her cheek, and the two share a first delicate kiss.

Yori nervously makes a confession to Justin during their moonlit stroll back to the car. "Ever since we first met back at the hot springs, I've felt this undeniable attraction to you. Yes, you're cute, but it's more than that. You have this mysterious presence, an aura like no one I have ever come across. I don't know what it is exactly, but there is something about you that I'm drawn to. Does that make any sense?"

For a moment, Justin wants to share with Yori the details of what's going on, but he decides it's not a good idea for now. "Yes, it makes perfect sense, and I'm glad to hear you say that. I too have felt the chemistry between us ever since we met."

They stop in front of the car and engage in a much more passionate kiss than the first one. After making the drive back, Yori pulls in front of the hotel entrance to let him out and promises to make his remaining time on the island memorable. She leans over to give him a hug, and they end the night agreeing to meet the next day.

In the morning, Justin meets Yori downstairs for their trip to Tairo Pond. On the drive over, they stop by a local restaurant to pick up some box lunches for a picnic. When they arrive at the pond, Yori spreads out a large beach blanket on the grass, and they spend some time casually chatting about the local wildlife over lunch. However, there is more mutual flirting going on than anything else.

"Let's go for a quick hike, and we can swim on the way back," says Yori.

Justin stands up and reaches out to assist her to her feet. He tosses the rubbish in a nearby trash can, and they take off on a leisurely stroll. Along the way, they spot a variety of birds, commenting on their individual appearances and songs. They soon return from the hike and rest on the blanket, pleasurably rolling around in the grass. Just as things are getting a bit too risqué, a rambunctious young family comes parading around the corner.

"Let's go for a swim," Yori says.

She strips down to her bathing suit and dips under the cool, fresh water, resurfacing to wipe her face dry. She wrings out her long black hair, smiling at Justin and encouraging him to come swimming by curling her index finger back and forth.

In an animated manner, he looks around in all directions with both arms extended, points back at himself, and dives into the water. When Justin surfaces, he swims up to Yori, and they embrace in a romantic hug and kiss, feeling wonderfully alive. They stare deeply into each other's eyes, then break out in a game of water splash.

The afternoon winds down, and they decide to dry off. Yori clutches her towel. "It's chilly for summertime."

"Yeah, it definitely feels cooler out right now than it has the past couple of days."

"Hey, I've got an idea. The hot springs closes early today for maintenance, but only on the men's side. The women's side was done last week. Do you want to go warm up in the pool? I have a key."

"Oh, I can see that you're a bit of a risk-taker. I like that about you. I'm in."

They get back into the car and drive over to the hot springs where Yori pulls around back to park. "We can enter through the side door over there. Don't worry, I know the maintenance guys. They wouldn't say anything."

Yori unlocks the door, and Justin follows her inside the dark facility. She reaches back to grab his hand and quietly escorts him to the women's locker room. Loud grinding sounds can be heard in the men's section from the maintenance crew cutting pieces of tile.

She carefully leads him to the edge of her favorite pool. "The crew is busy remodeling one of the showers and should be at it all night." She sits down in the water to soak up some warmth.

Justin takes his time getting accustomed to the temperature but eventually sits down on the second step. "This feels fantastic. Thanks for spending the day with me. I had a great time!"

"You, sir, are quite welcome."

Yori swims up to Justin and wraps her arms around him. He pulls her in closer for a kiss and they briefly cuddle together in the soothing hot water before sitting along the edge to look at the stars and cool down. Rather than press their luck, Yori fetches them a couple of towels to dry off, and they quickly get going without being noticed. Feeling warm and refreshed, neither Justin nor Yori have any intention of ending the night this early. Instead, when they return to the hotel, he invites her up to his room.

"I'll meet you there shortly," she says. "Let me change into some dry clothes and check in on my grandparents. They go to bed fairly early and might even be asleep already."

"OK, sounds like a plan. I'll see you in a bit."

Justin gets out of the car and walks upstairs. A short while later, Yori knocks on the door, bringing with her some candles, fresh berries, and an iPhone playing music. She is wearing his UCSC hoodie and some skimpy white jean shorts. Justin stands leaning his head against the doorway, smiling, and invites her in. She steps into the room under his arm and he smells her lavender-scented shampoo as she brushes past. He looks down the empty hallway in both directions and gently closes the door.

Justin is woken early in the morning by the sound of chirping birds and the day's first sunlight. He checks the time and gets up to take a shower, accidentally knocking over a plastic cup on his way out the door. The noise wakes Yori, and she decides to go downstairs, figuring Justin could use some hot tea and toast for the long day ahead. She jots him a quick note: "Come find me downstairs when you are ready to go. I'll make us a little breakfast. Y."

After returning from his shower, Justin reads the note and finishes packing for his trip to Hawaii. He double-checks to make sure the nine stones and gifts are secure, takes one last look around the room, and grabs his luggage. When he gets downstairs to the front desk, Yori's grandmother graciously thanks him for visiting, and wishes him safe travels. He sets the keys on top of the counter and turns to see Yori's grandfather standing near the exit. The old man rolls his eyes and opens the door. When Justin walks through the doorway, her grandfather smiles and pats him on the back. "Stay genuine, young man."

Justin looks around for Yori and finds her sitting on a stone bench under a big shade tree. They make eye contact and exchange a wave. He sets down the bags and walks over to her. She greets him with the most terrific smile he has seen in a long time, and he sits next to her. "Good morning, Yori. Before I forget, I just want to thank you for the fantastic time yesterday. I really enjoyed spending the day with you and will remember our time together forever."

Yori hands him a cup of tea. "Good morning, Justin. I, too, had a wonderful time yesterday. You are a terrific person who made me feel special, and I appreciate that very much." She removes the plastic wrap covering a ceramic plate of fresh berries and toast.

"How are you doing on time this morning?"

"We should probably get going to the airport fairly soon. Thanks for breakfast. This looks perfect."

"You're welcome. I figured you could use some food in your belly for the day of travel."

Justin sips some tea and throws a couple of berries into his mouth. He begins missing Yori even though she is sitting right in front of him. Their short time together has affected him in a wonderful way he never thought possible, and his stomach squirms like a kid on a roller coaster. "So, what are your plans for the rest of summer?"

"Nothing too much. I might visit some friends in Tokyo, but that's about it."

"I know this might sound crazy, but why don't you come visit me? I'll be stopping off in Hawaii for a couple of weeks before returning to California. I'm not sure how long it would take you to coordinate the travel visa and all that. But I would really like to see you again somehow, someway, hopefully maybe soon. What do you think? Or not. Maybe?"

A big grin forms on Yori's face and she starts clapping her hands and stomping her feet in excitement. "Yes, yes, yes, I want to go! My family vacationed in Oahu when I was six years old, although I don't really remember very much. But we never made it to Maui, and I've never been to the mainland United States." She calms down from the initial shock. "My answer is yes. I would love to come see you. My mom and dad won't be fond of the idea, but I live with my grandparents, and they are much more understanding. Especially my grandmother. I'm sure she will even pay for my flight and help me process the paperwork. She has traveled all over the world and is good at that sort of thing."

"Really, that's fantastic. I'm so glad to hear you say yes. My parents have a place for us to stay in Maui; otherwise, we can rendezvous in California and do some sightseeing. A couple of friends and I rent a beach house in Santa Cruz. We can hang out there in between a road trip or two. What do you think?"

They stand up in mutual excitement, and Yori jumps into his arms, giving Justin a giant hug. Her legs are wrapped around his waist, and she gives him a kiss on the neck.

After finishing breakfast, Justin sets his bags in the car, and Yori gives him a ride to the airport. She pulls up to the curbside drop-off, and Justin gets out of the car. He leans in through the window to give her one last kiss goodbye. "It has been great meeting you, and thanks again for everything. Hopefully, our paths with cross again soon."

"I'm so happy to have met you, Justin. As soon as my grandmother helps me process the paperwork, I will call you with the details."

Justin notices his hoodie lying on the back seat of the car. "Why don't you go ahead and hang on to that for now? But promise me I'll see you wearing it again soon."

Yori gives him a mysteriously sexy smile. "Oh, you will see me wearing it soon, that I promise you." She blows him a kiss and rolls up the window. Justin puts his right hand over his heart, extends his left one outward, and rolls his head back as she honks the horn twice and drives away.

7

THE VALLEY ISLE

A female flight attendant begins talking over the loudspeaker in a delightful Hawaiian accent. "Aloha, and welcome to Kahua Mokulele O Kahului, or Kahului International Airport, on the beautiful island of Maui. The local time is two twenty-seven p.m. and the temperature outside is a pleasant eighty-four degrees. For your safety, please remain seated with your seat belts fastened until the captain has turned off the Fasten Seat Belt sign. This will indicate that we have parked at the gate, and it is safe for you to move about the cabin.

"Please check around your seat for any personal belongings you may have brought on board today, including cell phones, laptops, tablets, and carry-on bags. Remember to use caution when opening the overhead bins, as heavy items may have shifted during the flight. If you require deplaning assistance, please remain in your seat until all the other passengers have exited. One of our crew members will be happy to assist you.

"The baggage claim facilities are located on the ground level. As you exit the gate area to the ground level via the escalator or elevator, turn right. Checked luggage will be available at carousel C. On behalf of the airline and flight crew, I want to thank you for flying with us today and wish you the warmest aloha and mahalo."

Moments later, the plane comes to an abrupt stop, and passengers begin stirring about the cabin in anticipation of offloading. The brief flight from Honolulu to Maui went as expected, and Justin has now completed the last leg of his long day traveling from Japan. He sends Melia a text letting her know the airplane has landed and that he should be ready for a curbside pickup shortly. She is waiting in the cell phone lot for his call and will provide him with a lift back to their family's home in Kihei, where they grew up.

Justin disembarks the aircraft onto the jet bridge and makes the slow walk through the white-walled, windowless corridor. He reads a reply text from Melia, confirming she will see him soon, responds to her with a thumbs-up emoji, and steps out into the crowded airport gate. After grabbing his luggage from the carousel, Justin walks outdoors, and his hat nearly blows off in the stiff trade winds. Luckily, he reaches up just in time to secure the cap back onto his head and steps out curbside. He spots a four-door black Toyota Tacoma waiting at the stop light for pedestrians to cross and easily identifies the truck belonging to his sister by the pink hibiscus flower decals on the upper corners of the windshield.

When they make eye contact for the first time in more than a year, Melia starts to smile and wave from inside the truck. She pulls over in front of Justin, who opens the door and tosses his luggage inside. They exchange an enthusiastic greeting of hugs and hellos, followed by Melia giving him a big, smacking kiss on his cheek and signaling her way back into traffic.

Ever since they were young children, the siblings have always maintained an exemplary relationship well respected and admired by their inner circles. They grew up sharing many of the same hobbies and interests, most of which revolved around the outdoors and preferred the companionship of family to trust and rely on. Especially once they became teenagers and the various ocean activities involved elements of danger, including skimboarding, surfing, and spearfishing. Melia is a lively, reliable young woman with a caring and compassionate side.

"So, tell me, tell me. How was Japan?"

"Japan was fantastic! I had a wonderful time over there, meeting our distant family members and exploring the islands. The food was amazing, and I met a special girl named Yori."

Melia zips past a silver convertible rental car stuffed with tourists and luggage. She is eighteen years old and a recent high school graduate with plans to attend the UH Maui campus in the fall. "You will have to fill me in on all the juicy details. I can't wait to hear more about her and your vacation."

"For sure. I have a couple of wild stories to share with you. Where are Mom and Dad today?"

"At work, but they said to tell you hello. Mom usually gets home around five thirty or six. But Dad works late; he won't be home until after nine. Are you hungry? Do you want to stop to get something to eat?"

"No, I'm good. I just want to go home, shower, and snooze for a few hours, if that's cool."

"Definitely, I totally understand. You had a long day. Maybe if you are up for it, we can hit Big Beach tomorrow. Do some skimboarding early in the morning like old times." Melia is eager to spend some time with her big brother whom she looks up to and admires.

"Skimboarding sounds perfect! Maybe we can grab some fried rice afterward."

Melia adjusts the radio to a popular station broadcasting Hawaiian and reggae music. They end up discussing Justin's plans for his trip to Hawaii on the drive home. He mentions wanting to hike Haleakala here on Maui, island-hop to the Big Island, and finish vacationing in Kauai prior to returning to California. Justin purposely leaves out anything to do with the nine stones, figuring he needs more time to absorb what has happened.

When they pull into the driveway of the family property, Justin receives a text from Kaito, requesting that he call ASAP. He takes a quick shower, changes into some comfortable clothes, and gives him a jingle. After three rings, the call goes to voicemail, and he hangs up the phone, figuring Kaito will eventually get back to him. Sure enough, Kaito calls right back, and Justin answers on the first ring. "Hey, Kaito. I just landed on Maui and received your message. What's going on?"

Kaito speaks in a very somber voice. "Hi, Justin. Unfortunately, I have some very bad news to share with you today. Grandfather Yoshiaki, your great-uncle, died this morning in his sleep. I spoke to Grandmother Mana, and she said he was feeling unusually tired yesterday afternoon, so she encouraged him to turn in early for some additional rest, and he did. When she woke up this morning to work in the greenhouse, she found him lying cold and motionless."

"Oh my gosh, how awful. He seemed so energetic and healthy when we saw him last week."

"Yeah, it's devastating news for everyone here. Yoshiaki was well respected and loved by not only family and friends but many others in the community. Would you mind doing us a favor and sharing the news of his passing with our family in Hawaii?"

"Yes, of course."

"In his will, Yoshiaki mentioned the desire for a quick funeral, and Grandmother Mana is going along with his wishes.

The arrangements have already been made for tomorrow, with only a few people attending."

"Oh man, that's just terrible. My condolences for your loss. I know you loved him very much, and he will be sorely missed."

Kaito goes on about how he will need some additional time to recuperate from his wounds and mourn the loss of Yoshiaki. He encourages Justin to go on with the next phase of the journey without him and, hopefully, they can reunite down the road. Kaito has become concerned about how each of the encounters, in one way or another, has led to someone in their party becoming injured. First Miya twisted her ankle, then Kat's leech bites became infected, plus Justin's snakebite on the forearm, and his own concussion and stitches.

"I can't help but wonder if somehow these are all related and are consequences of the encounters," says Kaito. "More than just accidents and coincidences. And now, with the passing of Yoshiaki on the same day you left Japan with the nine stones, I don't know. I'm worried."

Prior to ending the call, they agree to speak again next week to revisit the conversation. Justin closes his eyes, recollecting the valuable time he spent with Yoshiaki, and dozes off. He wakes up to find his mother standing in the doorway, softly calling out his name. She has black, shoulder-length hair and is dressed in dark-blue scrubs. Sakura works as a registered nurse for the local hospital and just returned home from the day shift.

He slowly gets out of bed to meet her at the door, and the two exchange a heartfelt hug. She stopped off to pick up some dinner on the way home and invites him over to the main house. They spend some time catching up over a few slices of pizza and salad. Eventually, Justin breaks the news to her about Yoshiaki's passing, and although Sakura hardly knew her uncle, she sheds a tear when hearing of his death.

She wipes her eyes with a tissue. "I'm so proud of you for reaching out to your extended family and taking the initiative to meet them by flying to Japan. Thank you for sharing, and I'll inform the rest of our family he has passed."

Melia walks barefoot through the kitchen on the travertine-tile floors. "Hey, Justin. I didn't know you were awake. Pizza? Yum!" She helps herself to a piece and sits down next to him.

"Let's go to the skate shop and pick up a new skimboard for tomorrow. We need a second one for you to ride. They close soon, but we can make it if we hurry."

"Right on, let's go, then. Thanks for the pizza, Mom."

"You're welcome. Have fun, you two. By the way, your father has to work late tonight; he won't be home until eleven."

When they enter the skateboard shop, a young man working behind the counter looks up. "Hey, howzit?"

Melia walks over to him. "Aloha. I was in here the other day and you guys had a couple of skimboards. Could we take a look at them?"

"I believe we have two more. Let me show you." He walks them over to the far corner and removes two boards tucked away behind some shoeboxes.

Justin picks up the ocean-blue one and gives it a look over. "We'll take it."

They follow the clerk back to the counter where he proceeds to ring them up. Justin tosses in a block of surf wax and waits for the transaction to process.

"Good to go. Mahalo for coming in today." The clerk hands him the board, wax, and a receipt.

They walk across the street for a rainbow shave ice with a sunset view before driving home. Justin shares several stories with Melia about college in California and his trip to Japan. He leaves out anything to do with the magical stones, encounters, or gifts, even though something inside of Justin urges him to be truthful. She senses something is up but doesn't press the issue.

After watching Justin yawn four times in a minute, Melia tells him to get some sleep, and she will see him in the morning. They embrace in a goodnight hug.

"It's so good to see you, my brother. Sleep well. I love you."

"I love you too, sis. See you in the morning."

Justin wakes up from a good night's sleep feeling refreshed and ready to hit the beach. He slips on some camouflage board shorts and a white T-shirt, grabs his sunglasses, and walks out of the guesthouse. He enters the main home through a sliding glass door and spots Melia sitting on the couch drinking a cup of coffee. She offers one to Justin, but he passes and instead opens up the refrigerator and snatches a bottle of coconut water. They momentarily small talk while enjoying some apple bananas, load up her truck, and take off.

After a brief drive, they arrive at Makena State Park and pull into the first of three entrances that access Big Beach. The large paved parking lot has ample room for nearly one hundred vehicles plus an overflow section that spills out onto the side of the highway next to the food trucks. The beach park has picnic tables, portable restrooms, and trash but lacks shade trees. However, the "Makena cloud," which stretches from the top of Haleakala to the island of Kahoolawe, is often overhead cooling the sand and providing much-needed relief to sun-scorched visitors.

They make the brief walk from the parking lot to the beach and plop down in the sand to analyze the shore break. Melia spots a section that suits her eye and points it out to Justin. "Look how the waves collide together right there, creating an explosion of water. I want to launch over that!"

Melia is a very athletic young lady who can proficiently handle a skimboard, surfboard, and skateboard. She has tremendous coordination, footwork, and timing, a specific set of skills honed during her youth and regularly put on display when visiting the beach. She welcomes challenges presented to her and tends to feed on the adrenaline of competition.

The siblings alternate turns riding small incoming waves. The weather and tide at Big Beach are calm today, not the usual pounding shore break that can be too dangerous even for highly skilled riders. Justin uses the newly bought wooden skimboard to glide across the water and sand for distance, mixing in an occasional spin or two but nothing overly fancy. He never reached the skill level of Melia and has no problem admitting she is the superior rider.

Justin embeds his skimboard sideways six inches into the sand and carefully sits on the edge, calling it a day. He guzzles down some coconut water and watches Melia carving up the shore break with punishing cuts and slashes on a custom fiberglass board. Her ability to gracefully catch air off the wave attracts attention from several tourists, and a small crowd forms to observe. The dozen or so spectators ooh and ahh as she flips off the board and comes crashing into the water at the end of each ride. When Melia finishes her last run, two young girls visiting from the mainland United States ask to have their photograph taken with her. She is flattered by their request and graciously accepts by placing an arm around each of the kids, so their mom can take the photo.

Melia sits down in the sand next to Justin and wipes her face with a dry towel. He hands her a coconut water. "You're a dragon on that skimboard! I can't believe how well you can ride now. Wow, I mean, really, that was impressive."

"Thank you, thank you. I've been practicing a lot the past year or two."

"I can tell. That was rad when you launched way up in the air and leaped off into a cannonball."

Melia polishes off the coconut water. "The ocean is clean today. Do you want to go diving before we get lunch? I brought the gear just in case."

"Yeah! Good idea. I haven't been spearfishing in a long time. What do you say we check out the third entrance and scavenge the left side for tako?" Justin says, using the Japanese word for octopus, which many Hawaiians have adopted as their own.

They stomp back across one hundred feet of warm sand, weave down a dirt trail through the kiawe trees, and return to the truck. They drive south for a half mile and pull over on the side of the road. Justin lowers the tailgate to remove a black mesh net dive bag containing masks, snorkels, fins, a dive float, and two collapsible three-pronged spears. He carries the bulky pack down to the shoreline where they gear up for a swim.

He wraps the black floatline around his waist and secures it with a heavy-duty metal clip. The twenty-foot line of super-strong parachute cordage is connected to a red seven-liter hollow core float by a large swivel for maneuverability. The polyethylene outer shell of the float is the same material that kayaks are made from and can cut through the surface water quite well. A twelve-inch-square waterproof red flag with a diagonal white stripe is attached to the float and warns others of divers in the water. The float gets dragged behind a swimmer during the dive and often gets used as a place to attach speared fish.

They enter waist deep into the warm Pacific. Justin uses the bungee cord attached to the end of his three-prong spear and launches the spear high up into the air. He watches the pole hit a peak height and come arching back down in the crystal-clear water where he intends to retrieve it momentarily. He then scoops water up in his cupped hand and splashes it across his face for a slight taste. After making this small connection with the sea, he gives Melia a thumbs-up and they submerge.

With visibility a good thirty feet in all directions, Justin swims out to where the three-pronged spear entered the water and quickly spots the bright-yellow pole embedded in the sand. He looks back to double-check that the float is pulling correctly, glances over at Melia on his left, and reaches out to tug on the four-foot fiberglass shaft. After easily dislodging the metal spear tip from the ocean floor, Justin surfaces to take a few deep breaths and goes back under. He notices a group of scattered rocks and coral not too far away and signals to Melia they should investigate the area by pointing in the direction with his spear. She nods in approval and gives a thumbs-up.

They explore the section of the reef where the water depth varies between ten and twenty feet. The calm, clear ocean is exploding with life and they encounter several of the usual suspects throughout the dive including yellow tang, trumpetfish, peacock grouper, goatfish, unicorn fish, and even the lagoon triggerfish, also known in Hawaiian as the tongue-twisting humuhumu nukunuku apua'a.

Melia recognizes a prized food species swimming into view and signals Justin to the surface. They come together, and she spits out the snorkel's rubber mouthpiece.

"A few parrotfish just swam in. I'm going to stalk them and see if I can get off a shot."

"I'll be right around here if you need my help."

With Melia busy trying to close in on the small school of skittish parrotfish, Justin spots a large Hawaiian green sea turtle, also called a honu, and swims over to the endemic reptile for a closer look. He feels a connection with the majestic creature while momentarily gliding alongside the animal and notices a shiny silver fishing hook pierced through the upper corner of the turtle's beak and can't help but wonder what happened. Although a green sea turtle's diet consists mainly of algae and seagrass, they have been known to bite a shore fishermen's line on occasion or become accidentally snagged.

When Justin starts running out of oxygen, he salutes the turtle out of respect, and propels himself upward by rhythmically kicking his fins one at a time until breaking through the surface for a much-needed breath of fresh air. He looks back down just in time to see the honu power stroking into the abyss by using a movement like that of a bird flapping its wings.

Melia pops up directly in front of Justin, startling him, and they agree to spend a few more minutes in the water before calling it a day. She has been unable to get a shot off at the parrotfish, but the school remains nearby, and she goes down after them in one last valiant attempt. He watches her dive down twenty feet to the ocean floor, lay out on top of a coral head, and remain motionless to blend in with the environment. Three juveniles swim right by her in reach of the spear tip, but she allows them to pass without confrontation, hoping to lure in a larger one. Her patience soon pays off when a sixteen-inch green-and-yellow bullethead parrotfish comes into view.

Unfortunately, Melia has run out of breath and becomes frustrated that she must surface for some air. So she kicks her way up, deeply inhales and exhales three consecutive times, and plunges back down to the reef. She spots the same parrotfish feeding on a dull-yellow coral head near the white sandy ocean floor. Instead of attempting a direct attack, Melia methodically moves around the coral to slip behind the fish and prepares her three prongs for a shot. She holds the looped bungee between her thumb and index finger, stretches out the cord midway down the spear, and grabs hold of the shaft, arming the weapon.

Meanwhile, Justin has spotted the telltale signs of an octopus in the vicinity and dives down to the bottom for a closer look. He temporarily hovers above a small rock formation observing a softball-size excavated hole in the sand where several broken crab and mollusk shells are scattered about. He moves within a few inches of the opening, notices something swirling within the crevice, and instantly recognizes the brown and tan colors of an octopus. After he gently inserts the three-pronged spear tip into the hole, a long tentacle extends up the shaft and attaches itself with a double row of powerful suckers.

Justin starts carefully tugging on the pole in an attempt to yank the octopus out through the shell-lined entrance. One, two, three, no luck. Octopuses have eight legs, which they can spread out within the hole, creating quite the challenge for predators attempting to remove the intelligent creatures. After a brief pause, he grabs the three-pronged shaft with both hands and readies himself for one final tug. Much to his surprise, the octopus easily pulls out through the opening on his fourth attempt, revealing the fascinating invertebrate.

Justin lifts the fiberglass pole upright, noticing the octopus has not been impaled with the sharp three prongs but instead clings on by choice. He worries the creature will escape at any moment and reaches out with one hand to firmly grab hold of a long dangling tentacle. The octopus easily slips through his grasp by pulling its arm free and slaps Justin on the wrist, adding insult to injury. The eight-armed magician then detaches itself from the yellow pole and floats downward, landing on some rocks below. In a chameleonlike manner, the sea creature instantly changes skin color from a swirly brown and tan to a deep solid mahogany and remains motionless, attempting to blend in. Defense sensory organs on their arms allow them to perfectly mimic the color and textures of surrounding corals.

Knowing the slippery creature could flee at any given moment, Justin prepares his spear to shoot, and swiftly fires from close range, hoping to pin the octopus down. The lightning-quick animal propels itself upward, twisting in circles to avoid the metal tips and comes to a complete stop midwater. Justin reaches out to snatch the octopus with his hand but misses, and the eight-armed magician slaps him across the face in an unusually comical manner. The mystical underwater creature completely stretches out its eight, three-foot-long tentacles in all directions, creating an image of rays protruding from the sun. Seconds later a cloud of black ink floods the ocean, and the octopus uses a powerful blast of water to propel itself out of sight.

In the meantime, Melia has positioned herself just above and behind the parrotfish in an ideal spot. She remains perfectly still, hovering close to the coral, and executes a perfect shot to the head, instantly stoning the fish. After surfacing to admire her catch, she swims over to Justin and is eager to share the news. Catching a mature parrotfish with a three prong is no easy task, and Justin congratulates her for the impressive accomplishment. She holds the fish just out of the water still on the spear tip and completes the short swim back into shore next to her proud, empty-handed brother.

Once on the shore Justin closely follows behind Melia, stepping on top of each and every footprint she leaves in the sand. En route to the truck, they walk past shadows cast from coconut palms swaying high above, step over fallen branches of the spiky kiawe trees, and disrupt a flock of foraging myna birds. He drops down the tailgate and heaves the dive bag into the truck bed.

"Great job spearing that fish!"

"I'm so thankful and stoked to have landed it. We just leveled up our lunch game big-time."

"Let me get your pic before we ice down the parrotfish. Hold on really quick."

Justin fetches his cell from the glove box and takes a photograph of Melia grasping the spear with the fish still attached and another one of her holding the colorful bluish green fish upright by the gill plate.

Melia lays the parrotfish into the red portable cooler, completely covers it with ice, and securely replaces the hard-plastic lid. She closes the tailgate, wraps a towel around her waist, and jumps into the truck next to Justin. They call in a to-go order of fried rice and chow fun noodles from a well-known local café and flip a U-turn onto the slightly congested two-lane highway. After a brief drive, she slows down, flips on the turn signal, and pulls into the restaurant parking lot. "Glad we called in the order. Did you see that line out front as we drove by?"

They step out of the truck and stroll down a narrow walkway to the casual restaurant boasting ocean views. Nearly one hundred people are dining outside on patio furniture underneath brightly covered umbrellas and another twenty-five are standing in line to order. Justin holds open the front door for Melia and follows her into the restaurant where they pay for the food. He carries two large Styrofoam boxes out to the car, and they cruise back home.

Justin walks inside carrying the food to find his father sitting behind a desk paying bills online. "Hey, Dad. What's up?"

His father, Landon, removes his glasses and spins around in the high-back desk chair. "Justin, you're here! How was the beach this morning?"

"Good, superfun. The water was clean, and Melia speared a nice uhu."

Landon walks over to Justin, shakes his hand, and pulls him in for a hug. "Where's your sister?"

"She's rinsing off outside in the shower. You hungry? We're going to cook up the fish and have a big lunch."

"Yeah, I could eat. If you want my help, I don't have to be at work for a couple of hours."

Melia comes barging in with the fish lying on top of the cooler lid and sets it down near the kitchen sink. "Hey, Dad. Of course, we want your help. Would you mind preparing the fish for us?"

Their father walks over to have a look at the parrotfish and gives Melia a congratulatory hug. "Nice catch, honey. I'll prep the fish if you two don't mind getting the grill fired up."

Landon retrieves a professional seven-inch fillet knife from his chef's knife bag, sets the parrotfish onto a large cutting board, and carefully removes the insides. He rinses the carcass clean with water, pats it dry with a paper towel, and sprinkles salt and pepper on both sides. He then places a large piece of aluminum foil on the kitchen counter, puts a green ti leaf inside, and lays down the fish.

Off to the side, he mixes some mayonnaise with pesto in a small bowl until smooth and smothers the mixture all over the scored fish. He minces a bit of garlic and dices some Portuguese sausage, green onions, mushrooms, and Maui sweet onions, then tosses everything together in a small glass bowl. He stuffs the fish with the mixture, lays a second ti leaf on top, and tightly wraps it all up to form a pouch.

They go out back to grill the fish and discuss the morning adventure at Big Beach. At one point, Justin texts his mom a picture of Melia holding the parrotfish and another of their dad moving the foil pouch with a pair of long silver tongs. Once the fish has fully cooked, Landon removes it from the grill and sets it down on a serving platter. They gather around the patio table and indulge in a tasty midday meal consisting of the grilled stuffed fish, fried rice, and chow fun noodles.

"That was fantastic. Thanks for lunch, you guys," says Landon. "I had better get going. We are expecting a packed house tonight at the restaurant. Have a good afternoon, and I will see you either this evening or tomorrow."

Later that afternoon, Justin receives a call from Yori, explaining she will need a few weeks to obtain a visa to travel to the United States. They devise a plan to rendezvous in California rather than Hawaii because he will have returned to the mainland by then. She is ecstatic about seeing him and visiting the US mainland for the first time. When she confirms her arrival date in Los Angeles, Justin will book a flight into LAX the same day, so they can meet at the airport for a road trip up the coast.

He hangs up the phone and notices a text from Brandon, one of his roommates in California, who also happens to be visiting family this summer on Maui. Like Justin, Brandon was born and raised on the island, and the two good friends chose to attend the same college after graduating high school.

"Whazup, Justin! Wanna go deep-sea fishing tomorrow morning? My uncle captains a boat out of Maalaea Harbor and has a couple of empty spots."

"Yeah, I'm in."

"I'll pick you up at five a.m."

8

HOUSE OF THE MOON

Early the following morning, Justin takes a hot shower to wake up and prepares for the fishing trip. He retrieves a pair of travel mugs from the cupboard and runs some disposable pods through the single-serve coffee maker. He pours a little non-dairy liquid creamer into each cup, drops in a couple of sugar cubes, snaps on the plastic lids, and walks out front. Brandon is waiting for him, and they set out on the drive to Maalaea Bay. The small boat harbor is a popular departure point for several ocean activities and home to the Maui Ocean Center. During the occasional large southerly swell, local surfers gather at the harbor to ride a wave called the freight train. The right-hander runs off the breakwall, over a shallow coral reef, and is considered one of the world's fastest rideable waves.

They arrive at Maalaea and park on the wharf facing the boats with shops and restaurants behind them. Brandon's uncle walks over to say hello and invites his nephew and Justin aboard the forty-one-foot custom fishing boat named *Sea Glass*. He introduces them to the deckhand and waits for a family of four to show up before going over some basic protocol. Once everyone settles into a seat, the deckhand unties the dock lines from the wooden pier, and they slowly pull out of the small harbor. A mother, father, and two middle school–age boys sit inside the roomy salon around the L-shaped lounge while Justin and Brandon find a place outside at the stern.

The old friends make small talk about the peaceful morning weather while observing the deckhand make some necessary preparations to fish. They watch him remove a large white tackle box from an exterior storage compartment, unsnap the hinged lid, and carefully select three distinct artificial lures for big game saltwater fishing. He first attaches a ten-inch metal head lure with a bright pink skirt to the massive Penn gold reel and rod containing one-hundred- pound monofilament line. Afterward, the deckhand rigs up smaller metal head lures with multicolored skirts on each of the outside lines containing slightly smaller reels and lighter test line. This presents a smorgasbord of options for predatory fish looking to strike.

Justin changes the subject from fishing for a moment.

"I want to visit the Big Island and Kauai before going back to Cali. You know, play tourist for a few days and hit some spots. Do you want to come along and join me for some good times?"

"Nah, I can't go, brah. I'm leaving for the mainland next Monday," replies Brandon.

"Oh, OK. Well, what about a hike up at Haleakala this weekend instead?"

"Damn, you're always the adventurous one. You know the elevation is ten thousand feet up there, right?"

Justin knows Brandon welcomes outdoor activities and should be up for the challenge. "You scared?"

"Nope. All right. I'm in, but only for one night."

The deckhand gets the fishing underway by dropping the lures into the water one at a time. He lays his fingers across the spool, sliding the drag lever down into position, and slowly releases the line. The artificial fishing baits are staggered at distances of fifty, seventy-five, and one hundred feet behind the boat to help avoid tangling during hookups and when maneuvering the vessel.

* * *

During the boat ride to the bottom-fishing grounds, two separate strikes occur on the smaller lures, and each of the young kids on board gets to land a fish. They soon reel in a pair of five-pound skipjack tuna to break the ice.

The trolling continues to McGregor Point, just over a mile away from Maalaea Bay, passing an old lighthouse and thirty-four windmills scattered on the West Maui Mountains. They cruise around the cliff, hugging relatively close to the shoreline. After traveling west for another two miles, the boat veers away from Maui and the deckhand reels in the trolling lines. When the captain slows the boat to a complete stop a mile offshore, all six anglers are handed light reels and rods for bottom-fishing. They attach finger-size strips of cut squid to bait the hooks and drop the lines one hundred feet down to the ocean floor using four-ounce lead weights. After feeling the weight reach the bottom, they crank up on the reel three or four times to bring the rig off the ocean floor which puts the bait in line with the fish and helps to avoid tangling up in the rocks and coral.

The boat drifts over the fishing grounds waiting in anticipation for strikes to occur. The first go-around doesn't even produce a single nibble, and the captain informs everyone to reel in the lines so he can reposition the boat for a second go at it. The move pays off in dividends when everyone except Brandon lands a fish. The husband and wife each reel up a two-pound bluestripe snapper. Their kids bring up a pair of bright-pink Hawaiian hogfish, a close relative to the parrotfish that can be recognized by their elongated snout, protruding lips, and sharp teeth. Meanwhile, Justin pulls in a yellow-stripe goatfish, a species that gets its name from two long chemosensory barbells that protrude out of their chins like whiskers on a goat.

Brandon joins the party with a bang by hooking into something sizeable, and his line begins peeling off the reel. He waits for the initial run to end and sets in for a battle of man versus fish. Eventually, man wins the battle, and the fish succumbs to exhaustion, gradually floating up to the surface. The deckhand steps in to assist by gaffing the fish behind the head and hoists it out of the deep-blue water onto the deck. "Uku," he yells out. The deckhand uses a small wooden bat to whack the gray snapper and put it out of its misery.

After some successful bottom-fishing, the boat captain calls it a day and encourages the anglers to reel up their lines. He waits until the poles and gear have been securely stowed away before steaming ahead on the boat ride back to Maalaea Harbor. Along the way, he instructs the deckhand to release the trolling lures once again to test their luck at enticing some open water big game to bite. Their persistence pays off when the large gold reel begins peeling off line.

The deckhand excitedly cries out, "Hook up!" He looks over at Justin. "Sit in the fighting chair. I'm going to set the pole in the holder, and I need you to hang on to it. Don't start reeling until I have cleared the other two lines from the water."

Justin scrambles into a white-cushioned plastic seat with a matching backrest and teak wood accents that is fixed to the deck of the boat by a metal base. The chair can swivel and rock or be positioned at an angle and is equipped with a footrest and rod holders for use when landing large fish. He waits for the deckhand to remove the trolling pole from the railing holder and watches him place it into the rod holder on the fighting chair in between his legs. Justin tightly grabs ahold of the large sturdy fishing pole with both hands and watches the deckhand quickly reel in the other two lines and clear them out of the way.

The boat slows down to an eventual stop and Justin begins fighting a large fish several yards out in the water. He gradually settles in to a slide routine to regain line by lowering the rod tip, sliding forward on the seat, and reeling. The objective is to relieve some line pressure for ease of retrieving yet maintain a tight line to the fish. He then cups one hand over the reel face and pushes back with both legs, bringing the rod up to its maximum effective angle. Justin slides forward, repeating the procedure to bring the fish close to the boat.

Brandon is standing behind Justin, patting him on the back, and closely watching his good friend winning the battle. "Good job, Justin! You almost got him. Hang in there."

The deckhand stands to Justin's right, holding a long wooden gaff, verbally coaching him through the excitement, and watching with anticipation to identify the species. He loudly calls out after witnessing the fish surface in a splash of water ten yards behind the boat. "Big kine ono!"

The deckhand encourages the onlooking anglers to move inside the cabin. "Everyone, stand back. I'm going to bring the fish in. They have extremely sharp teeth that can cut your leg wide open if they decide to flop around." He leans over the railing with one hand on the leader line and a gaff in his other. "Reel in. Again. Again. Wait. OK again. Stop!" He uses the leader line to guide the fish close to the boat and swiftly harpoons the fish on the first attempt. "Way to go, Justin, nice one!" The deckhand yanks the fish up and over the railing with the gaff and strikes it twice in the head with the small bat.

Justin's forearms are burning from reeling in the twenty-pound ono. He leans back in the fighting chair, mesmerized by the sunlight reflecting off the ocean, and becomes lost in the dreamy moment. With the boat bobbing up and down in the rolling swells, a feeling of content overwhelms him. He watches a puffy, fast-moving cumulus cloud roll over the West Maui Mountains. The cloud formation suddenly morphs itself into the face of a young woman with long flowing hair racing out to sea. Then just as quickly as the woman appears, the wind speed picks up and blows the image back into a cotton-candy fluff ball.

Justin closes his eyes, envisioning a wooden plaque hanging in his parents' living room: Live by the Sea, Love by the Moon. He feels a real sense of being humbly grounded by his moral compass and thankful for the chance to catch such a nice fish. His eyes open to see the deckhand washing away fish blood, using a wide-mouth hose that draws water from the ocean. He receives a round of congratulations from the Canadian family on board, and even the captain wanders back from the wheelhouse for a look. After icing down the fish, they resume trolling for a few more minutes prior to reeling in the lines. When the boat arrives back at Maalaea Harbor, the deckhand cleans the catch, hands everyone a plastic bag of fillets, and assists the anglers off one at a time.

"Thanks for inviting me on the trip today, Brandon. I've always enjoyed boat rides and that feeling of freedom exploring the open ocean. Landing a few nice ones never hurts either!"

"Yeah, no worries. Good times today, for sure."

They arrive back at his parents' house, exchange a quick smack of hands, and Justin grabs a bag of fish. He walks inside the house, sets the bag inside the refrigerator, and reads a note left on the kitchen counter. "Hi, Justin. Hope you had a blast today with Brandon. Grandma invited all of us up to the house tomorrow for dinner. Hopefully, you caught some fish to bring along. Anyways, Mom and Dad are working, and I'm out with friends. See you tonight. Love ya, Melia."

Justin crumbles the yellow paper into a ball, jukes an invisible defender, and uses both hands to launch a high-arching shot at the rubbish can. Swish. With an empty house and no one coming home soon, he decides now would be an ideal time to experiment. He wanders over to the guesthouse and retrieves the nine stones and three recovered gifts from a stash spot high in the bedroom closet.

Justin sits out back on the patio furniture to analyze the hardened lump of tree sap, the bag of star sand, and the delicate scroll. He picks up the stone marked Haleakala in kanji on one side and a bird's head on the other. Remembering his parents have a bird book inside, he grabs it from the house and thumbs through several pages before stumbling on a section regarding Hawaiian honeycreepers. He identifies the bird on the stone as an iiwi, or scarlet honeycreeper, by the distinct slender, down-curved bill.

He removes a second stone from the pouch marked with Kauai on one side and a lizard etching on the other. Ever since first laying eyes on this rock back in Japan, Justin assumed the reptile to be a common gold dust gecko seen throughout the Hawaiian Islands. However, upon closer review, he notices an unusual flap of skin hanging beneath the creature's lower jaw called a dewlap and quickly associates the feature with the anole lizard.

Justin interlocks his fingers behind his head, inhales a deep breath of fresh air through his nose, and holds it for several seconds before exhaling from his mouth. With his eyes closed, he begins repeating the same breathing exercise several times in a row, incrementally extending the duration of each breath hold. On the ninth inhale, Justin is engulfed in an extremely relaxed demeanor as his heart rate slows and his mind calms. His concentration level deepens, and he becomes flooded with a flash of cloudy visions. He envisions a beach sunset where a pair of tilting tiki torches are burning, a conch shell blows, and three coconuts crash down into the sand.

While still holding his breath, Justin's eyes open, and a strong gust of wind blows through the backyard, mysteriously interacting with the vegetation. He suddenly develops the ability to identify each plant species in sight including their detailed biological structure, reproduction, and lifespan, specific information typically only a botanist would know from years of research and time spent in the field. He glances over at a wooden bowl of seashells on the patio table instantly accessing similar information about the creatures that once lived in the protective outer layers.

Now almost out of breath, Justin sees a large bat-shaped black witch moth land on a concrete wall of the house. The mystical-looking insect has a six-inch wingspan colored in mottled brown with hints of iridescent pink and purple. Although they are associated with death in the folklore of many cultures worldwide, the black witch moth is viewed positively in Hawaiian mythology. It represents a loved one who has just died and is an embodiment of the passer's soul returning to say goodbye.

Justin has become increasingly uncomfortable because of the lack of oxygen but for whatever reason senses a need to fight through his temptation to breathe. He trembles to a near-panic state but settles down and pushes beyond his comfort zone. His eyes feel heavy, and electrical charges pulsate through his limbs.

The moth flutters along the wall secreting saliva in an intricate pattern of interlacing lines and never-ending loops.

Seconds after finishing, a sudden gust of wind blows through the yard and carries the moth away, leaving Justin gasping for air. He awakens from the dreamy state, mentally exhausted but with clarity and a renewed sense of purpose. He can no longer recall the detailed information as was the case in the trancelike state, yet he now comprehends the process of tapping into it. By implementing some basic breath-hold techniques, Justin can temporarily enter an extremely focused state of mind, granting him access to the information each gift provides. However, this level of concentration lasts for the length of the breath hold only, and his last attempt came in at seventy seconds.

Justin gathers up the nine stones and gifts and walks inside the guesthouse to collapse on the bed. He falls into a deep sleep but is woken up later that evening as a deep rumbling echoes in the distance. He looks outside to see dark-gray clouds slowly approaching over Haleakala from the northeast and hears the sound of raindrops bouncing off the rooftop and tapping on the window. A cool draft blows in through a slightly cracked kitchen window. "Brrr." He reaches out for a throw blanket, changes the television to a channel broadcasting Hawaiian music, and settles down for a session of internet surfing.

Afterward, he boils water in a saucepan for hot tea. His mother keeps the guesthouse well stocked with supplies, including a nice selection of Hawaiian-grown coffee and specialty tea bags. "Chamomile, Earl Grey, green tea, Scottish Breakfast, and spiced chai. Definitely spiced chai."

He pulls off the lid from a small metal container, takes a deep whiff of the spicy vanilla goodness, and removes one of the pyramid-shaped tea bags. He drops it into a glass teacup and carefully pours in some steaming hot water. After allowing the brew to steep, he discards the bag, drips in a tablespoon of locally harvested honey, and adds a splash of milk. He stirs the glass using a tiny green porcelain spoon and takes a sip.

A new song starts up on the music channel, and the rhythmic sound of a strumming ukulele fills the airwaves. He instantly recognizes the famous medley of the songs "Somewhere Over the Rainbow" and "What a Wonderful World" by Bruddah IZ, and he grabs the remote to turn it up.

Justin opens the front door for a closer look outside at the stormy weather. He sits under the small covered patio drinking the hot tea and catches a lovely scent of night-blooming jasmine coming from a nearby bush. Water droplets fall from the rooftop ledge, and he hears a series of irregular pitched twitters over the calming music. The insect-like chirps resemble kids' sneakers squeaking on a gymnasium floor.

Several dozen tiny greenhouse frogs suddenly emerge from a pile of leaves and start hopping up and down on the concrete walkway in rhythm with the ukulele chords. The little frogs dance between the raindrops, jumping one foot high off the ground in all directions.

As the strumming ukulele continues toward the song's ending, so does the seemingly well-choreographed dancing-frog number. Justin looks on, bobbing his head left and right in quiet laughter as the lyrics fade away to a brief instrumental ending.

Zap! A bolt of lightning illuminates the sky, temporarily brightening the surrounding area, closely followed by a thunderous roar that sends the orchestra of frogs scattering in all directions. Within seconds the entire group has disappeared without a trace, leaving nothing more than a memory behind in the puddles. He feels a renewed sense of vitality from his animated encounter with the tiny frogs, basking in the moment before going back inside.

The following afternoon Justin, Melia, and their parents drive over to old Wailuku Heights for a fish fry with the grandparents. They bring along his catch from deep-sea fishing that will be nicely complemented by some fresh produce grown at the property. Grandfather Hayato and Grandmother Airi are both avid gardeners who meticulously care for their well-manicured yard where they grow a variety of fruit trees and vegetables. The property is located at the top of a steeply paved road that backs up against the West Maui Mountains with sweeping bicoastal views.

Grandmother Airi answers the door, delighted to see her loved ones. She invites everyone inside after greeting each of them with hugs and kisses.

"Oh my gosh. I'm so happy you are here, Justin! I haven't seen you in such a long time. You know, your grandfather and I are so very proud of you. Now, come in, come in. If you don't mind, please put the fish in the kitchen."

"Where's Grandpa Hayato?"

"Oh, honey, he's out back fooling with the yard. Feel free to go look for him. He talks so much about you and has been really looking forward to seeing you today."

Justin's dad is holding the bag of fish. "Would you like me to prepare the batter and coat these beauties for the fry?"

"That would be wonderful, my dear. Mahalo!"

Grandmother Airi fixes everyone a glass of freshly prepared minted lemonade, and the gang heads out back. They sit around an eco-wood outdoor patio set telling stories and watching Grandfather Hayato throw a tennis ball to his four-legged friend. She calls out to him in a gracefully charming voice, and he immediately looks over, noticing the family's arrival. Hayato waves back in excitement and reaches down to stroke their pet dog, Sandcastle, a chestnut red basenji.

Grandfather Hayato approaches the table full of energy, smiling broadly, and in a glorious mood. He exudes confidence, positivity, and compassion that is undeniably evident through his mannerisms and eloquent tone of speech. He is a charming, handsome man who possesses a way with words and the ability to carry on a conversation from now until eternity if you let him.

"Hello, everyone. Welcome and so good to see you." He walks over to securely hug Melia in the way only a loving grandfather can hug his grandchild. "My dearest Melia." Her mother is sitting right beside her, and she stands up to embrace him next. "Sakura, beautiful as the day I first laid eyes on you."

Hayato strolls around the table, passing by Grandmother Airi on the way over to see Justin. He gently places a hand on her shoulder, and she reaches out to grab ahold of his arm as they lock eyes and smile. "And you, sir. It's an honor to have a world traveler in the family. Your grandmother and I are thrilled to see you. Welcome home, Justin." They exchange a firm handshake followed by a warm hug. "Now sit down and tell us all about your adventures overseas."

Justin shares a couple of stories from college life in California before mentioning the unexpected passing of Yoshiaki. The mood at the table quickly changes from pleasantly interactive to quietly gloomy, and the family mourns his loss. Thankfully, Landon shows up just at the right time, carrying two hotel pans full of medium golden-brown fried fish and speaks to them in an English accent. "Your dinner is served."

The family indulges in the delicious meal while enjoying one another's company. At the end of dinner, they jointly clear the table and move inside to relax in the living room. Justin remains out back with Hayato, tossing the ball to Sandcastle.

"I usually take the dog for a walk about this time every evening, but my back has been acting up lately. Would you mind taking him out to burn off some energy? He seems to be really fond of you today for whatever reason."

Justin tosses the ball to Sandcastle, and the dog makes a leaping catch. "Yeah sure, no problem. Where should I take him?"

"Remember that dirt path at the end of the street that leads back into the mountains? Take him over there for a bit. He loves exploring the tree line." Grandfather Hayato walks inside to get a twenty-foot retractable dog leash and attaches the metal clip to his collar.

"We'll see you later. Come on boy, let's go!" Justin starts jogging and Sandcastle trots right alongside him. They skirt around the house to the front yard and walk past three neighboring properties en route to the path that cuts across a small field disappearing into the tree line. The rapidly setting sun has already vanished out of sight behind the mountains and will soon dip below sea level. However, the full moon has just risen above Haleakala and should provide plenty of illumination for the brief evening stroll.

The two companions march through the field to a sloping forest tree line where Justin unclips the excited dog to explore. He leans up against a banyan tree observing the strong prey drive deep within Sandcastle. The anxious canine eagerly sniffs along the ground, picking up several scents left behind, and suddenly bolts into a nearby bush, flushing out a pair of long-legged white cattle egrets. The scurrying waterbirds hustle out of the bush and take flight just in time to avoid the clenching jaws of the pursuing predator. Like many in the heron family, cattle egrets have a massive wingspan and can easily glide great distances.

Justin keeps an eye on Sandcastle, who is busy combing through an area roughly half the size of a football field. At one point he sees the dog in hot pursuit of a mongoose, and the two animals scamper off into the brush. He becomes concerned when Sandcastle fails to reappear and calls for his return but to no avail. So, he walks over to where the dog fled and stops at the forest edge to avoid entering the canopy of increasing darkness. He whistles and calls out. "Sandcastle, come here, boy."

Seconds later, he hears a high-pitched set of whistling and chirps coming from a songbird hidden within a nearby tree. Justin remains still and scans the branches, looking for the noisy culprit. He spots a small bright-crimson bird with black wings, white undertail coverts, and a long, downward-curving bill matching the etched image on the stone.

The bird drops down a couple of branches and continues singing in what seems like an attempt to communicate with him. Justin tries to imitate the song by whistling back at the bird in a similar tone. Suddenly, a lovely woman's voice can be heard chanting a sweet Hawaiian melody. Justin instantly feels overwhelmed by a surreal sensation. Without hesitation, he steps into the calling forest, drawn to the soothing sound.

Meanwhile, the bird follows closely behind Justin, bouncing from shrub to shrub, wildly squawking up a storm, and suddenly darts past him to land on a flowering ohi'a lehua evergreen tree. A frosty whirlwind swirls into the area out of nowhere, clearing away the fallen leaves in its path. The vortex concentrates into a bright sphere resembling the moon, bursts into a puffy white cloud, and morphs into the female Hawaiian lunar deity, Hina.

Justin stands frozen in time, mystified by her presence, grace, and sensuality. She is dressed in a white-and-silver wrap that drapes over her left shoulder, eloquently flowing down to her midthighs. She wears a headband lei made of purple-and-white orchids that holds back a thick lock of long, straight black hair that dangles down to her waist, accented by a matching lei around her neck. She has soft, dark-honey colored skin with warm orange-red undertones and stunning facial features emphasized by piercing brown eyes and sultry lips.

The Hawaiian word *mahina* means moon, moonlight, and/or month, which are symbols usually associated with women. *Hina* is a name variation given to the Polynesian goddess who represents female energy, strength, and conviction. In Hawaiian culture, Hina takes on many identities, including the mother of Maui and goddess of corals and fisherman, but she is also closely associated with the moon, communication, cycles, and mediation. She is a personification of the feminine and known for her willingness to give.

Hina is carrying a rolled-up pure-white kapa cloth made of pounded bark. She unties a bit of string holding the kapa together, lightly tosses it upward with a flick of her wrist, and magically commands the kapa to unravel. As the cloth straightens out, it makes a snapping noise resembling the popping sound of a rolled-up towel when whipped. The kapa flutters down beside the ohia tree, emitting a faint light that radiates a couple of feet off the ground.

She sits down at one end of the kapa and signals for Justin to join her. "Don't be afraid. Come and sit. I am Hina, and you have nothing to fear."

He sits across from her on the smooth linen. "Pleased to meet you, Hina. My name is Justin."

She raises her arms up to shoulder height, causing light from the linen to enclose them in a cocoon from the outside world. "I have a story to share with you today. May I borrow that string around your neck?"

Justin unclips his fishhook necklace and reaches out to turn over the twisted cord. When he places the piece of jewelry into her open palm, a bright wave of light splashes outward and gets absorbed down into the cloth.

Hina gives him back the hand-carved wooden hook, lays the cordage down on the cloth, and removes some twine from her headband. She then ties the two pieces together in a true love knot; a type of knot that consists of two interlocked over-hand bowknots made from two cords that sit close together when tightened.

Images begin projecting from within the cocoon of light resembling a movie theater surround screen. Each clip lasts for several seconds, showing various people engaged in daily life. Justin can truly feel each of their individual emotions through-out the different scenes of love, affection, and friendship. An aging married couple strolls through the park hand in hand. Children run and laugh in a game of duck, duck, goose. Twin sisters, separated at birth, reunite forty years later. A family wel-comes the birth of their child. Four generations of women pose for a holiday photograph. An entire city in celebration after their team just won a world sports championship.

Human beings possess a wide spectrum of emotions that have traditionally been broken down into six broad categories: anger, disgust, fear, happiness, sadness, and surprise. However new scientific studies suggest there might be twenty-seven types of interconnected emotions that can represent a feeling. The expanded list now includes admiration, adoration, aesthetic appreciation, amusement, anxiety, awe, awkwardness, bore-dom, calmness, confusion, craving, desire, disgust, empathetic pain, entrancement, envy, excitement, fear, horror, interest, joy, nostalgia, romance, sadness, satisfaction, sympathy, and tri-umph. Some of the emotions such as anger and happiness are not even on the new list, but these feelings can originate from other emotions such as envy and satisfaction. Also, multiple emotions can overlap and be elicited from one specific event rather than just one single feeling.

The last image fades away leaving Justin speechless and with a greater understanding of sentiment. He makes spirited eye contact with Hina, still sitting frozen by her inspirational presence. After a few mystic seconds tick by, she releases Justin from the charm and instructs him to pick up the true love knot. "As you continue through this journey of life, remember to never forget the complexity of human emotions. The more you seek to understand others, the more they will seek to understand you, and in doing so humankind shall benefit moving forward. Lead by example, do what is right, and be the change you wish to see in the world. Did I mention peace, love, and sandy feet?"

Justin and Hina share a brief laugh, and the cocoon light fades away, leaving only a faint illumination coming from the cloth.

"I must go now," she says. "Take care of yourself."

"Wait. Why? I have so many questions to ask you."

"The answers you seek lie within your heart, mind, and soul." Hina slowly dissipates back into a concentrated sphere of light hovering several feet off the ground.

Justin grabs the true love knot, steps off the cloth, and watches it become absorbed into the ball of light.

"Take me with you."

Her voice projects from the sphere. "It's not your time. You still have much to achieve. Be brave and *malama pono*." Her voice fades away saying, "*Ua ola loko i ke aloha*," meaning "Love gives life within."

Before Justin can respond, the tree limbs part ways overhead, and the sphere of light blasts off toward the full moon. He stands motionless for several seconds, staring up at the clear night sky as Hina streaks away like a reverse shooting star. The moment she vanishes, Justin feels something press up against his thigh, and he looks down to see Sandcastle standing on his two hind feet leaning up against him. He pets the dog's head. "Hey, boy. I thought you might have gotten lost." Sandcastle makes a whimpering sound, drops down on all fours, and excitedly spins in three circles chasing his tail. "What do you say we get out of here?" The dog replies with a yodel of approval.

9

HOUSE OF THE SUN

The following morning, Justin, Melia, and Brandon take off on an overnight camping trip to Haleakala National Park. The thirty-seven-mile drive from sea level to the ten-thousand-foot volcano summit is the world's highest elevation gain in the shortest distance. They work their way upcountry to the small town of Kula and hang a left onto Highway 378/Crater Road for the eleven-mile stretch to the park entrance. The highway is slow going with numerous driving hazards that include an inversion cloud layer at seven thousand feet, steep turns, oncoming downhill bike tours, heavy traffic, slippery pavement, and the occasional bout of altitude sickness.

They arrive at the entrance to the park and pay twenty-five dollars to explore the remote wilderness encompassing more than thirty thousand acres. Brandon pulls over at Hosmer Grove campground, so they can use the restrooms and stretch their legs before tackling the remaining ten-mile drive to the summit.

Justin has a quick look around while waiting for Brandon and Melia to use the facilities. He walks past the designated camping area where some tents are pitched in the grass.

Three people are sitting on a picnic table drinking coffee, and another family of four departs on the hiking trail. A homeless man in his sixties slowly pushes a shopping cart. The thin, medium-height man is wearing khaki shorts, a flannel shirt, and a green bucket hat drooped over his shaggy head. He has on dark sunglasses, sports a full gray beard, and unlaced hiking boots without socks.

The homeless man walks right past Justin calmly speaking. "Did you know scientists estimate there are one billion, trillion stars in the observable universe?" Without waiting for an answer, the man continues pushing the shopping cart repeating a phrase. "Patience is a virtue, expect the unexpected. Patience is a virtue, expect the unexpected. Patience is a virtue, expect the unexpected."

They drive to the Park Headquarters Visitor Center to pick up a camping permit. The original plan was to stay overnight at one of the three cabins located in the summit area, Paliku, Kapalaoa, and Holua. However, the cabins require a reservation six months in advance, so they opt for tent camping instead. Both Holua and Paliku also have primitive wilderness campsites with pit toilets and undrinkable water. The trio has decided to visit Holua, which requires a seven-mile hike down the Sliding Sands Trail.

They reach the Red Hill summit overlooking the Haleakala Observatory site, an area off-limits to the public. The complex is Hawaii's first astronomical research observatory and features several dome buildings that house high-powered telescopes and multiple research facilities.

They loop around the uppermost horseshoe lot and drive back down less than a mile to park at the Haleakala Visitor Center. After exiting the car and strapping on their backpacks, Justin, Melia, and Brandon set out on the long day of hiking.

The summit weather can be unpredictable at times with varying temperatures. Fortunately, they are venturing out on a pristine day with clear blue skies, light wind, and warm weather. A much-welcomed sight considering their next four hours will be spent trekking over loose cinders and rocks along the three-thousand-foot drop in altitude to the campsite that is located at seven-thousand-feet elevation.

A park employee waits to greet them at the Sliding Sands Trailhead. "Aloha. How y'all doing today? Looks like you three are setting off on a big hike! You guys picked a perfect day to experience all this natural beauty."

"Look at that, amazing!" says Melia.

She gets her first glance at the panoramic views down into the erosional valley of Haleakala's summit region, which is peppered with young cinder cones and lava flows that blanket the depression floor. There are a dozen cinder cones in view; each one is the site of an eruption, and each one has its own crater. Much of the alpine cinder desert valley is colored in an earthy natural-clay pigment with ashen tones except for the eastern ridges that are painted green by a lush fern forest.

Melia and Brandon engage the park employee in a brief conversation about what to expect on the trail. Meanwhile, Justin spots a nearby Haleakala silversword in full bloom and moves in for a closer look. The unusual plant's low-growing, dense rosette form resembles a bouquet of swords in a circular arrangement of silver, spiky, fleshy leaves. The silversword can live up to ninety years, flowering only once in a lifetime by sending up a spectacular stalk covered in hundreds of vibrant purple flowers that soon die, scattering dry seeds into the wind.

The hikers set off on the initial part of the trail where the ground underfoot turns to cinders, and the trail's signature switchbacks drop steeply away from the main park road. Plant life is quite sparse with an occasional silversword popping up alongside the path but not much else. About a mile into the hike, they encounter a small flock of foraging chukars, a small exotic upland game bird in the pheasant family. The half dozen birds simultaneously look up when they approach and bolt across the landscape like roadrunners.

Brandon takes a drink from his water bottle. "My uncle hunts those birds and claims they are good eating."

"They kind of look like little turkeys. What kind are they?" asks Justin.

"I forget the name."

Melia watches the pheasants speed away. "Chukars."

"Yeah, that's it. Chukars," replies Brandon.

"Supposedly in Indian mythology, the chukar is deeply in love with the moon and stares at it longingly."

Brandon laughs. "What? Did you just make that up?"

"No. The park ranger guy mentioned it when I asked him about the wildlife we can expect to see today. Weren't you listening? He also said we should have a spectacular view of the full moon tonight."

Justin can see Melia is frustrated and chimes in to keep the conversation light. "What else did he say we might see?"

Melia lets out a grumbly sigh and looks over at Justin. "Nene goose, pueo, the seabird Hawaiian petrel, bats, rodents. Not much else can survive up here in this harsh environment."

"Pueos live up here? Cool, I hope we see an owl!" replies Justin.

They continue descending along the switchbacks for another couple of miles, passing an occasional hiker or two heading back out in the opposite direction. The trail gradually becomes rockier as it passes through lava fields, sidesteps a giant rust-colored cinder cone and bottoms out on the volcano floor. They come to a metal hitching rail used by guided horse-back tours and veer left at a major signposted trail junction that points northeast to Holua. After walking a mile on the softer cinder trail, they reach a small crest that rolls downhill to the next major four-way junction.

Justin reads from a map. "According to the directions, we are supposed to turn here at Halemauu Trail."

Melia and Brandon move to either side of him for a look at the map and concur. They trek north on the Halemauu Trail for two miles, passing through a section known as Silversword Loop. The easygoing side trail rolls gently up and down through a naturally occurring garden of silversword plants before con-tinuing another mile to the Holua cabin area. They walk by an empty ranger cabin to discover the already flattened campsite set on a small ledge overlooking the volcanic floor.

Brandon removes his backpack, drops it on the ground, and lies down in a patch of dry grass. "I'm so glad we finally made it. My feet are killing me." He takes off his hiking boots to massage his feet.

A large orange tent that appears to be unoccupied is set up on the right-hand side of the campground. So, Melia walks to the opposite end.

"This looks like a good spot. What do you think?" She removes her pack. "Let's get our tents set up."

Justin walks next to Melia. "Yeah, I agree. This should be fine." He removes a small bag containing the two-person tent, dumps out the contents, and puts it together.

Melia crawls inside to relax. "Nice. I like it! Home sweet home."

Brandon sits up in the grass looking exhausted. "I just want to chill here for a minute. That hike really wiped me out."

"Throw me your one-man, and I'll set it up for you," says Justin.

"Thanks, bro." Brandon locates the tent and tosses it to Justin, who proceeds to quickly erect the camouflage tent.

"There you go, all set. Relax inside and drink lots of fluids. You're probably dehydrated. I brought along some Gatorades if you want one." Justin reaches down to assist Brandon to his feet and hands him the purple sports drink.

"I'm going to crash for a while. Thanks, Justin, I appreciate the help." Brandon drags his backpack into the tent and zips it up.

Justin lies down next to Melia in their tent and the two siblings fall asleep. When Justin wakes up, he grabs some granola bars and two bottles of water.

Melia yawns and stretches. "Where are you going?"

"I was thinking about sitting on that ledge overlooking the summit. Wanna join me?" He points to a nearby rocky outcrop.

"Sure, that sounds like fun. I'll meet you over there in a few."

Justin finds a flat spot on the rocks to sit down, and Melia joins him shortly after. They munch on some peanut butter granola bars while taking in the scenic sunset view. A cloud layer has begun to form across the volcano floor behind them.

"Absolutely breathtaking," says Melia. "I'm glad we decided to make this trip. Well worth the long day of hiking."

"Yes, I agree. Quite spectacular indeed." Justin looks over at Melia, and he can see she is visibly shaken. "Quite moving, right?"

Melia wipes her eyes and sniffles. "What? Oh yes. It's beautiful. Can I talk to you about something personal?"

"Yeah, sure. Anything."

"Ever since we were little kids, the two of us have shared a deep connection. Through good times and bad, you have always been there for me, and I have always tried to be there for you. No one on earth knows me better than you, my brother, and I know you better than anyone else. Our love is genuine and pure. So, when I say what I'm about to, consider the source and try to answer honestly." A tear streams down her cheek.

"You are becoming a different person in a way I can't explain and don't understand. I feel it in my bones. Please tell me what's going on. I'm worried about you, Justin." Another tear rolls down her face. "I tried sharing my feelings with your friend Brandon over there, and he thinks I'm crazy. But something happened when you were in Japan, and you have not been the same since." Melia wipes her eyes and tries to gather herself.

Justin leans in to give her a hug and shares the story of his trip to Japan. He tells her about the inherited pocket watch from Great Grandfather Saito, the nine stones he found with Kaito, all four mystical encounters, and the magical gifts.

With her hand on her chin, Melia piercingly stares at Justin with her best poker face, amazed at what she just heard.

"What? You don't believe me?" exclaims Justin.

A few seconds later, she grabs him for a giant hug, kicking her heels on the ground in excitement. "Believe you? Yes, of course I believe you. Can I see the gifts you were talking about? Where are they? How do they work? Oh my gosh—this is amazing! I knew it. I knew it! Wait till Brandon finds out. Won't he feel stupid."

"Calm down, calm down. They are hidden at the house. I'll show them to you tomorrow when we get home. But you can't tell Brandon or anyone else, for that matter. This has to remain a secret."

"Who else knows about it?"

"Just the two of us and Kaito. Promise me you won't say a word of this to anyone."

"Yes, I promise."

They sit quietly together, staring at the setting sun until he breaks the silence. "What do you say we go see how Brandon is doing?"

Justin stands up and turns around to see his gigantic shadow cast down upon the cloudy valley below. He waves his arms back and forth with a big smile on his face, watching them stretch out from what seems like forever. He taps Melia on the shoulder, encouraging her to have a look. She stands up to witness the optical illusion of their humongous shadows casting across the summit floor, surrounded by colorful rings of light, and they both begin to laugh.

This shadow illusion is known as Brocken specter, anticorona, Brocken bow, mountain specter, and mountain glory. The name Brocken originated from the highest peak in the Harz mountain range of Northern Germany known for frequent fogs. This specter appears when the sun shines from behind the observer, who is looking down from a ridge into fog or mist. The light projects an enormous shadow of the observer upon the clouds, opposite of the sun's direction, and often in a triangular shape. Around the shadow in the mist appears a halo of rainbow colors. Native Hawaiians called this natural phenomenon *hookuaka*, meaning a view of the soul.

10

THE PRESERVE

Two days after the Haleakala hiking trip, Justin and Melia pack their bags and board a flight for the Big Island of Hawaii. They touch down at the Kona International Airport midday and are picked up by Melia's friend, Anuhea. The two girls grew up together on Maui, attending the same elementary and middle schools. Anuhea has invited them to stay at her family's home in the Kailua-Kona district on the Western Slopes of Hualalai, one of the five volcanoes that form the island of Hawaii.

From the moment they step into Anuhea's car, the two girls start chatting at an incredibly fast pace, almost too quickly for Justin to comprehend what they are saying. He listens in bewilderment to the eerily frantic speed of their conversation and doesn't even attempt to get a word in. How can two people cover so much information in such a short time? Incredible. Really, quite astonishing. Never in his entire life has he heard two people talk so fast.

After exiting the airport, they hang a right onto Highway 19, one of three state routes that form a circle around the island, often called the "Hawaii Belt." The drive to Kailua-Kona travels along a harsh, semibarren lava field road overlooking the glistening Pacific Ocean in the distance. The rocky terrain is home to a large population of wild goats that can be easily spotted foraging for grasses and other vegetation in the hardened black lava.

Without skipping a beat, Anuhea shifts the conversation Justin's way, finally acknowledging his presence.

"Hey there, Justin! Wow, it's been a long time since I last saw you. How have you been? Melia said you go to school in Cali nowadays and mentioned you just went to Japan. Sounds exciting! So, what brings you to the Big Island?"

"Hello, Anuhea, good to see you. Yeah, you know, a little R & R and the chance to play tourist for a couple of days."

"Right on, right on. Big Island is mo bettah, so they say."

"I also wanted to get a look at the ancient koa trees in the Kona Hema Preserve. Over in Japan, I had the opportunity to visit Jomon Sugi, the nation's oldest living tree, and it has sparked my interest in the living titans."

"Righteous! I can feel your passion. We can definitely make that happen. The preserve is only an hour drive from our house. By the way, I've got a surprise for you two. My auntie arranged for us to have a private tour of the seahorse farm today. It's just up the road on our way home. What do you say?"

Melia chimes in. "A seahorse farm? Oh my gosh, how cute is that? I love seahorses. That sounds like fun."

"Really, a seahorse farm? I've never heard of one, but that does sound rad," replies Justin.

"Good, good. I'm glad to hear you two are up for it. I'm excited! In fact, we'll be there at the next turn."

They pull onto the crushed stone gravel parking lot and stop in front of three white picnic tables sitting beside a single-story sky-blue building. Justin holds the door open for the two girls and follows them inside the spacious, air-conditioned gift shop.

A lanky young man with long brown hair tied into a bun intro-duces himself as Liam and explains that he will be their tour guide through the facility. He is wearing a black shirt that has an image of a red seahorse and says, "Stars of fairy tales, legends, and Greek mythology." Apparently, his mother and Anuhea's aunt are good friends, having known each other for many years. He is soft-spoken and very friendly. "Do you have any questions before we get started? No? OK. Follow me right this way."

He leads them down a small corridor that opens into a large, tarp-covered outdoor facility containing several separate sections. They visit circular tanks of various sizes that resem-ble stand-up swimming pools, each housing different seahorse species at varying growth stages. Several employees can be seen cleaning the white PVC pipe running in every direction and testing the water conditions inside the tanks.

"Besides caring for all these seahorses around us, or the canaries of the sea, as some refer to them, we also raise banded pipefish, Banggai cardinalfish, and clownfish," says Liam.

"Banggai cardinalfish? Those sound cool. Can you show us some?" asks Melia.

"Yes, follow me."

Liam continues speaking as they walk to the marine fish section. "At the end of the tour, we have an exhibit set up with several glass aquariums for viewing each of the species up close. Although we don't breed them here at the farm, there are a few leafy sea dragons in one of the tanks, an endangered relative of the seahorse."

After showing them the marine fish, Liam brings the group back to a chest-high, kiddie pool–size circular tank where they feed live brine shrimp to some yellow-spotted seahorses. Then they visit another tank where they get a chance to hold a mature specimen. Seahorses grasp objects with their curled, flexible tails and often anchor themselves to vegetation. However, in this case, a finger will do just fine.

Their tour concludes at the glass aquarium exhibit, adjacent to the gift shop, were Liam goes into his concluding speech.

"So…hopefully, you can see we are both 'a different kind of farm' and an educational facility that offers a better understanding of the ocean environment to those willing to listen. Keep in mind that humankind has now fished ninety percent of the fish from our oceans in the last fifty years alone. How much longer will the remaining ten percent last? We need sustainability in the food we eat and sustainability in the animals we keep as pets. It takes a conscious effort by fish suppliers, retailers, and consumers alike to stop bleeding our oceans dry."

Justin sees the red seahorse on Liam's shirt fluttering about ever so gently. His eyes crinkle in disbelief, and he wonders if he is imagining the animation that abruptly stops.

Liam continues. "We are endangered species conservationists and invite you to get involved. Thank you for visiting our eco-farm today. It's been nice meeting you three. The restrooms are right over there and when you are done looking at the aquariums, you can exit back into the gift shop through that door. Have a good day! Mahalo!"

Melia grabs Anuhea's hand. "What an interesting place! I have to use the bathroom before we get going. Will you come with me?"

They disappear into the women's restroom, leaving Justin behind to wander about the aquariums. He approaches a tank of variously colored dwarf seahorses nicknamed pixies and kneels for a closer look at the tiny, delicate creatures that measure one and a half inches.

According to Guinness World Records, the dwarf seahorse is the slowest moving fish on earth with a top speed of five feet per hour. They swim upright, propelling themselves by using the dorsal fin and maneuver about by using pectoral fins located on either side of the head.

Justin closes his eyes inhaling through his nose and exhaling through his mouth. He does this several times in a row, lengthening the interval between each breath until reaching a thirty-second pause. On the ninth inhale, his eyes open, and a calming sensation flows throughout his body as he enters the trancelike state.

The pixies begin to interact with one another in an unusual manner, and all nine marine animals in the twenty-five-gallon tank form a single-file line and start swimming in unison. They stop just in front of the glass near Justin's nose and spread out to form a perfect circle. He delightfully grins at the colorful little creatures who return his gesture by forming a happy face with two seahorses representing the eyes, one as the nose, and the remaining six a smile. Justin places his fingertip on the glass, draws a triangle, and pulls his hand away to observe the tiny fish follow suit. He then swirls his hand in several circles and the pixies commence a majestic underwater dance.

Melia returns from the restroom alone and notices Justin gazing into the dwarf seahorse aquarium. She can see the pixies' unusual movements and quickly realizes Justin must have something to do with it. "Stop harassing the locals."

Justin is startled by her unexpected touch and takes a deep breath, instantly returning to a normal state of reality. Simultaneously the seahorses resume their typical behavior pattern and disperse within the tank.

Anuhea joins them in the aquarium room, and they visit each of the various tanks. At the end of the line, they funnel through the exit door into the gift shop. Justin purchases a souvenir T-shirt, buys each of the girls a set of seahorse earrings, and puts some cash into a donation jar supporting ocean awareness. They make the remaining drive to Kona and stop off for some lunch at a well-known fish-and-chips hotspot to indulge in some onion rings, steamed clams, pickle chips, and beer-battered mahi-mahi. When lunch concludes they drive across town and up the sloping lush green hillside to Anuhea's family property that includes a coffee farm.

Justin and Melia are shown to a guest room in the family home where they will stay for a couple of nights while on the island. After they drop off their bags, Anuhea walks them down to a small barn that houses farming equipment, and they jump into a four-wheel drive, all-terrain vehicle for a tour of the property. Anuhea drives, Melia rides shotgun, and Justin sits behind them on one of the two rear seats of the hunter-green quad. They drive down a dirt road, passing the production facility, to a sprawling coffee orchard of three thousand small trees decorated in tiny arabica cherries.

On the ride back, they stop off at the production facility where Anuhea introduces them to her family and a couple of the farm's employees. The crew runs light this time of year but will double in size during the next few months to harvest and process the ripening cherries. Anuhea shows them the drying racks, hulling machinery that removes the parchment layer, a bagging area for exporting milled beans, roasting machines, and a packing room for grounds and whole beans. The tour concludes at the gift shop and tasting room where they sit down at a patio table to enjoy a cup of freshly brewed coffee.

"My cousins are planning a barbeque at their place this evening and invited us over to join them if you two want to go. The boys tend to be a bit rowdy at times, but there should be plenty of good food, music, and laughs."

Justin sits quietly as the two girls fall right into another session of high-speed chatter. After patiently listening to them for a while, he politely interrupts their conversation and offers to pick up some produce to go along with dinner. Anuhea suggests a local farmer's market on the edge of town and lends him the keys to her car. They plan to meet up at her cousin's house located on the same property later that evening.

Justin drives over to the outdoor market set in a parking lot of the shopping center. A handful of vendors are selling produce, flowers, food, clothing, and miscellaneous souvenirs to a mixed crowd of locals and tourists. He purchases some tomatoes, avocados, toasted coconut crisps, dried mangoes rolled in sweet and tangy li hing mui powder, and a dozen mountain apples.

Justin returns to the car and sets the bag of items down on the passenger seat. He cranks the air-conditioning to full blast and pulls out his cell phone to text Yori.

"Thinking of you and wanted to say hi. I'll be returning to CA in about a week. Did you hear anything on the visa and whatnot?"

She replies, "Justin! Funny you would ask me that today. My travel arrangements were stamped for approval this morning, and I am booking a flight into LAX in ten days."

"Really? That's fantastic. I'll make sure my return trip matches your arrival date."

Yori sends him a final message containing a selfie of her winking an eye, puckering her lips, and showing her long black hair pulled into a ponytail.

Justin scrolls through his contacts to find Melia and sends her a text. "Hey, sis. I decided to take a short drive up the coast. Hope it's OK to borrow Anuhea's car. See you later this evening."

Melia replies, "She said no worries, and we'll see you tonight."

Justin searches for the Kona Hema Preserve and plugs the coordinates into a mapping application on his phone. The preserve is thirty-five miles away and will take just over an hour to reach. He tunes the radio to a local reggae station and sets off south. Upon reaching his destination, Justin parks in front of a posted sign reading Kona Hema Preserve that is staked into the ground alongside a locked yellow swing gate. An additional sign attached to the gate indicates the preserve is off-limits to the public and that trespassers will be prosecuted. The entire perimeter is lined with wire mesh fencing to prevent access.

Justin steps out of the car, flips the door closed behind his back and stares at the gate pondering what to do next. After analyzing the situation, he figures the risk is worth the reward and decides to enter the preserve for a closer look. He attempts to climb over the yellow swing gate, but multiple cars roar by on the highway in opposite directions, and he backs away to reconsider his options. After scanning the area in both directions, he walks over to a section of the fence line that slopes downward and temporarily curves out of sight behind a small cluster of young koa trees. "That looks like a better spot."

Justin attempts to jump the fence by swinging his right leg over the smooth wire. He cries out in agony after clipping his heel on the sharp metal post corner. A patch of skin the size of a dime is flipped back and lightly bleeding.

Something buzzes by his left ear that sounds like a gas-powered Weedwacker. He turns his head to follow the fading noise, and he sees what looks like a black bumblebee flying off. Seconds later, another insect buzzes his right ear, followed by another past his left, and another one past his right.

Justin hobbles down the fence line to a papaya tree where the black bumblebees are gorging themselves on overripe fruit.

However, he moves in for a closer look and realizes those are not bumblebees but rather large beetles. He reaches out to pick one off the tree and holds the bug in his palm. The hefty insect is the size of his upper thumb with long slender legs and a raylike antenna on its head. The black-bodied bug is splotched with white markings and coated in a bronzy-metallic sheen.

Justin realizes the beetle image found on the stone matches the oriental flower beetles drawn to the fermenting papaya. He locates a chink near one of the fence posts, pulls back on the loose wire to enlarge the opening, and carefully slips through into the preserve. A Hawaiian hawk glides by overhead making a loud screech en route to landing in a tree. Several colorful songbirds, a colony of hoary bats, two short-eared owls, and a flock of crows swoop into the same tree, causing quite the ruckus.

In the blink of an eye, four larger-than-life Hawaiians dressed in loincloths suddenly appear around the tree. Justin realizes those aren't regular men at all but rather native Hawaiian deities. Kane, Hawaiian god of wild food and the forest, and father of the other three men, is wearing a magnificent red-and-yellow feather helmet and grips a long koa-wood spear with his right hand. Next to him stands Ku, the god of war, who proudly displays a giant boar tusk necklace and is wielding a flaming mace said to contain the souls of those he has slain. Next to Ku is Lono, the god of cultivated food, peace, learning, and music. He clutches an intricately decorated ukulele in one hand, dangling the instrument by its head. Finally, standing next to him is Kanaloa, god of the ocean, healing, and the underworld. He is holding a freshly pulled uhaloa plant in his left hand, a species of flowering shrub with medicinal properties, commonly called sleepy morning.

Ku speaks to him in a raspy voice. "What brings you to this sacred land?" His thundering tone causes the crows to squawk and stir in the tree.

"Well, for whatever reason, I felt compelled to visit these ancient trees and explore this untouched ecosystem."

Ku is unhappy with his response and harshly replies. "So, you decided to trespass in this protected forest for your own personal satisfaction? How dare you!" He jabs the fiery mace forward in an aggressive manner, causing additional flames and smoke to burst out from the tip.

Justin freezes with the smile cleanly wiped from his face and tries to ease the tension. "Whoa. I apologize for entering the preserve uninvited like this, and I mean no disrespect. If you want me to leave now, I can go."

Kane interrupts in a deep, stern voice. "Ku, that's enough."

Lono takes two steps forward and addresses Justin in a neutral manner. "Somehow you have successfully navigated to this point of the arduous journey bestowed upon you. Well done. He points to a rocky ledge nearby. "But if you want to leave here today with that which you seek, show us your courage and jump into the freshwater pool below."

Kane solemnly says, "If you survive the fall—and that is a big if—you will be gifted one of these four objects we hold before you."

Justin cautiously walks to the edge, peers over the sheer drop-off, and sees a relatively good-size freshwater spring far below. "You want me to jump off from way up here and land way down there in that small pond? That must be fifty feet."

Kanaloa jokingly responds, "You better aim for the middle."

The men start laughing loudly, causing the crows to squawk and stir again.

Justin defiantly replies, "And if I say no?"

Kanaloa gives Ku a devious look and turns back to Justin "Maybe he throws you over."

Ku makes a grimacing face, and the men burst into laughter.

* * *

"I choose option number one." Justin takes several steps back and wipes some moisture from his brow. "Here goes nothing." He sprints toward the edge and leaps.

Lono calls out. "No cliff is so tall it cannot be climbed."

Justin descends into the gorge feet first with his arms flailing helplessly, free-falling for nearly two seconds before impacting the fresh water at a speed of thirty-five miles per hour. Fortunately, he timed the jump correctly and lands near the middle of the spring pool unharmed. Although he is now fifteen feet under water and disoriented. Justin gathers himself and swims up toward the light. An intense burning sensation fills his lungs as oxygen drains from his body with each stroke and kick. Eventually, he breaks the surface, gasping for air, and he shivers out of the valley as twilight falls upon the preserve. He fumbles toward the ohia lehua tree where the deities once stood and is surprised when he instead finds four wooden tiki statues. The intricately decorated ukulele Lono held now rests on the ground leaning against his tiki.

"What do we have here?" Justin picks up the guitar-like instrument for a closer look. The vintage four-stringed ukulele is made from deep-auburn, tiger-striped koa wood with shark-teeth tuners and Polynesian artwork across the back of the body. Also, a familiar symbol has been etched around the sound hole. "That is the same marking from the pocket watch and knife."

Justin strums the ukulele a few times with his bare thumb and fingertips high up on the neck to create a creepy crawly sound. The hair-raising noise incites a state of panic in the tree, causing the bats and birds to disperse into the darkening forest. He walks over to the fence and stops with one foot through the opening. His head rotates around for one last look at the tikis, but the wooden statues have vanished.

Back at the car, Justin sits in the driver's seat holding the ukulele. He hears a low rumbling sound of oversize tires on the highway, followed closely by a Jeep of laughing teenagers that goes whizzing by. He examines the ukulele in the light and notices a folded note within the instrument's sound hole. Justin slips his finger in between the strings to fish out the letter.

"This special ukulele is much more than a simple musical instrument. It's a representation of the arts, an expression of sentiment done by people with skill and imagination. These various acts of creativity have brought joy to the world in many forms including music, literature, painting, sculpture, drama, acting, and dance. Take pride in accepting this gift and know you are now sworn to protect its secrecy. Oh, and one last thing. Be sure to pay a visit to Kalakaua Beach on the island of Kauai. But be forewarned that the road you travel is a treacherous one. Lono"

The note disintegrates in Justin's hand. He gently sets the instrument down on the passenger seat and grabs his cell phone. After reprogramming the mapping application to the coffee farm address, he starts the ignition and pulls out on the highway. Still damp and cold from the spring water, Justin cranks on the heater and makes the long drive back to Kona.

Upon arriving at Anuhea's family property, a stocky young man wearing a hoodie and board shorts approaches Justin outside the car and speaks to him in a vibrant Hawaiian accent. "Hey, whatz up braddah? You must be Justin. I'm Anuhea's boyfriend, Pika. She mentioned that you borrowed the car to play tourist this afternoon."

"What's up, Pika? Good to meet you."

"I'm headed around back if you want to join me."

"Go on ahead without me for now. I need to change into some clean clothes. I'll see you over there shortly."

"Shoots. Catch ya later, brah."

Justin waits for Pika to fade around the corner, and he snatches up the ukulele from the passenger seat. He walks over to the adjacent house where their guest room is located, changes into some dry clothes, and stashes the instrument in his luggage. Afterward, he drifts over to the backyard barbeque party looking for Melia among the guests. She is lounging in a beach chair by the blazing firepit, sitting with Pika, Anuhea, and one of her poofy, curly-haired cousins.

Melia calls out for him over the pulsating reggae beats. "Justin! You finally made it back." She points to a buffet table of potluck dishes ranging from kalua pig and poi to chicken long rice and laulau. Starving from such a long afternoon, he loads a plate with the traditional Hawaiian cuisine and joins the group.

"What's up, everybody?" Justin eagerly digs in to the food, scarfing down half of his meal.

"How did the car hold up?" asks Anuhea.

He wipes his mouth with a napkin between bites. "Oh, the car held up great today. Thanks for letting me borrow it."

"You were gone for a long time. Where did you end up going?" asks Melia.

"Well, I first checked out the farmers market." Justin takes another bite of the kalua pig and closes his eyes to enjoy the tender, juicy slow-cooked pork. "Mmm, that's so good," he says under his breath and continues. "But I figured you two had a lot of catching up to do, so rather than hurry back to the coffee farm, I went for a long drive to the preserve."

Melia looks sharply over at Justin but restrains herself from scolding him in front of the group. She wonders why he went out there alone and is concerned that something might have happened. "Do we still need to visit there tomorrow?"

Mesmerized by the dancing flames, Justin looks up at Melia. "No, I don't see any reason for us to make another trip out there. We can do something else instead."

Anuhea claps her hands together. "I've got a great idea. Let's go zip line tomorrow! I know someone who can get us a discount." She looks over at Pika sitting beside her and smacks him on the knee a couple of times. He works for a local company that operates helicopter tours over the volcanoes and runs zip lines through the tropical forests.

Justin finishes eating dinner and gets up to throw away his paper plate. He returns to the firepit and whispers into Melia's ear. "The preserve visit was successful. We'll talk more about it later."

She glances over at him with a surprised look on her face, and he returns the gesture with a smug smile.

"So, are we a go with the zip line?" asks Anuhea.

Melia is not fond of heights but reluctantly agrees. "All right, but under one condition. No helicopter tours. I absolutely draw the line. Seriously, I'll get sick and puke."

Anuhea laughs but replies sympathetically. "Ahh. You got it. No helicopters."

An advertisement comes on the radio mentioning a list of local artists scheduled to perform at an outdoor music festival in a couple of weeks. Anuhea speaks passionately about her desire to attend the event and convinces Pika to buy them a pair of tickets on his phone at once. Following suit, the group discussion turns to famous musicians from the state of Hawaii including Bruno Mars, Jack Johnson, and Rylee Anuheakeala-okalokelani Jenkins, better known as Anuhea.

"So, tell me. Do you know or are you related to the famous singer/songwriter Anuhea Jenkins?" asks Justin.

"No, I do not know her, and we are in no way related. But I do admire her as a person, especially for what she has accomplished in her musical career. As you probably know, Hawaii is a small state full of prideful people. We should never forget to pay tribute to locally born artists who push the envelope, break through, and succeed in mainstream, mainland-driven industries."

Her poofy-haired cousin lifts his hand in a fist and comically shouts out "Represent!" causing Pika to laugh hysterically.

"Will you two morons shut up. I'm being serious over here, and you imbeciles don't even know what day of the week it is! Not you, Justin—those idiots."

Pika remembers spotting a ukulele through the car windshield earlier when speaking with Justin out front. "Hey, Justin. Did I see you had a ukulele in the car?"

Justin is hesitant to answer. "Yeah, why do you ask?"

Anuhea bites the lure, jumps right in, and rapidly fires off a sequence of questions. "What? You have a ukulele? Can I see it? Do you mind if I play a little?" She first learned how to strum the four-stringed version back in junior high school and has even written a song or two. Nothing on a professional level like her famous counterpart sharing the same first name, just something she enjoys doing in her free time.

"All right, all right. Let me go get it. I'll be right back." Justin retrieves the ukulele from his luggage and sits down next to Anuhea. He reaches out to hand her the instrument but pulls the ukulele back before she can grab it. With a serious look on his face, he leans in and quietly speaks to her in a sincere voice.

"Promise me you will be careful with it."

Anuhea smiles. "I promise, Justin."

He returns the smile, hands over the ukulele, and light-heartedly responds, "By all means, have a look and play us something special."

Anuhea reaches out with both hands to receive the ukulele and admires its uniqueness. She picks it up with her right hand and cradles the body high against her chest like a mother cuddling a newborn child. She then places her left thumb behind the instrument's neck and begins some simple up-and-down strumming to warm up. But she suddenly stops playing and looks over at Pika. He responds with an air guitar gesture and sends her a glance of encouragement to proceed.

Anuhea slides to the edge of her seat, takes a deep breath, and closes her eyes to clear her mind. "I call this one 'Sandy Sunday.'" She breaks out in an original, finger-picking, palm-muting, slappy, funky jam.

> Sitting under a palm tree, toe tapping the sand
> listening to some reggae beats, on Hawaiian land.
> We had all gathered down, on the beach to play,
> and get the most we can, on a Sandy Sunday.
> The sun shone brightly, the trades blew lightly
> the surf picked up, ever so slightly
> Wahine, kane, keiki, and kapuna
> enjoying themselves like the big kahuna.
> But that's when it dawned on me, what tomorrow brings
> Another day of work and school, my least favorite things
> So rather than get caught up, with the Monday blues
> I'll make the best of today; this is what I choose.
> I'm not even thinking about that right now
> Can't think about that no, no

I'm not even thinking about that right now
Can't think about that no, no
I'm not even thinking about that right now
Can't think about that no, no.

The group gives Anuhea a round of applause. She rolls right into another original melody and follows that up with a popular cover. "That's all for me. Thanks for the test drive." After the third song, she hands the ukulele back to Justin and reclines in a beach chair.

Melia congratulates her with a shocked look on her face. "Anuhea! I had no idea you could play the ukulele and sing like that. You have such a lovely voice." She gets out of her chair and walks over to give her friend a hug. "Good job. I'm so proud of you."

"Ahh, thanks, Melia. That really means a lot coming from you."

Justin wakes up the following morning and wanders down to the coffee tasting room to find Melia and Anuhea eating some pastries. He pours a cup of the house roast, adds a splash of cream, stirs in two rough-cut brown sugar cubes, and joins them on the patio. In between sips of the hot brew, Justin internet searches Kalalau Beach in Kauai and realizes they are in for a difficult road ahead. The only way to land access that part of the rugged Na Pali coast requires traversing the eleven-mile Kalalau Trail, one of Hawaii's most difficult. The steep, rocky trail crosses above towering sea cliffs, weaves through five lush valleys, and abruptly drops down to sea level at the secluded beach. The other option to access Kalalau requires a seven-mile rough water paddle with surf launches and landings. Justin figures he will let Melia decide which one they will tackle when they arrive on Kauai.

11

KALALAU BEACH

"I can't believe you talked me into this, Justin!" exclaims Melia.

"Relax and focus. You can do it! When I count to three, jump into the front of the kayak and get situated. I'll push us away from shore and hop in behind you. Remember what the instructor said, getting through the surf zone is tricky and requires timing, powerful forward strokes, good side strokes, and teamwork!"

Melia takes a couple of deep breaths and watches a set of three-foot-high waves come through. She is standing in waist-deep water holding on to the sides of an orange tandem sea kayak. Rumbling white water from the breaking waves rushes past them, causing a misty spray to splash up against their sun-blocked faces.

"Here comes the set wave!" says Justin. "Once this one rolls by, we're going for it!"

Crash! The wave breaks twenty-five feet in front of them and comes tumbling by. "One, two, three!"

Melia puts both hands down on top of the kayak and prepares to hoist herself up into the front section. She lifts her body upward by extending her arms like a push-up, swings one leg over the side, and rolls into the shallow seat. "I'm in!" She looks over her shoulder and grabs ahold of the leashed paddle.

"OK good. Here we go!" Justin digs the soles of his feet into the sand for leverage and uses a combination of lower- and upper-body strength to push the kayak away from shore. He jumps into the rear portion and spins around to face forward. "All right, I'm in! Let's go!" They begin paddling away from shore with grit and determination. "Spear the approaching waves with your paddle."

"Yes, I know. A spearing motion presents the least amount of resistance to the force of the water." Melia spots a new set of waves forming on the horizon and calls out with a slight sense of hesitation in her voice. "Do you see those waves coming at us? Justin, Justin! Paddle faster, or we're going to get crushed!"

He looks up to see the approaching swell and plunges his paddle deeper and faster into the churning ocean, alternating sides with each stroke. The wave face starts to form, and he calls out in an encouraging tone, "We're gonna make it. We're gonna make it! Dig, dig, dig!"

Melia screams out in exhilaration as the kayak goes up and over the wave just before it breaks.

"Cheehoo! Keep paddling until we get past the surf zone!" exclaims Justin.

They pour on the steam for a little bit longer and topple over the second wave with slightly less drama than the first. Justin falls into rhythm with Melia, and they uniformly coast over the third and fourth waves to reach the staging area where three other kayaks bob up and down waiting for them. A Spanish couple in their twenties ride on a tandem, two middle-aged female endurance athletes on another, and the group's quirky instructor, Tristan, rides solo.

Two days ago, Justin and Melia left the Big Island for Kauai. Once on the island, they had a back-and-forth conversation weighing out the eleven-mile hike versus an arduous seven-mile paddle. Melia chose the kayak trip mainly because of her fear of heights. Just the thought of crossing over the several hundred foot–high ocean cliffs makes her sick. So, they arranged a two-night expedition with a company that provides guided tours and met with the instructor, Tristan, yesterday for a lesson on open-water paddling. After class, they spent one night in a small hotel and showed back up this morning ready to paddle.

When they reach the waiting kayaks, Tristan coaches the group. "Way to go, you two! I'm glad to see someone paid attention yesterday. Listen up, everyone. We have a challenging three-hour paddle ahead of us, but fortunately, the weather is in our favor. The water looks calm, and the prevailing trade winds should kick up to give us a boost. Can I get a quick thumbs-up from everyone to confirm they are ready to get a move on?" He waits for a sign from each of the six group members and continues. "Good. Now listen up. I'll set the pace as we pull away from Ha'ena Beach Park. Stay close together but not too close and work as a unit with your team member. The paddler in front should control the rhythm, and the rear paddler should follow along. Now let's scram out of here!"

The strenuous first leg of paddling goes about as smoothly as anyone could have expected, considering the circumstances. About an hour into the grind down the cliff-lined coastline, a pod of spinner dolphins pays the group a visit and swims alongside the kayakers. The small, acrobatic marine mammals take turns breaching out of the water nose first, twisting their bodies as they rise into the air, spinning anywhere between two and five revolutions before crashing back into the ocean on their sides. A delightful sight indeed, watching frolicking dolphins leap with power and speed.

Sometime later, gentle trade winds begin blowing from the northeast at ten miles per hour. Even though it's helping, any wind on the water complicates matters. At this speed, it starts pushing the kayaks around and generating waves two to three feet high in open water. Realizing the group could use a break, the instructor guides them close to shore and dips inside a calm sea cave for some relaxation and hydration. They casually float around in the sheltered cavern, feeling satisfied as a group with their accomplishment of reaching the midway point.

Tristan's voice echoes off the rocks. "Are we rested and ready to venture on?"

Justin and Melia are reclined in their kayak, feet dangling in the water, and give a thumbs-up. The two endurance athletes also seem ready. They are taking turns drinking from a water bottle, and one of the women shouts out with a thumbs-up. "We're ready!"

Tristan calls out to the young couple from Spain. "How about you guys?"

They had decided to go for a quick swim in the mellow sea cave and seem to be having a bit of trouble getting back into the kayak. Eventually, the couple figures it out when the guy manages to pull himself up and subsequently instructs his girlfriend to do the same. She struggles, yells something nasty at him in Spanish but somehow manages to get back on. They quickly make up and give the thumbs-up.

Tristan has seen just about everything during his four years of guiding kayak tours along the Na Pali coast, and this is nothing new. He simply shakes his head and laughs. "All right, listen up. Nice job on the first half of today's paddle. I saw some good teamwork and communication out there today. Let's keep it up and stay focused on the task at hand. As you saw a few moments ago, the trade winds kicked in as expected. Now, the winds are at our back and should help. But remember, variable winds and ground swells can cause flip overs, and that's a bad thing. So, stay alert, read the water, and stick together as a unit. Other than that, we should be fine. Now let's get back out there and have some fun, people! Who's with me? People?"

Tristan leads the group out of the sea cave, followed closely by the young couple, and then the endurance athletes. Justin and Melia patiently wait their turn to exit the narrow opening and slowly paddle out once everyone else has cleared the way. When their kayak passes through the mouth, a green sea turtle surfaces for air on the way into the cave. Coincidentally, the honu has a shiny silver hook embedded in its upper lip and winks at Justin right before diving back underwater. He turns around for another look and watches the animal power glide into the calm, clear waters.

With all four kayaks now out of the cave, the gang resumes paddling at a steady pace. They venture past Hanakapiai Beach, meaning bay sprinkling food, where several dozen people are known to have drowned. Strong rip currents, high surf, and vicious shore breaks make the beach extremely dangerous and unsafe for swimming.

The next hour of paddling is by far the most difficult, and the group realizes why many people feel this might be the roughest and most grueling kayak trip on the planet. Variable winds, increasing swells, tugging currents, general fatigue, and the relentless sun all factor into wearing down the body and mind. At one point, the endurance athletes see Melia struggling and pull next to her with some words of encouragement. Whatever they said seems to have worked, and she kicks it into another gear with a jolt of energy. Eventually, the rough water subsides, and Kalalau Beach comes into view for the first time. With their destination now in sight, a general sigh of relief trickles over the kayakers. They hunker down and grind through the final stage of paddling with soggy skin, burning muscles, and a desire to kiss the sand.

Tristan leads them close to shore and stops just outside the surf zone to give a refresher on landing their kayaks. After the brief lesson, he leads by example and is the first to attempt the challenge landing in a shore break. His years of experience come to fruition, and he successfully maneuvers onto shore and drags his kayak high up onto the large sandy beach. He gives a thumbs-up and waves the next group in.

Of the three remaining parties on the water, the endurance athletes are by far the most experienced kayakers and have agreed to go second. They time the waves right and successfully make it ashore without incident. Tristan gives them a hand with pulling their kayak away from the water and signals for someone else.

"By all means, have at it!" says Justin.

The Spanish couple accepts his offer and paddles directly toward the beach. Their kayak catches the wave at a bad angle and flips over, sending them both into the breaking surf. Fortunately, they bounce up unharmed in the shallows and start laughing as they turn the kayak over and drag it onto shore. Once high up on the sand, they give a thumbs-up.

Melia turns to Justin feeling one last burst of enthusiasm. "Let's show these fools how we get it done Maui style and charge it." They paddle hard into the surf zone, instantly catching a midset wave that transports them all the way to shore. After hitting the beach, Melia hops out first, followed by Justin who grabs the bow handle and drags their kayak high up on the sand.

Tristan slowly claps his hands together several times. "Way to go, everyone! Way to go! Welcome to Kalalau! Why don't we set up camp under that good-size milo tree just above the beach? The branches provide a lot of shade throughout the day, and we're gonna need it. Our kayaks should be fine where they are, but let's haul up all the gear and supplies."

Justin removes two waterproof dry bags from the kayak's internal storage compartment and hauls them up to the make-shift campsite. He constructs a two-person tent, unravels the sleeping pads, and tosses in some light blankets and a couple of small pillows. Melia strings up a blue tarp from the low sprawling branches for some additional privacy and protection from the elements. Feeling satisfied with their setup, the siblings relax inside their tent, munching on salami, cheese, and crackers, and reminiscing about their epic morning spent on the sea.

Tucked far away in the Na Pali Coast State Park, the isolated Kalalau Valley is surrounded by two-thousand-foot-high cliffs. Although the remote area was occupied by native Hawaiians as recently as the twentieth century, it completely lacks any modern-day amenities such as plumbing and electricity. No roads, no cars, no stores, no cell phone coverage, and no internet service. Mother Nature at her finest. The lush, tropical valley spans half a mile wide, two miles long, and contains numerous unmarked hiking trails that lead in every which direction, taking willing explorers to an array of streams, waterfalls, and swimming holes. Bananas, guava, taro, orange, and mango trees can all be found growing wild alongside endemic flowering plants.

The flat-bottomed valley descends between fluted peaks that protrude atop red dirt ridges lined in green vegetation, eventually opening to a deep one mile stretch of sand known as Kalalau Beach. A blissful solitude for brave adventure seekers daring enough to dream an excursion to the faraway land. The serene Kalalau stream carelessly flows through the valley and empties directly into the ocean near the designated camping area, providing fresh water to drink and rinse off in. However, the cool water needs to be boiled or treated for drinking since virtually all Hawaiian streams are contaminated with leptospirosis that can cause flulike symptoms and fatalities in extreme cases.

Tristan approaches their tent wearing a pair of silver-framed Elvis sunglasses and a cutter-style straw cowboy hat. You know, the one where the sides curl up. He kneels to look through the zipped screen door, removes a long blade of grass from his mouth, and speaks to them in a southern drawl. "Howdy y'all. We're fixin' to fetch some drinkin' water from dat dere waterfall over there. Would either of you two turkeys like to join us on a little excursion?"

Justin cracks a half-hearted grin. "You remind me of my cousin Kaito, and I mean that in a good way."

"I've never heard of that Cairo fella you are referring to, but he sure sounds like a good ol boy. Now, if you don't mind, can we cut the chitchat. Some of us are rather parched, and we need to wet the whistle if you know what I mean. Are you two coming along or staying here to man the fort?"

Melia unzips the tent and steps out with a beach towel and water bottle, whistling a western gunslinger's song. "Ready when you are, Tex."

Justin reaches inside of the dry bag to remove a small container of water purification tablets he picked up yesterday at the sporting goods store. He grabs an empty two-liter water bottle, puts on some sunglasses, and crawls out of the tent. "To the watering hole!"

The seven campers march off on a short walk to the western end of the beach where fresh water flows into the ocean from a rocky streambed. They slowly traverse upriver, shaded by the tree canopy, listening to the harmonious sound of Ho'ole'a Falls. Moments later they arrive at the base of a cascading one-hundred-foot waterfall that gently flows down a red rock face and settles into a natural swimming pool. The group fans out across the narrow shoreline to fill their bottles and rinse off in the crisp cool water.

Justin searches the area looking for lizards in hopes of spotting one matching the stone etching, and he stumbles across a wood plank sign hanging from a tree branch with the phrase E kala mai ia'u written across it in charcoal.

"Hey, Tristan, do you know what this says?"

"The phrase means 'I'm sorry.' It pays homage to ancient Hawaiians who once ruled these sacred lands."

Justin continues exploring the nearby vegetation and comes across a bright-green gecko catching some warm sunrays on a large fern leaf. He eagerly leans in for a closer look but quickly realizes the lizard and stone image don't match.

Melia calls out excitedly from the pond's edge. "A baby turtle. How cute!"

"That's a red-eared slider," says Tristan. "The freshwater turtle was originally introduced to Hawaii in the pet trade many years ago and has since become an invasive species. Owners once purchased the silver dollar–size juveniles as cute little pets, unaware they can grow to nearly a foot in length, far too big for most home aquariums. So, people began releasing them into the wild."

"They're adorable!" exclaims Melia.

"Yes, but watch out. The slippery critters become somewhat aggressive in old age and have been known to bite."

She gingerly steps out of the knee-deep clear water and wraps herself up in a beach towel. "No one is biting me today."

Tristan calls everyone back over to the waterfall and speaks to them in an upbeat, goofy tone. "All right, gang, listen up. We still have a few hours of daylight left to explore. Please be careful and remember, we're all on our own out here. Help is at least a half a day away if someone were to get hurt. So be cautious and don't do anything stupid." He reaches down into the water with both hands and snatches up the turtle for a look. "I'm headed into the valley on a scavenger hunt for firewood since there isn't any near the campsite. Would anyone like to join me?"

Always in search of their next adventure, the two endurance athletes volunteer and move in beside him for a glance at the red-eared slider.

Tristan turns to address the Spaniards. "How about you two?"

Standing with their arms around one another, the young couple stares into each other's eyes, exchange a whisper, and the man named Alejandro answers him. "We're still beat from the long paddle ride. Would you guys mind if we went back to camp and chilled out?"

"No worries," replies Tristan.

Justin is feeling energized from the fresh water and encouraged by the gecko sighting. He glances over at Melia. "I'm in."

She can see the enthusiastic look in his eyes and reluctantly agrees, even though resting back at camp sounds like a better option. "All right, let's get it done."

The Spanish couple waves goodbye and walks downstream. They can be heard shouting out "mahalo" after disappearing behind a large rocky outcrop.

The remaining five adventurers set out along one of the unmarked trails that takes them away from the waterfall, cuts across the edge of their campsite, and detours into the valley.

They immediately start gathering up twigs, sticks, and small branches for tinder but can't find anything substantial enough to sustain a campfire all night. Right when they are about to turn back, a mixed flock of small foraging birds swoop into an open field, landing around a fallen tree hidden in the long, dry grass. Justin and Tristan high-step over to investigate. When they approach the dried-out trunk, a low-flying helicopter zips by overhead, causing the African silverbills, chestnut munias, and nutmeg mannikins to scatter.

Tristan rolls the dead tree back and forth with his foot. "Check it out! That's enough wood to burn all night and then some. Let's try to pick it up!"

"How much do you think it weighs?" asks Justin.

He lifts one side of the six-foot-long trunk and sets it back down. "Oh, probably a hundred pounds."

Justin grabs ahold of the other end. "On my count. One, two, three!"

They lift the log off the ground with relative ease and walk it back through the field to rejoin the women.

One of the endurance athletes speaks up. "Now that's what I'm talking about. Way to go, you two!"

On the return hike to camp, Melia spots an extremely well-camouflaged lizard hanging out on a thin tree branch and stops so the group can have a closer look.

Justin instantly recognizes the species. "Jackson's chameleon. I love these little guys."

He gently lifts the bright-green lizard and holds the docile reptile in his open hand. The chameleon has three horns on its head, one protruding from the nose, and one above each eye.

Melia questions if the species is correct, and Justin subtly shakes his head back and forth, indicating it's not the right type.

169

The scavengers return to camp and drop the wood in a pile next to the pit. Melia decides to lie down in the tent for a snooze, Justin and Tristan work on starting the campfire, and the endurance athletes go for a beach walk to look for the Spanish couple. They plan to meet back at sunset for dinner.

Once the fire is lit, Tristan fetches a pot from his dry bag to boil some water for tea. He dices up a ripe mango they found on the trail and slides the yellow chunks into the pot to add a natural sweetener. "Let's try to keep the fire at a slow burn this afternoon. The smolder and smoke should help ward off pesky mosquitoes and flies."

Melia wakes up from her nap and lies beside Justin in a black-and-white woven hammock. "Where did everybody go?"

"They're down exploring those prehistoric-looking sea caves along the coast. Do you want to go have a look?" Justin stayed behind at camp when Tristan left to find the others a little while ago.

"Why didn't you go with them?"

"I don't know. I guess I just didn't feel comfortable leaving you here all alone."

"Ah, thanks, Justin. You're the best! I feel a lot better after taking a nap. Let's go check it out!"

The two siblings fumble out of the hammock and stroll down the deep stretch of warm sand to the windy shoreline. They walk along, staring up at the gigantic rock cliffs that line the coast, ducking in and out of sea caves as they go. Some are deep and dark, others are wide and shallow, a couple have enough water to swim in, and one even has a rock garden. Eventually, they find the group in a secluded cove playing in the shore break and climbing on a fallen boulder that cracked down the center.

Melia and Justin plunk themselves down in the soft sand with their backs leaned up against the jagged rocks. They sit quietly, soaking up the magnificent convergence of mountain and sea, reminiscing and daydreaming, hypnotized by the captivating moment. Melia breaks the mellow silence with a random life question for her older brother. "How are we supposed to remain positive and focused in a world full of pessimism and doubt?"

Justin picks up a handful of the golden sand and slowly releases the granules into the wind. "I believe it starts with living life in the present rather than too far in the past or too much in the future." He scoops up another handful of sand to release. "We must try our best to ignore those who say we can't choose to associate with those who believe we can, ask plenty of good questions, and be confident enough to challenge the answers. Remember, ninety percent of what people worry about in life never happens."

"OK, but that's easier said than done with all the negativity out there."

"True but you need to tune it all out and choose to see the glass half-full." He tosses the sand up into the air and wipes off his hands." Let me put it to you another way. Imagine controlling your mood like the dial of a camping lantern. Each morning you wake up with the ability to adjust. You can leave the dial low on dim and gloomy, find a happy medium, or turn the knob up to bright and sunny."

"A conscious choice!" exclaims Melia.

"That's right, it takes a conscious choice to do what is morally and ethically right even if that goes unnoticed."

Melia picks up a wishbone-shaped piece of broken-off coral, gives it a quick look, and skims it back into the incoming tide.

Justin goes on to tell her a story from last semester when he was studying the types of evolution including convergent, divergent, parallel, and coevolution. "When the subject of adaptive radiation came around, which is the process of rapid evolutionary diversification from a single ancestral line into a multitude of new forms filling different ecological niches, it made me realize how we all must be willing to accept inevitable change in a positive light. Therefore, I came up with the phrase *adaptively radiant* as a way to describe this mental state of fortitude and perseverance."

Melia responds in an upbeat tone. "Adaptively radiant. I like it. To shine brightly and remain positive in the face of change. Thanks for the encouraging words, Justin."

With the afternoon closing in on the evening, the seven adventure seekers say goodbye to the peaceful cove and set off on the return walk to camp. Tristan comes up with the idea to build a wind chime made from scavenged materials, and they start collecting seashells, coral, and small sticks of driftwood. "We'll tie it all together with some fishing line back at camp."

While searching for shells in the ankle-deep shoreline, Justin sees a reddish-brown plump sea cucumber and kneels to pick up the harmless creature. He carefully holds the squishy marine organism in his palm, watching the filter feeder ooze water from its body. The Spanish couple comes over next to him for a closer look and Justin starts rattling off information in an unusual manner.

"There are ten thousand known species of sponges that can be found in all marine and many freshwater habitats. Shallow tide pools, deep ocean depths, rivers, streams, ponds, and lakes. You name it. The ancient and successful group of invertebrates have been living in the waters of this world for more than six hundred million years, give or take a millennium. My favorite is the Iouea, a fossil sponge that lived during the Cretaceous period of geological time from about sixty-seven million to one hundred forty-six million years ago. By the way, Iouea happens to be the shortest word in the English language containing all five vowels and the shortest four-syllable word in English. However, there are approximately one hundred and fifty words that use all five vowels only once and only twenty-seven words that use all five vowels in the correct order such as acedious, aerious, caesious, and placentious."

The couple stare at Justin in bewilderment and continue searching for seashells. Alejandro looks over at his girlfriend, Paula. "I have no idea what he just said, but it sounded really cool."

The group returns to camp and Justin takes charge of the fire by dragging a large section of the trunk over the smoldering coals. Meanwhile, Tristan fetches a roll of twenty-pound test fishing line from his dry pack and constructs the wind chime with assistance from the endurance athletes.

As the evening continues to unfold, the group gathers around the campfire for a simple dinner. Tristan suggests that they play a game of "What brings you to Kalalau?" something he traditionally does on the first night of each expedition. "The rules of the game are simple. We all spend a few minutes sharing a personal story of what brought us here today. It can't be a nine-word or three-sentence answer. That's too simple. Elaborate. When the person who's up finishes, he or she turns to the person to the left and asks, 'What brings you to Kalalau?.' The game ends at the conclusion of the last camper's personal story."

Tristan offers to go first and begins sharing his thoughts. He passionately explains his internal desire to explore ever since he was a child, the satisfaction he feels from challenging himself in dangerous situations, and how Kalalau is the ultimate reward for risk-takers.

"I recall my first trip here four years ago like it was yesterday. The intense beauty of the land, raw power of the ocean, and mysterious energy of this valley is second to none and hard to explain. Admittedly, I fell in love at first sight. So, I found a job working for a local kayak tour company and have been leading expeditions out here each summer ever since."

He looks around at each of their drowsy, sun-kissed faces, and turns to the Spanish couple. "So, what brings you to Kalalau?"

The young couple look at each other, exchange a few words in Spanish, and Alejandro begins speaking. "Paula and I have known each other for two years. We became engaged five months ago, but we have never lived together. So, she came up with the idea to spend the summer backpacking in America to become better acquainted. It's been exciting and challenging but worthwhile, and we have no regrets."

He looks over at Paula and they exchange another smile. "As for Kalalau, we actually read about the beach in a magazine at Honolulu airport and planned the trip on a whim." He goes on to mention how they are avid kayakers back in Spain and names a few of their favorite locations. When he finishes, Alejandro gently nudges Paula with his elbow. She turns to the endurance athletes and speaks to them in a heavy Spanish accent. "What brings you to Kalalau?"

The women jump in and out, sharing a story of climbing Mount Everest with a dear friend ten years ago. At the conclusion of the expedition, the three companions made a pact to visit Hawaii one day and hike the notorious Kalalau Trail. Sadly, their friend was diagnosed with stage-four breast cancer later that year and passed away shortly afterward. While on her deathbed, she reminded them of the agreement they came up with back at Everest and made the couple promise to fulfill her dream. Fast forward several years and here they are today.

A woman named Lacy finishes the story. "We brought her ashes along with us in a small metal container and plan to spread them out when the right moment presents itself."

Her partner, Angie, chimes in. "Lacy has a bad knee from a previous fall, and we decided the kayak trip would be slightly easier on her versus the hike."

The couple finishes up by mentioning their tight bond formed through physical fitness and the lifelong commitment each has made to one another. The two women shed a few tears and embrace in a long hug followed by a short kiss. Angie looks over at Melia, "So, what brings you to Kalalau today?"

Melia was moved by the women's story and takes a moment to gather herself. She wipes her eyes and compliments them on doing something so admirable. "Why am I here today? That's a good question." She clears one last sniffle and continues. "I was born here in Hawaii eighteen years ago, and I have spent my entire life growing up on the beautiful Valley Isle of Maui. It's my home, and I love everything about it. The ocean lifestyle, the warm weather, all the outdoor activities, and the food. Damn, do I love the food. But to me what makes Hawaii so special is the Aloha spirit. Simple acts of kindness such as letting a car pull out in front of you or greeting one another with genuine warmth. A contagious state of bliss the world needs more of."

She stops for a moment and looks over at Justin. "But, do you want to know what I really love most about Hawaii? My family, my o'hana. What they have taught me in life and what we have shared together is immeasurable. I am a lucky person to be part of such an amazing, eclectic group of people. I really am."

Melia's eyes water, and she tries to speak but the words just won't come out. Justin reaches out to hold her hand for support and she continues. "Without their guidance and love, I probably wouldn't be here today. Especially Justin." She begins to shed a few tears. "He has always been there for me ever since we were little kids, and I would do anything for him. When he asked me to come along on the trip, I said yes." The two siblings have a nice long hug and when they relinquish the embrace, she asks him the question. "Justin, what brings you to Kalalau?'

A loud hollering sound resembling that of a wolf call roars from deep within the valley, chilling the unsuspecting campers to the core. Justin looks around the campfire at the perplexed look on everyone's face, and he and Tristan stare each other down precisely as the howl repeats. "What the hell was that?"

Tristan cups his hands around his mouth and yells out at the top of his lungs. "Cut the noise. It's noisy!" He proceeds to coolly explain what they just heard. "Relax, everyone, relax. That's just Uncle Dave howling at the moon. The guy has been living all alone out here off the land for twenty years, mostly surviving on feral goats and wild boar."

He goes on to explain how several valley dwellers illegally live in the area despite the state park rules forbidding people from residing on the protected land. "Park rangers sweep through every month or two but there are so many hiding places out there, it's virtually impossible to find someone who doesn't want to be found."

Justin breaks an awkward silence to divulge his personal reasons for venturing out to Kalalau. He starts off by mentioning his desire to have a memorable summer that has resulted in trips to Japan, Maui, and the Big Island. "So, an acquaintance of mine suggested the journey out here to see what Kalalau is all about. Although it's been great so far, I can honestly say I am not looking forward to the paddle ride back."

The group members seem to agree with him as they each smile, nod, or softly chuckle. "But really for me, it's about the need to grow as a person and experience what this amazing world has to offer us. To cherish the special moments and create memories for a lifetime. You know, it's one thing to see pictures online or hear about other people's life experiences. But nothing comes remotely close to tasting that saltwater over there or touching this fine sand. To smelling that fire burn, hearing those waves break, and seeing that sky full of stars. So, why am I in Kalalau? Because I want to live my life to the fullest, and for me, that starts with stepping outside society's walls of confinement and experiencing this fascinating world firsthand."

Tristan slowly stands, stretching and yawning. "Good job, everyone, well done. Thank you for playing the game this evening, and don't forget to collect your parting gifts at the door. Now I don't know about you guys, but I'm exhausted. What do you say we call it a night and get some rest for the valley hike tomorrow?"

The exhausted campers agree with his idea of some much-needed sleep and disappear into their tents one by one. Justin decides to spend a bit more time around the fire and moves into the hammock for a better look at the stars. He listens to the tents rustle momentarily, but the noise quickly subsides, and the campsite turns quiet, leaving only the pleasant sounds of popping wood and crashing waves. Suddenly, he feels a jolt of energy zap through his body, and he makes a rash decision to revisit the waterfall in search of a lizard that matches the stone image. He retrieves a flashlight from the tent, grabs his water bottle to refill, and slips out of camp unnoticed.

Justin trudges down the extensive beach to the mysterious ocean. When he finally reaches the wet, compacted sand, a foul scent of decay blows onshore, overpowering his nostrils with the putrid smell of death. Figuring a dead animal must have washed in from the depths, he scans the area with his flashlight searching for the carcass, sending several small ghost crabs scurrying back into their burrows. Unexpectedly, the flashlight cuts out and won't turn back on. He flips the switch back and forth and taps on the side a couple of times, but it just won't work. Simultaneously, a cumulonimbus of clouds form in the otherwise pristine night sky, blanketing out the moonlight and causing darkness to fall upon Kalalau.

Justin fiddles with the flashlight batteries and is startled by a warm, far-carrying tone of conch shells blowing somewhere down the beach. He stands motionless, listening to the shell trumpets uniformly sound off several times in a row. At the conclusion of the horns, a brief silence is followed by the commencing of war drums that send a deep chill through his spine, and goose bumps across his arms. He squints down the shoreline to see a shadowy band of torchbearers emerge from the ocean, closely followed by a large group of apparitions dressed in battle gear. Some of the ghostly figures are clothed in decorative helmets, others wear cloaks, and all carry menacing weapons of death ranging from long spears to thumping clubs.

According to Hawaiian mythology, night marchers, or *huaka'i po*, are the deadly ghosts of ancient Hawaiian warriors that rise from the ocean and march to ancient battle sites or sacred places. Legend has it the regular-size men levitate out of the water, suspended in the air just high enough so that their feet do not touch, and come ashore to the tune of conch shells and beating drums. The ghostly figures continuously march throughout the night and vanish just before sunrise without leaving any evidence of their visitation. Ancient Hawaiians believed that any mortal man who looked directly at the night marchers would die violently unless he had an ancestor within the marchers' ranks or would lie facedown on the ground and project a mind message of respect, fear, and submission.

Having been born and raised in Hawaii, Justin is aware of the legendary mythological beings and wants absolutely nothing to do with them tonight. Considering the night marchers' distance down the beach, he temporarily contemplates sitting down and letting them pass but instead turns and bolts out of fear. He sprints up the rising dune to camp, stumbles over his own feet, and falls face-first into sand, spilling the loose batteries, flashlight, and water bottle. Justin frantically tries to collect everything but has trouble seeing in the dark and can't locate the AAA batteries. So, he leaves them in the sand and bear crawls the rest of the way uphill on his hands and feet.

He looks over his right shoulder to see a pair of skeleton hula girls dancing under a palm tree in the distance. The astonishing image causes him to awkwardly fall once again, only this time on firm ground, and he hyperextends his thumb upon impact. Justin rolls over onto his back, clutching his thumb with a grimace and witnesses a rare phenomenon called a meteor procession. This type of shooting star occurs when the meteor breaks up into several fireballs traveling virtually parallel to the surface of Earth.

With his mind racing a million miles an hour, Justin attempts to gather himself, tolerate the pain, and not succumb to nagging trepidation. He envisions the creepy thought of vengeful night marchers entering the campsite to wreak havoc but quickly swipes away the nightmare and refocuses. "Get up, get inside that tent, lie still, and think respectful, positive thoughts."

Justin rises to the occasion, thwarting off the looming fears and returns to the smoky campsite, sore thumb and all. He ducks inside the tent and lies down next to the peacefully sleeping Melia. He remains very still with his eyes closed, flashing back to each of the previous five encounters, causing his body to give out, and he fades into a deep sleep.

He wakes up early the next morning lying flat on his stomach with one cheek flush against the ground accompanied by a very sore thumb. Justin peels one eye open to observe a single brown anole lizard feeding on tiny black beetles along the ground just outside the tent screen. He watches the lizard gorge itself on several little bugs before hopping up onto a nearby rock and finishing off the last one held captive within its jaws. The anole leaps three feet across to a low-hanging branch, spins itself around to face the ground, and begins to protract and retract the yellow and orange flap of skin beneath its lower jaw. Justin pictures the matching river rock image in his mind and instantly knows the two are alike. He quietly sits up to avoid disturbing Melia and carefully slips out of the tent.

"Hello there, my little friend! I've been searching all over for you."

Justin clutches his throbbing thumb and continues observing the behavior displayed by the brown lizard. When his eyes refocus on the dim morning ocean in the backdrop, he witnesses a single-sail wooden outrigger canoe offshore maneuver into the secluded cove. With the campsite quiet and all the tents zipped up, he decides to walk down and have a closer look at the unusual watercraft. Although boats occasionally park offshore at Kalalau Beach, passengers are not permitted to come onshore without a permit and seeing one this early is rather remarkable considering the remote location.

Justin has trouble seeing clearly in the faint morning light, but there appears to be only one man aboard the outrigger that has stopped just outside the surf zone. A strong gust of wind suddenly comes blasting through the secluded cove, lifting Justin off his feet, and blowing him aboard the canoe. He stumbles upon impact but somehow manages to gain his balance and not fall overboard.

A tall, thin Hawaiian man stands in front of him flaunting long, wavy, black hair and ancient Polynesian garb. The man speaks to Justin in a deep voice with an upbeat tone. "Aloha. I am Paka'a, god of the sea and inventor of the sail. Welcome aboard my tiny seafaring vessel I call *Makani*." He follows up the brief introduction with an unusual Hawaiian chant that summons a gust of wind to blow them out to sea.

Lying in the canoe beside Paka'a is the Wind Gourd of La'amaomao, which was given to him long ago by his mother. The calabash or bottle gourd is said to contain his great grandmothers' bones along with all the winds of the Hawaiian Islands, each of which has a specific name linked to a section of land or a certain place. By learning the winds' names, chants, songs, and prayers, Paka'a has gained control of them and can call on the thirty-two winds of the compass at any given moment to help guide his vessel.

Once under sail, Paka'a demonstrates to Justin the specific winds that come from various directions at certain speeds and temperatures. He first calls on a warm northeasterly twenty-five mile-per-hour trade wind, followed by a stiff cold core westerly Kona, and an extremely violent lehua wind with speeds reaching eighty miles per hour. Justin tightly grips the canoe for dear life, fearing he might fall overboard during the unexpected, unorthodox sailing hiatus. At one point, his body slides partially over the side, and Paka'a reaches down to grasp him on the wrist, giving Justin a chance to regain his balance. Eventually, the skies clear, and the winds subside, allowing them time to discuss ocean currents around the islands as the beach comes back into view. The conversation switches gears, and Paka'a shares a story about the sail morphing into a modern-day rocket in reference to titanic means of exploration. He references humankind's history of Earth travel and what the future may hold.

"If the horseback was replaced by the oar, and the sail replaced the oar, and the gas engine replaced the sail, and rocket propulsion has replaced the gas engine, what will replace rocket propulsion? Humankind today believes rocket ships are the future of exploration just as humankind once viewed sailing in the same light. But the two are similar means of transportation to help perpetuate and fuel our desire to explore. Kindred spirits, if you will. Think about it. The sail and the rocket ship are blood brothers cut from the same stone. What helps spacecrafts land back on Earth? Sophisticated parachutes, a morphed version of the sail."

Paka'a carefully maneuvers the outrigger back into the secluded cove just before sunrise and diligently holds the watercraft in place directly outside the surf zone. He points at a floating gourd bobbing in the swells and suggests Justin retrieve it on his way into shore. Although the calabash is not the Gourd of La'amaomao, which remains in Paka'a's possession, it contains our desire to sail the winds, travel beyond the horizons, and a history of Earth exploration.

"The swim will be treacherous and difficult, but stay focused. Grab the gourd, fight through the strong rip currents, and battle the high surf. I'll be here watching you the entire time. Makani olu'olu e kai malie!"

Justin rises to his feet with a wobble, looks over at Paka'a one last time, and plunges into the deep-blue sea headfirst. His eyes open under water during the glide and he uses a pull-down breaststroke to swim as far as possible, surfacing directly in front of the gourd. He hauls the floating calabash into his possession and looks over his shoulder to give Paka'a a thumbs-up, but he has vanished along with the outrigger canoe.

With the calabash under his left armpit, Justin starts swimming into the sloshing surf zone and instantly gets pummeled by a large breaking wave. The force of Mother Nature slams him deep underwater, but he manages to resurface for a breath only to feel the crunch of another wave that forces him back under. When he surfaces a third time, Justin can see the current has started pulling him off course, and a state of panic floods into his body. He grips on to the gourd with both hands as a fourth wave crumbles over the top of him, sending Justin back underwater yet again. Exhaustion has now set in, and he opens his eyes looking up at the rolling wave passing by overhead. Then out of the blue appears a green sea turtle with a shiny silver hook in its upper lip. The honu intentionally swims close to Justin and he grabs ahold of its front fin with his hand. The turtle power glides them under the surf and into the shallows where Justin releases the sea creature and watches it swim away. He surfaces for a deep breath in the chest-high water, thankful to feel the sand under his toes.

Meanwhile, Melia wakes up from a terrific night's sleep feeling refreshed, rejuvenated, and ready to take on the world. She slips into some exercise pants, grabs her bottle of water, and takes off on an early morning beach walk in search of Justin. On her way down to the ocean, she scoops up some AAA batteries partially covered in the sand and stores them inside the silicone water bottle sleeve. When she finally reaches the waterline and can't see Justin in either direction, she realizes her best option is to remain on familiar ground. So, she sets off on a jog past the sea caves en route to the secluded beach, figuring if he doesn't turn up, she will double back and wait for him at camp.

Melia comes trotting around the rugged cliff face to enter the sheltered cove. She catches sight of Justin sprawled out on his stomach in the shoreline and instantly starts to agonize over what might have happened. His eyes are closed, and he doesn't appear to be moving. "Justin!" she frantically calls out to him from across the beach and takes off sprinting down the sand, scaring away two wading sandpipers. "Justin!" She calls out his name again and executes a perfect baseball slide next to him. "Are you OK?"

Justin's left eye opens to see Melia's face within inches of his own. He flips over onto his back, sits up, and wipes a clump of wet sand from his cheek. "I'm fine, although I probably drank half the ocean this morning."

"Well good, I think. I mean, what happened to you? Why would you go into the water alone? Are you hurt? Can you stand up? Maybe we should get you back to camp."

"Slow down. This ain't the mainland. I already told you I'm OK. Would you mind grabbing that bottle gourd behind you before it gets washed back out to sea?"

Melia turns around to see the decorative double-bulbed bottle gourd and snatches up the dried-out, hollowed container. She gives the golden-colored calabash a quick look and hands the lightweight canister to him.

"Merci beaucoup." Justin puts his hands down behind him in the sand, stretches out his legs, and leans his head back, staring out at the horizon. "Can I have a drink of your water?"

"Yes, sure, of course. Here have all you want."

He guzzles down half the bottle and hands it back to her. "You're never going to believe the morning I just had. I'm not even sure that I believe it."

"Did you find the lizard?"

He answers sarcastically. "Oh yeah, I found the lizard all right."

184

"Tell me more, tell me more! I want to know who, what, where, when, how, and why!" Melia feels a rush of adrenaline enter her bloodstream, and she eagerly waits to hear what Justin has to say.

"All right, I'll tell you what, help me stand up, and I will share the details on the way back to camp. I don't know about you, but I could go for some breakfast right about now."

Melia jumps to her feet, grabs Justin's extended hand with both of her own, and uses a combination of her legs, arms, and core muscles to pull him up just as the sun rises in the serene orange-peach sky. On their return walk to camp he explains what transpired last night, mentions the anole encounter this morning, and shares the story of having to retrieve the bottle gourd in the ocean.

"That explains the batteries." says Melia.

They return to camp and find Tristan stoking the fire. He tosses a handful of twigs onto the smoldering coals and drags over a section of the partially burnt tree stump. "Good morning. I thought you two were still asleep."

Melia speaks right up to save Justin the trouble of explaining. "We woke up early and went for a beach walk to see the amazing sunrise. Very inspirational."

Tristan sees the gourd Justin is holding and believes it to be a percussion instrument.

"Nice Ipu heke. Where did you get that from?"

"I found it floating in the ocean this morning. Cool huh?"

"I'll say." He returns to stoking the fire. "People have found all sorts of interesting artifacts out here over the years. Fish floats, old nets, miscellaneous debris. I once found an ice chest floating offshore that still had cold drinks inside."

The remaining members of camp start funneling out of their tents one at a time until all seven adventurers have

gathered around the fire. They eat a light breakfast while discussing their final full day at Kalalau Beach. Tristan then out-
lines the plan for tomorrow morning, starting with breaking
camp at sunrise and hitting the water early for the return paddle. He has already contacted a colleague of the tour company
this morning on a long-range two-way handheld radio to ver-
ify the weather for tomorrow, and the woman has confirmed
everything looks promising.

With breakfast winding down, Lacy and Angie mention
their desire to hike up Kalalau Trail today in search of higher
ground to spread their friend's ashes. Tristan offers to guide the
expedition and the endurance athletes welcome his expertise.
They invite the others to come along, but Justin and Melia
decide to stay back at camp.

Lacy looks over at Paula and Alejandro who are lying
together in the hammock. "What about you guys? Are you up
for a hike today?"

The sleepy-eyed couple exchange a few casual words in
Spanish, and Alejandro replies to her in English. "Yes we'd love
to tag along."

A short time later, the five hikers depart from camp on what
they estimate to be a three-hour round trip. Tristan looks down
at his watch to see the local time of 8:27 a.m. and jokingly says,
"If we're not back by high noon, send the search party."

Sometime later, a scruffy-looking bushman unexpectedly
wanders into camp, startling Justin and Melia. He politely
introduces himself as Uncle Dave and asks to speak with Tristan
in a heavy pidgin accent. Justin explains to the man how Tristan
went on a hike this morning but will return to camp around
lunch time. Uncle Dave agrees to come back this afternoon and
hands Justin a large ziplock bag full of fresh goat jerky. Apparently, Tristan was supposed to bring him some basic supplies

as a swap out for the dried meat. The two men exchange a fist bump and Uncle Dave disappears out of camp with a sneaky feral cat following close behind him in the shadows.

Melia makes sure Uncle Dave is completely out of sight prior to commenting. "Interesting guy. Likable enough but definitely an oddball and somewhat out there, if you know what I mean."

"I hear you. He's a little peculiar, but aren't we all. I can see where the guy is coming from and understand his perspective. You know, some people simply refuse to conform to societal standards and choose to live a simplistic lifestyle. Certainly not for everyone but there is something admirable in that train of thought."

Justin and Melia fall right into a conversation about how to spend their last couple of days on Kauai and brainstorm sightseeing spots to visit once they return to civilization. He mentions his desire to check out the Kilauea Point National Wildlife Refuge, but Melia is more inclined to spend her time lounging around the magical Hanalei Bay. They scheme out a plan to visit them both before having to catch a flight back to Maui three days from now. A trip home for Melia but nothing more than a layover for Justin en route to California.

The five hikers eventually return in good spirits and with arms full of tinder and scavenged fruit. They drop the wood in a pile near the campfire and line the fruit on a low-hanging branch.

"How was the hike?" asks Justin.

Lacy and Angie tell him all about their adventurous morning walking through the lush tropical valley on their way up the trail. Lacy does most of the talking with Angie jumping in to provide specifics.

"We saw a couple of really pretty red birds near the waterfall," says Lacy.

"Northern cardinals," adds Angie.

"And a small flock of cute little green ones with white circles around their eyes."

"Japanese white eyes."

"And all sorts of other ones throughout the day."

"Francolins, white-rumped shamas, Kauai creepers, and—oh shoot, what was their name again? Small Kauai thrush!"

"It was awesome. Plus we found a perfect little flat ledge up on the cliff to spread out her ashes."

At the conclusion of their story, a group of nine kayaks appear out on the water and begin landing onshore one at a time. Tristan explains how their expedition is led by his good friends and coworkers from the tour company and mentions that the large party will be joining theirs to form a supergroup. "What do you say we walk down there and give our fellow thrill seekers a hand?"

Justin steps into the warm sand somewhat saddened that his time visiting the Garden Isle will soon come to an end but at the same time, enamored of the thought of getting to see Yori soon. He visualizes holding her close with their fingers intertwined.

12

MORRO BAY

An employee of a fast-food restaurant calls out numbers from behind the counter amid the hustle and bustle of a busy airport lunch scene. "Order number one forty-eight."

Justin leans up against a wall, scrolling through emails, when his number is called out. He slides the phone back into his jeans pocket, weaves past a few waiting customers, and hands over the ticket in exchange for a red plastic tray of hamburgers and french fries. "Can I please have some ketchup?"

The woman points left. "Right over there, sir. Order number one forty-nine."

He snatches up a couple of extra napkins, uses a large pump dispenser to squirt some ketchup into small paper cups, and sits down at a freshly wiped empty table. With his mouth watering for a taste, Justin bites into the juicy cheeseburger. A woman approaches carrying two sodas and sits across from him. He cleans the drippings from the corner of his mouth and looks up as Melia helps herself to a box of fries and a burger.

"How's the food?"

Justin gathers up three french fries, dips them into the ketchup, and devours the hot, crispy shoestrings. "So good"

Melia unwraps her hamburger, takes two consecutive bites, and washes them down with some ice-cold root beer. "I know this might sound weird, but I'm super excited to be here at LAX. This airport is crazy busy compared to Maui. Look at all those people!"

"Welcome to the mainland." Justin continues eating his cheeseburger.

"Anyways, thanks again for inviting me. I'm thrilled with the opportunity to see California and support you during the final stages of this journey ahead."

Justin pops the remaining bite of cheeseburger into his mouth, chews it up, and swallows.

"Yeah, I'm glad you were able to come along."

Melia finishes her hamburger and crumbles up the wrapper into a ball. "I can't wait to meet Yori."

"She's fantastic! A real outgoing, energetic girl who lights up a room in her own mysterious way. Have you ever heard the saying 'When someone shows you who they are, you should believe them the first time'? From day one, minute one, I could tell she was special. Special in a way that's hard to describe, and now I can't stop thinking about her. Thinking about the brief time we spent together and what the future holds for us. I can't wait to see her today. Can't wait," he gushes with red cheeks and passion.

"Aww, Justin. She touched your heart! I have never heard you speak of someone in that regard."

"I know, right?" He checks the time on his cell. "Her plane should be landing any minute now. Let's finish up with lunch and go wait for her at the gate. You're really going to love her. She's great!"

Justin polishes off the remaining french fries, slurps down the last of his beverage, and dumps the tray of garbage into a trash can on their way out of the restaurant. He escorts Melia over to a nearby gate in the international terminal, and they sit in coin-operated massage chairs. Five kneading minutes into the muscle rub, passengers begin offloading and Justin eagerly stands in anticipation. He analyzes the face of each person exiting, reading their individual moods and body language one by one. A crabby businessman in dire need of his vacation followed by a newlywed couple on their honeymoon. An emotionally drained father carrying his sleeping child alongside his exhausted wife pushing their restless toddler in a stroller. An elderly couple sharing a laugh followed by a very tall man troubled by his stiff back.

Nineteen passengers later, Justin spots Yori's familiar face, and the two make eye contact from halfway across the terminal. She instantly lights up with excitement, grinning from ear to ear, and hurries over to him through the crowd. They embrace in a long, meaningful hug, and she whispers into his ear, nibbling on the lobe. "You make me feel alive!"

Justin caresses her long, thick black hair, which has been woven into a braid, and smells an intoxicating scent on her neck as she leans close. Just before they release from the sentimental embrace, he whispers back. "I missed you."

When he turns around to introduce Yori to Melia, Justin is dumbfounded to find Kaito standing there wearing a dark-blue vintage T-shirt that reads "I'm going back to Cali" in gold lettering.

"What the heck are you doing here, Kaito? I'm mean. Wow! I didn't expect to see you today, but I'm glad you made the trip." The two cousins engage in a cool-guy handshake followed by a brief one-armed back-slapping hug.

"It's good to see you too, Justin. My apologies for showing up unannounced like this, but Yori and I thought you would appreciate the surprise."

Justin looks over at her with crinkled eyebrows and a confused look on his face, trying to figure out exactly what is going on. "But how did you two—? What a minute, I'm confused." She responds to him with shrugged shoulders and a wry smile.

Kaito jumps in to explain how Yori found him on social media after the three of them became acquainted on Miyake-jima. She was genuinely concerned with his overall health and wanted to find out how he was recovering from the injury. They soon began discussing the passing of Grandfather Yoshiaki, and her thoughtful words helped him sort through the dark time of sorrow. A week later, she mentioned planning the vacation to visit Justin in California and they came up with the idea for Kaito to accompany her on the trip. So they processed the travel documents together and coordinated the flights.

"Well, however it all worked out, I'm glad the four of us are here today." Justin introduces Melia to Yori, and the two instantly hit it off like old friends. He gives them a minute to become somewhat acquainted, listening quietly as they chat up a storm, waiting for the appropriate moment to step in for another introduction. "Melia, you remember Kaito."

Melia turns to Kaito with a bright smile, and he waves her in with both hands for a friendly hug. Although the two cousins haven't seen each other in nearly ten years, they share a mutual feeling of comfort and familiarity, and an apparent bond forms in the moment.

At the conclusion of introductions, the galvanized pack of four meanders their way through multiple airport corridors and down a pair of escalators, eventually stumbling upon the carousels to collect their luggage. They catch a shuttle bus from the airport to the rental car facility where Justin completes the paperwork as the others giggle curbside babysitting the bags. He pulls the car around and encourages the women to sit while the men load up. Justin waits for the rear car doors to close and quietly opens a conversation with Kaito to keep the details private. "Did you mention anything to Yori about the nine stones, encounters, or gifts?"

Kaito tosses his carry-on bag into the trunk. "Not a word, my cousin."

"Good. Let's keep it that way for now. I'll fill her in when the timing is right."

"How much does Melia know?"

Justin loads a suitcase into the trunk. "Melia knows just about everything. She helped me get through the encounters in Hawaii and has been a real lifesaver. I couldn't have done it without her. She'll keep quiet."

Kaito loads another bag. "Did you tell anyone else?"

Justin shakes his head no. "How about you?"

"Nope, the secret remains at three for now." Kaito closes the trunk, walks around to the passenger side of the car, and asks Justin one last question before opening door. "Where are the special gifts?"

Justin walks around to the driver's side, stops at the door, and winks as he responds. "Safely in the trunk. I'll share the details with you in Morro Bay. Shall we get going?"

A big grin forms on Kaito's face. "Road trip!" He opens the car door, hops into the passenger seat, and slams the door shut. Justin watches him turn to the women in the back seat and say something humorous that causes them to break out in laughter.

With the car packed up and passengers buckled in, they embark on a four-hour drive along the scenic Pacific Coast Highway from southern to central California. The car buzzes with excitement as they discuss the week's itinerary that includes stops in Morro Bay, Santa Cruz, Mono Lake, and Death Valley.

Eventually, exhilaration fades to exhaustion, and conversation fades to silence, leaving Justin alone in his thoughts when the others fall asleep.

Midway through the drive, Justin pulls over to stretch his legs at an unincorporated community in Ventura County called Mussel Shoals. He veers off the moderately congested freeway onto Old PCH that parallels Highway 101 in search of a place to park along the picturesque rugged coastline. They drive down a narrow road, passing by the Cliff House Inn and Shoals restaurant, two dozen modest oceanfront homes, and the long Richfield Pier that leads out to Rincon Island. Ultimately Justin stumbles upon a small gravel parking lot across the street from the beach and whips into an open spot.

Justin leaves the car running and walks across the street to an old park bench overlooking the ocean. The other three are still sound asleep, clearly tired from their long day of traveling, and he figures it best not to wake them. He spends a few peaceful minutes taking in the fresh air and scenic views, visualizing what lies ahead on the remainder of their voyage.

Yori suddenly sits down and snuggles up against him, interrupting his moment of meditation with her pleasant voice. "Did we make it to Morro Bay already?"

Justin wraps his arm around her as clouds roll by covering up the sun. "No, not yet. I was feeling a bit confined in the car and needed a quick breather."

They sit quietly watching surfers catch head-high waves adjacent to the pier.

"This place is beautiful. Where are we?" she asks.

A woman walks past them carrying a bright-orange Frisbee. She takes several steps into the sand and flings the disc low and far along the ground to her eagerly waiting dog that chases after it.

"Mussel Shoals Beach. We're about halfway to Morro Bay."

Yori sits up to look Justin directly in the eyes. "Thanks again for inviting me on this trip. It's all I have thought about ever since the day you asked me. *Arigato*." She sends him a touching smile and leans back against the bench looking out at the ocean.

He continues staring at her with a lump in his throat and an odd sensation in his stomach. Something about that glowing smile touched him deeply, and he thinks about them being married someday. On one hand, a very odd feeling to have for someone he met just last month, and on the other, nothing has ever felt so right. "You're welcome. I'm thrilled you said yes and were able to make the travel arrangements. We're going to have a great time these next two weeks, that I promise you."

"My parents think I'm crazy for coming to see you in California. Especially my dad. He's worried sick and believes you might be a weirdo murderer or something."

Justin starts laughing. "What?"

"Seriously. He went on about how you were planning to kidnap me and will demand a king's ransom for my return. I think he watches too many crime shows."

Justin continues laughing in sympathy for her father "Ahh. Poor guy. He must be sick right about now. People can convince themselves to believe just about anything."

"Oh, he'll be fine. My dad has always been a worrier. I tried explaining to him that we made a special connection, but he just doesn't understand or doesn't want to understand. I can't figure out which one."

"Your father sounds like a good man trying to protect his daughter."

They continue to enjoy one another's company, engaged in a discussion about visiting Morro Bay for the first time together.

Eventually, Justin suggests they hit the road once again to finish the second leg of their coastal drive. Yori notices Kaito has moved into the back seat next to Melia, so she makes her way to the front passenger door. His face is squished up against the glass, eyes closed, uncomfortably asleep and dreaming on the outskirts of la-la land.

A short while later, Yori dozes off, joining the other two sleeping beauties in dire need of some additional rest. Justin slept well on the plane ride over from Maui earlier today, but he too is starting to succumb to fatigue from the long day of travel and visualizes a nice comfortable bed waiting for him at the hotel as his reward for captaining the ship.

Over the remainder of the drive, they pass through the city of Santa Barbara, detour off the Pacific Coast Highway, and head inland through the Los Padres National Forest. They skirt the Cachuma Lake Recreation Area, cruise through the old Danish-style town of Solvang, and continue across the Santa Maria Valley, which was the homeland of the Chumash people for thousands of years. The final stretch of road takes them back to the coast, venturing through Pismo Beach, home of the spectacular monarch butterfly grove where thousands of animated orange-and-black butterflies annually migrate, seeking shelter from the freezing northern winters by clustering together in a grove of eucalyptus trees. Highway 101 then veers away from the coast yet again, taking them inland to the city of San Luis Obispo before they change freeways one last time and take the CA-1 N, completing the drive into foggy Morro Bay.

Justin locates the quaint little seaside bed and breakfast where he has a room booked and carefully maneuvers the vehicle into a narrow parking place facing the harbor. The car doors fling open with anticipation and excitement, and the group gets their first whiff of the cool, crisp evening air that smells slightly salty with a hint of seaweed. The temperature hovers in the fifties, bringing about unusual sensations of cold fingers and frosty cheeks. Sounds of pigeons cooing, sea lions calling, and water sloshing up against the dock fill the air.

They make their way inside the cozy hotel lobby to check in. A professionally dressed, well-spoken woman in her thirties escorts them to their quarters, the Bay Suite, which features two queen beds, two couches, a kitchenette, and a fireplace topped off by incredible views of the harbor.

After getting cleaned up, Justin lies down on one of the beds and falls sound asleep, completely wiped out from the extensive day of traveling. The others decide to allow him some much-deserved quiet time, electing Yori to write a note explaining they went for a walk in search of dinner and will return shortly. She locates a pad of writing paper from the coffee table and scribbles him a quick message. "Dear Justin. Thanks again for driving. We stepped out for a little shopping and to find some takeout. Sleep well, Yori."

Justin wakes up to an empty room, growling stomach, and a note left by the crew. He reads the message from Yori and sits outside on the weathered wood plank patio overlooking the dimly lit bay. A foghorn blows in the distance, and he counts out the twenty-five seconds between intervals while scanning the various boats anchored to the moorings in the harbor. A fifty-foot, two-story riverboat comes floating past on a dinner cruise filled with rambunctious passengers laughing, waving, and enjoying themselves in an otherwise calm, still night.

Buzz, buzz, buzz. His cell phone starts to vibrate with an incoming text message from Melia stating they are on the way back with Chinese food for dinner. He continues watching the riverboat pass by and comes up with the idea of taking a harbor cruise tomorrow. A boat ride should provide an ideal opportunity to view the surrounding area from offshore and hopefully reveal an osprey hideout in the process.

Melia calls out from the hotel room door. "Hey there! You hungry? Come get something to eat."

Justin turns around to see Kaito and Yori slip past her into the room carrying brown paper bags of food. He replies in a groggy voice, clearly still fatigued from the long day of traveling. "You're back. Yeah, I definitely can eat something." He slowly rises to his feet and gingerly walks over to Melia who holds the door open for him. Right before he enters the hotel room, a car door slams in the distance, simultaneously causing the horn to chirp once as the lock mechanism engages.

They gather around a circular dinette set to indulge in the Chinese cuisine that consists of kung pao chicken, sweet and sour pork, egg rolls, lo mein, and white rice. The conversation is light during dinner with the women sharing a story about shopping for souvenir T-shirts down the street. At the conclusion of the meal, Kaito hands everyone a fortune cookie, and they take turns cracking open the crispy sugar delights to read the messages inside.

Kaito elects to go first, and he reads off the quote in a deep voice. "Society prepares the crime; a criminal commits it." The others ooh and ahh.

Melia goes next, eating the cookie prior to reading off her message written on the small white piece of paper in red block letters. "Wealth awaits you very soon." She claps several times in approval and gives Kaito a high five.

Yori breaks her cookie apart into tiny pieces, nibbling on the little bites as she quietly reads the fortune to herself with a broad smile and then out loud for the others to hear. "The love of your life is stepping into your planet this summer." She looks over at Melia and the two smirk and chuckle.

Finally, Justin completes the circle of fortune by cracking his cookie in half and pulling out the message. "If you feel you are right, stand firmly by your convictions."

After cleaning up the dinner rubbish, they find an old movie to watch on TV and thumb through the tourist brochures looking for exciting things to do in Morro Bay. Justin chimes in with the idea of a harbor cruise, and they quickly agree with his suggestion and elect Kaito to handle the reservation. He jumps right on it by locating a company online that offers one-hour nature tours of the bay and books four seats on a thirty-foot pontoon boat that departs tomorrow at 10:00 a.m.

Early the following morning, the crew picks up continental breakfast from the hotel lobby, and they sit outside on the patio furniture overlooking the harbor. They sip on hot beverages while discussing the lively morning scene out on the water. Approximately seventy-five anchored boats are now visible in the daylight, mostly sailboats, some of which have tall masts towering nearly forty feet high. The vessels have various locations marked on their sides including Morro Bay, Portland, and San Francisco, along with wild names such as *Transparency*, *Nonsequential*, and *Zero-Sum Game*. Many display reflective party streamers to deter the plethora of migratory seabirds that frequent the area and can be heard hooting, hollering, gasping, and screeching.

Justin watches sea lions climbing on top of a floating structure that contains three towers that mimic the three much-taller smokestacks at the harbor's PG&E power plant. The massive sea mammals lounge on the small platform basking in the sun but only the biggest and boldest ones. With space for fewer than ten, the floating oasis is prime real estate for those individuals in need of a break from the frigid waters that hover in the midfifties this time of year. Additionally, sea otters occasionally break the water's surface feeding on sea urchins, clams, and abalone. The otters can be difficult to spot, and it takes a keen eye to catch a glimpse of the furry little critters.

Kaito speaks up, encouraging them to get a move on. "The boat departs soon. We can walk to the slip from here, but it might take a while."

They set off walking on the Embarcadero to the boat launch, passing by several small hotels, a multitude of ocean-front seafood restaurants, souvenir shops, boutiques, museums, art galleries, an ice-cream parlor, and outfitters for boating on the bay. Old wooden docks dot the shoreline where colorful flags proudly wave from pillars and poles.

The harbor cruise gets underway at maximum capacity with a boat full of twenty passengers and a two-person crew. When the hard-top pontoon pushes away from the dock, a man's voice starts projecting over the loudspeaker, narrating the scene and interacting with the tourists on board. After a brief introduction and safety meeting, he asks the guests where they are visiting from today, commenting as several individuals call out their hometowns, which include places such as Los Angeles, San Diego, and Orange County. When Kaito mentions Yori is visiting from Japan, the narrator declares her the winner for being the individual who traveled the farthest and tosses her a sea lion stuffed animal as the prize.

The boat slowly cruises from one end of the bay to the other, with the narrator filling them in on historical information and local wildlife. He mentions the migratory patterns of birds that annually visit Morro Bay from as far south as Mexico and as far north as Canada. "At any given moment you can see ducks, geese, gulls, herons, pelicans, and various birds of prey such as hawks, eagles, peregrine falcons, and ospreys." He goes on to mention the 581-foot-high Morro Rock located just north of the harbor, explaining how it's a volcanic plug that connects to the shore by a causeway, making it a tied island. "The Chumash and Salinan tribes have considered Morro Rock a sacred site for millennia. It's protected as the Morro Rock State Preserve, and it's illegal for the general public to climb."

The guide goes on to describe the estuary on the southern coastal part of Morro Bay that includes Los Osos Creek and Chorro Creek filtering into the Pacific Ocean. He mentions the dune that protects the estuary from open ocean swells and how the shallow open water of the bay is tidally drained. "Dune habitat dominates the western and southwestern edge of the bay, called the Morro Dunes National Preserve, which has its own distinct avifauna and is inaccessible by land."

Melia raises her hand to ask a question, and the narrator signals her to proceed. "Can you describe an estuary? I'm not that familiar with the term."

"Yes, of course, no problem. For those of you who couldn't hear the question, the young lady from Hawaii asked what is an estuary. The term refers to a partially enclosed coastal body of brackish water where at least one river or stream flows into it and freely connects to the open sea. Think of it as a transition zone between rivers and marine environments."

When the cruise concludes and the passengers begin debarking, Justin approaches the narrator to pick his brain on locating an osprey, the animal found on one of the nine stones. The man obviously knows a thing or two about local wildlife and hopefully can steer him in the right direction to see the elusive bird of prey. "Ospreys can and have been observed all throughout the Morro Bay area including the mud flats, harbor, Morro Rock, and salt marsh. However, my suggestion to you would be either to rent a kayak and paddle to the more remote locations of the estuary or take a walk along the El

Moro Elfin Forest Natural Area. The easily accessible board-walk trail is less than a mile long and teeming with life."

After exiting the boat and returning to their rental car, the group decides to venture over to Morro Strand State Beach for a close look at the jagged Morro Rock. They find a place to park in the crowded lot of tourists sprinkled with locals and set off trudging in the cool sand littered with large brownish-orange stalks of kelp containing fist-size bulbs of salt water. Sections of the seaweed are wider than a baseball bat, several times longer, and are covered in sand flies eager to inspect the drying vegetation. An immense amount of the seaweed grows offshore and regularly floats inside the bay, moving in the direction of the tidal current.

They walk north down the three-mile stretch of protected beach passing by a cozy family picnic, two joggers sporting colorful attire, a proud father assisting his young daughter with flying a dragonfly kite, and various other beachgoers taking in the simplicity of a sandy coastal day. As they approach a huge patch of kelp, Kaito recognizes something intertwined in the seaweed and reaches in to remove an old soccer ball. The four companions spread out, kicking the ball back and forth in preparation for an entertaining game of boys versus girls. When Melia slide tackles Kaito, stripping him of the ball, and scores the winning goal, she receives a standing ovation from a local surfer who just came ashore in a full body wetsuit.

The group engages him in a brief conversation about the local surf scene. He mentions how Morro Strand contains several sandbars that create a variety of breaks. "If you stay near the Rock, a conveyor belt of rip current zooms you outside with minimal effort, but everyone hits that spot. Although I enjoy the Rock, you can easily find rideable zones without competition anywhere up and down the beach."

When Melia mentions being a surfer girl from Maui, the guy goes bonkers, ranting and raving about his desire to surf the Hawaiian Islands someday. "It's always been a dream of mine to visit Hawaii and surf some of those famous waves. You're a lucky person to live there, no doubt. I'm so jealous of you right now." He picks up his surfboard and starts the long walk back up the sand. "Have a good time in Morro Bay."

Melia starts to exaggerate a shiver. "It's chilly out here. Do you guys wanna get going?"

On their return walk to the car, Melia and Kaito run ahead kicking the soccer ball down the shoreline. About one hundred yards from the parking lot, Justin reaches out to grab Yori's chilly hand and gets jolted by static electricity when their fingers come into contact.

Several paces later, Justin notices a small white disc lying beside a clump of kelp and bends down to snatch it up. "Hey, check it out! A sand dollar." He brushes off the loose debris from the sun-bleached sea urchin skeleton and hands it over to Yori for safekeeping. "A gift to you from me and the sea."

"Oh my gosh, how cute! I love it!" She takes a long look at the sand dollar and momentarily holds it close to her heart. "I'm going to keep this as a memento from our time here in Morro Bay."

The courting couple continues collecting additional sand dollars, throwing back the broken or chipped shells, but keeping a handful of intact ones. Eventually, they regroup with Kaito and Melia in the parking lot to discuss options for the remainder of the day. Justin desperately wants to visit the Elfin Forest, but the women oppose his idea and suggest the Museum of Natural History instead.

Kaito settles their minor dispute with a simple resolution. "Why don't we drop the women off at the museum, and then we can hit the trail. The two of us should be able to complete the loop in about an hour, and we can pick them up on our way back to the hotel."

They unanimously agree with his suggestion, pile into the car, and proceed over to the museum. Yori walks around to the driver's side and knocks on the window for Justin to roll it down. "Text me when you are on the way to pick us up."

"You got it. Have a good time, and we'll see you after a while."

The men wait for them to enter the building before driving across town to the Elfin Forest trailhead. They set out on the clockwise loop with Justin sharing three brief stories about his Hawaii encounters. He fills Kaito in on the details as they observe ducks, cormorants, and egrets frolicking in the blue water from Bush Lupine Point. With no ospreys in sight, the cousins continue to Sienna's View, pausing to witness numerous waterfowl at play but not their specific bird of prey. So, they push onward to the pygmy oak grove where two-hundred-year-old California live oaks provide a shady shelter with their sprawling branches covered in hanging moss.

"Let's chill out on that bench for a bit," says Justin.

Kaito nods his head in agreement and they plop down to rest.

Justin picks up a long blade of grass, places it into his mouth, and bites down gently to taste the bittersweet stalk. He leans back on the wooden bench, tilting his head toward the sky, inhales a big whiff of the briny air, and wonders where tomorrow will take him. While he stares into a cloud of morphing faces, the sun makes a dramatic entrance, temporarily blinding him with flashes of light and bright spots. Now engulfed in a confused state of vertigo, Justin closes his eyes to allow the sensation of whirling and loss of balance to pass.

He doesn't mention anything to Kaito about the incident and quickly suggests they get going. With a pounding headache and pale face, he tries to stand but quickly falls flat on his face. Looking up now, he sees the world from a grounded point of view, eye level with the leaves, sand, rocks, dirt, and dust.

"Are you all right? What happened?" exclaims Kaito.

"I'm fine. It's nothing to worry about." Justin sits up and tries to regain his composure. He cracks a joke to lighten the mood. "I stood up too fast, felt a little light-headed, and my knees buckled."

Kaito reaches down and places both hands under Justin's armpits, hoisting him up in one swift motion. They decide to call it a day, considering the circumstances, and complete the boardwalk trail loop without further incident. Back at the car, Kaito offers to drive, allowing Justin an opportunity to recover on their way to pick up the women at the museum.

Upon returning to the hotel, a thick marine layer has formed around Morro Rock and is slowly spreading across the harbor, bringing a calming sensation into the bay. The air has cooled, and wildlife disperses as birds scatter, otters hide, and sea lions dive. A lone kayak fisherman rows his way through the channel, hoping for an afternoon bite, while Justin leans up against the railing overlooking the water. He watches a large gray seabird thrash and splash its wings along the waterline, fluttering upon takeoff as gulls loudly callout in approval.

Back inside the hotel room, Melia and Yori are chatting about visiting Tidelands Park at the south end of the Embarcadero while Kaito engages in some mindless channel surfing on the couch. Justin comes stumbling through the door and plants himself down on a bed to scroll through his cell phone.

Yori calls out from the couch. "Melia and I are going to the park just up the street. Would either of you like to join us?"

"I'm beat," says Justin. "I kind of just wanna chill before we go out to dinner."

Yori blows him a kiss from across the room and turns to Kaito. "How about you, sir?"

"To the park!"

Kaito, Melia, and Yori arrive at Tidelands, a two-acre public play area that stretches right along the bay. Children can be seen enjoying themselves throughout the sand play area, which centers around a giant pirate ship climbing structure. The nautical theme park has seal statues, a whale's tale, and crow's nest displayed among the well-maintained lawns, barbeques, and picnic tables. A set of stairs leads down to the mud flats on one end and a side tie dock with a fish-cleaning station on the other.

They wander down to the empty wooden boat dock to witness a school of small fish swimming past, skimming along the long seagrass that grows just beneath the water's surface. Clams, worms, and shrimp mingle within the jillions of living sand dollars that conceal large portions of the clear, shallow bottom. When two gray seagulls glide in to see what all the commotion is about, Kaito runs after them flailing his arms to scare off the curious birds looking for a quick snack. After hanging out on the dock, they walk up to the park, waving at a paddleboarder who coasts by in the thickening fog.

Back at the room, Justin wakes up from a siesta in a cold sweat and jumps into the shower for a refresher. By the time he finishes getting ready for dinner behind a closed bathroom door, the others have returned to the hotel room and are busy preparing for the evening themselves. They have a 7:00 p.m. dinner reservation at an award-winning seafood restaurant located just up the street on the waterfront.

A short while later, the warmly dressed foursome departs for an evening stroll down the Embarcadero. The fashionable women walk ahead of the two men, who hover behind a few steps, engaged in a private conversation. Kaito mentions to Justin that he inherited twenty-five thousand dollars from Grandfather Yoshiaki's will and offers to cover their expenses from here on out. "If we don't have any luck finding an osprey tomorrow, I'll pay for another night or two at the hotel if they have a vacancy or find us somewhere else that does. There's still a lot of ground to cover in and around Morro Bay. Maybe we should consider hiring a local guide."

Justin doesn't like the idea of involving anyone else. "Let's see where tomorrow takes us first. I would prefer to rent some kayaks and paddle around the harbor before we call in the cavalry." The cousins agree to explore the estuary via kayak and devise plan B, which entails contacting a local expert.

They arrive at the crowded restaurant, check in with the receptionist, and have a seat in the waiting area for their name to be called. Several people-watching minutes tick by until their turn comes up, and a young man escorts their party to a corner table overlooking the bay. He hands each of them a menu, fills their glasses with ice water, and mentions that the waiter will be with them shortly.

While they thumb through the dinner menu, a well-dressed, sophisticated, middle-aged woman shows up to take their order. She fills them in on a couple of specials, answers a few of their seafood-related questions, and enters each of their meals into a handheld tablet. Yori orders the roasted organic chicken, Melia opts for a bread bowl of clam chowder, Kaito selects the cioppino, and Justin decides on a strip steak, medium rare. The server recommends some oysters on the half shell and Dutch-style mussels for the appetizers, which they gladly tack on.

As the chefs prepare their meal, Melia reads out loud from a laminated tabletop document chronicling the history of Morro Bay's commercial fishing industry dating back to the nineteenth century. The document mentions early days of a growing abalone fishery followed by robust times of sardine, groundfish, salmon, and albacore fishing in the twentieth century. Soon thereafter, a fleet of commercial passenger fishing vessels began serving the thousands of visitors and locals as commercial fisheries continued to evolve. Nowadays, Dungeness crab, market squid, lingcod, oysters, sablefish, Pacific hagfish, and shortspine thornyheads have become a staple of the local twenty-first-century harvest.

Before they know it, two plates of skillfully prepared appetizers arrive, accompanied by a large wooden bowl of Caesar salad and a basket of freshly baked breads. The party of four indulges themselves in some delectable side dishes, bonding in laughter while consuming the gourmet starters in the midst of a noisy crowd of ravenous diners. Moments after completing their first course, three bussers simultaneously appear to clear the clutter and prepare the table for dinner. The impeccable service continues when the main course arrives in a precarious balancing act performed by the waitress and her server's assistant. At the conclusion of dinner, they bypass having dessert at the restaurant, and instead decide to get an ice-cream cone down the street. The waitress drops down the hefty bill, which is snatched up and covered by Kaito who receives a warm round of appreciation from the others.

They exit through the restaurant doors and spill outside onto the damp boardwalk. On their way to get some ice cream, they stumble upon an arcade full of classic games and step inside the densely packed room for a bit of fun. Justin and Yori make a beeline to three pinball machines lined up against the back wall, contemplating whether to try Tales from the Crypt, Star Wars, or Lord of the Rings. Yori picks Star Wars but explains to him that she doesn't know how to play pinball, inviting Justin to demonstrate as she stands in front of the machine. After inserting a few quarters to start the action, he moves in behind her, wrapping his arms around her waist with his hands on top of hers. He goes on to explain the concept of pinball and shows Yori how pressing down on the side buttons controls the flippers. After sharing a brief intimate moment, Justin steps back and Yori explodes like a pro gamer, racking up points at an incredible rate.

"Are you trying to hustle me?" he says, watching on in amazement.

Yori goes on to explain how immensely popular arcades are in Japan and that she used to frequent them quite often in her teens. After achieving a top ten all-time score on the pinball machine, she jumps up and down clapping her hands in excitement and turns around to plant a big kiss on Justin.

Meanwhile, Kaito and Melia inspect an array of vintage video games that include Paperboy, Joust, Frogger, Double Dragon, Mortal Kombat, and a one-lane Skee-Ball alley. They sit down at opposite ends of a retro cocktail arcade game machine to test out their skills on a competitive round of Mrs. Pacman. Melia triumphs in the end, narrowly beating out Kaito's score, notching another victory for the girls who share some giggles on their way into the ice-cream parlor next door. They reappear moments later, each carrying a waffle cone topped off with double scoops. Melia enjoys a specialty flavor imported from Canada called Tiger Tail, an orange-flavored ice cream with black licorice swirls, and eats the top scoop before giving the remainder to Kaito. Yori chooses green tea over vanilla bean and shares with Justin as they talk about an out-of-order Zoltar fortune-telling machine, reminiscent of the old carnival days.

After an enjoyable night out, the foursome set off on their return walk to the hotel room feeling fuzzily satisfied from the dinner and desserts. Kaito unleashes an improvised song he swiftly titles "Bow Down in the Presence of the G.O.A.T." after hearing the story of Yori handling her business on the pinball machine. His goofy, rap-inspired melody ebbs and flows between Japanese and English, bringing a host of chuckles and laughs from the others as he compliments her game, dubbing Yori the Greatest of All Time.

Immediately upon returning to the bayfront inn, Melia snaps a photograph of the group posing alongside a lit company sign and quickly texts the group selfie to her mother. She remains out front to give her mom a call, and the others file into the room.

Sakura speaks to Melia in a concerned voice. After all, her eighteen-year-old daughter has ventured off to the mainland for the first time without parental supervision. "Are you having a nice trip, honey? Are you being safe? Please tell me your brother is looking after you and that everything is OK."

"Yes, Mom, everything is fine. We're having a great trip so far, and Justin has my back. Try not to worry about it."

"Remember, you're first semester of school starts in three weeks. Please be home on time."

"Yes, Mother, I'm aware. I have a plane ticket reserved in two weeks that departs out of San Francisco. Justin has already promised he will take me to the airport."

Their conversation continues in a similar fashion until Melia decides she has had enough lecturing for tonight. "All right, Mom, gotta go now. You're breaking up. I'll call you from Santa Cruz in a few days. Ta-ta."

Meanwhile, Kaito lies sprawled out on the couch flipping through the TV channels and comes across an entertaining standup comedian. Justin and Yori are snuggling on a loveseat in front of the fireplace for warmth, quietly talking between themselves.

When Melia enters the hotel room through the heavy front door, Kaito bursts out in laughter from a joke being told, inciting her to jump on the couch next to him. The two cousins share in some laughs for a few moments, but she is tired from the long day and soon crashes on the corner bed. He stays up to watch the comedy show but falls asleep ten minutes into a Western, leaving only the two lovebirds awake.

Justin and Yori sink farther into the couch, cozying up together under a supersoft cotton throw blanket. He apologizes for the crowded hotel room and assures her of some additional privacy once they get to Santa Cruz. "Originally, I had planned on just the two of us here in Morro Bay, but obviously things have changed." She watches his lips closely while he speaks.

"But we have a good-size house in SC with plenty of room for everyone to spread out."

Yori whispers into his ear, sending a tingling sensation down Justin's spine. "Stop talking and kiss me."

His hand slides around the back of her neck and they passionately kiss as sparks fly. While still lip-locked, she places her chilly hands on his toasty cheeks, and the kissing intensifies. He caresses her upper back, slowly working his hands down her sides, and glides his palms across her lower curves for a firm squeeze. Suddenly, a humorous line from a classic film causes them to start laughing, and they realize the moment must end for now.

He kisses her neck one last time. "Maybe we should call it a night."

Yori tightens her ponytail and gives him one last peck. "Yes. To be continued. Enjoy the couch." She quietly slides into bed and bundles up in the soft linens.

Justin shuts off the TV, turns down the fireplace, and crashes on the love seat with his feet dangling over the edge.

13

THE DUNES

Justin wakes up in the middle of the night and has a hard time falling back to sleep. He slips on a light jacket and slides out the front door to the patio overlooking Morro Bay. The weather is calm, cool, and clear with dim lights from the boardwalk casting long shadows on the relatively still, pitch-black harbor water. He sits down on a damp, all-weather Adirondack chair, which has a flat back, contoured seat, and wide armrests, rubbing his sleepy eyes and yawning. Thoughts of Yori cross his mind in the peaceful quietness.

A series of sharp whistles can be heard approaching in the darkness and something flies overhead chanting. "*Cheep, cheep. Yewk, yewk.*" A large brown-and-white raptor glides past him, lands on a high-pitched corner of the adjacent rooftop and starts to bob and weave its head as it scans the shallows. The distinguished bird of prey stands twenty-four inches tall with an impressive five-foot wingspan and possesses a menacing curved beak, large white feet, and deadly black talons.

Without warning, the stealthy carnivore crashes down feet first into the water causing several pigeons to scurry from the dock. It immediately resurfaces empty-handed and flaps back up to the same high perch. On a second go-around, the raptor finds success in its uncharacteristic night stalk, temporarily hovering above the waterline before diving in with open talons. The bird resurfaces with a plump orange rockfish in its grip, flutters over to an old wooden rowboat tied off to the dock, and starts devouring the prized catch. When Justin stands up and leans over the railing for a closer look, the disturbance startles the raptor, triggering the bird to look up and release a loud shrieking call of disapproval. The bird's irises start glowing a mesmerizing golden brown, sending goose bumps down Justin's arms when he realizes the species. "Hello there, Miss Osprey."

The bird rips one last chunk of meaty flesh from the rockfish, inhales the lumpy bite, and flies away to finish her meal in privacy. Justin watches the raptor disappear halfway across the bay and can faintly see its radiant, glowing eyes when the osprey comes to rest across the water on a sand dune high point. He estimates the distance at three hundred yards and brainstorms a daring idea to borrow the rowboat and paddle over for a closer look. So, after quietly retrieving a flashlight from his backpack, he walks down to the desolate small boat dock and bravely rows off on borrowed time. After witnessing dinghies navigate the bay with ease during daylight hours, he feels confident in his capabilities to make the jaunt across. However, at the same time he realizes attempting this alone and at night is unwise but goes for it anyway on a whim.

Things start to get a little dicey halfway across with the harbor lights fading farther away on each pull of the double oars. Justin whispers under his breath. "Why didn't I wake up Kaito? Stupid, stupid, stupid." He eventually makes it across and drags the rowboat safely ashore.

With his vision limited under a moonless night sky, Justin removes the small flashlight from his coat pocket in an attempt to shed some light on the Morro Dunes National Preserve. He scans across hills of rolling sand that are grown over by grasses and brush, searching for the elusive osprey that seems to have disappeared under the cover of darkness. All of the sudden, he begins to hear a twanging, metallic sound in between the deep foghorn intervals that resembles, *"daweeed, daweeed, daweeed, daweeed"* and a tiny western snowy plover appears on the sandy knoll some forty feet away. The petite cosmopolitan shorebird looks down at him from the mound and repeats her alarm call numerous times in a much louder tone. Several seconds after the noisy announcement, dozens of additional plovers become visible on the dunes and start spilling downhill toward him like an army of marching ants.

Justin stands still, dumbfounded by the birds' unusual movements, and unsure what to do next. He shines the flashlight to his right, looking for an escape route, unexpectedly seeing several infuriated brown pelicans closing in. He looks over to the left hoping for a clear path and gets startled by a committee of vultures hobbling toward him. To make matters worse, his feet sink ankle-deep into the muddy shoreline when he tries backpedaling out of the predicament, leaving him stranded and vulnerable. While the angry birds encircle him, Justin calls out in an abrasive voice. "What do you want from me?"

The foghorn sounds off in response to his question, closely followed by the materialization of a winged figure from the shadows that screeches out. *"Fraaank. Fraaank. Fraaank."*

Hoping for the best but fearing the worst, Justin nervously taps on the dimming flashlight as a gigantic, long-necked creature swoops down and comes to a gliding halt in the sand. The gray-bodied predatory wading bird has slender brown legs with a white neck and head that is accentuated by a black headdress and a strong, dagger-shaped pinkish-yellow bill. The bird's height first appears equal to an average man but shrinks down considerably to just over three feet tall as it approaches and starts speaking in a sarcastic old man's voice with a stereotypical New York accent.

"Back up everyone, make room. I said, back up." The bird follows that up with a tremendous, earth-shattering "*Fraaank*" to silence the crowd. "Now, that's better. When I, the mighty gray heron speaks, you, the mixed flock of hooligans should listen."

The silly, animated bird dawdles over to Justin like a court jester on stilts, pushing his way past the squabbling vultures. "Sorry about those birdbrains. Do you mind me asking what the hell you are doing out here all alone at night? Just kidding. That was rhetorical. But in all seriousness, what brings you out here?"

He tries to explain. "Well, we're on a quest to find an osprey in Morro Bay and I finally saw one moments ago. So, I followed it over here in that rowboat and—"

The heron cuts him off. "I know how you got here, Captain Obvious. Let me rephrase the question. Why are you here, and specifically what are you looking for?"

Justin responds in an uncertain manner. "I'm investigating an unsolved riddle that our ancestors left behind?"

"That's right. Now you're talking my language. Go on."

"And will hopefully learn a thing or two about myself during the process?"

"There you go. There you go! What else?" replies the heron excitedly.

"And I will earn a valuable gift for completing your challenge?"

"Gift? What gift? I know nothing of a gift or a challenge, but maybe you would like to hear a message I brought along instead?"

Justin scratches his head in confusion and tries to move around, but he can't get out of the wet sand. "But I thought—"

The heron interrupts him again. "You thought what?"

"I thought—Oh, never mind."

"You thought you would mosey on out to this sacred soil and be gifted almightiness on your good looks and charm alone?"

"No, not exactly. I figured you would first challenge me with a riddle, rite of passage, or something along those lines."

The heron loudly shrieks in hysterics calling out "*Fraaank.*" He eventually settles back down and continues. "Well, you thought wrong, half-Japanese man from Hawaii who lives in California."

Justin's mood sours. "All right, well, my bad. Help me out of this foot trap, and I'll be on my way. Sorry to bother you, talking bird from the East Coast who migrated west."

The onlooking birds hoot and holler in glee, but the heron quickly silences them with another ear piercing "*Fraaank!*" before he responds. "Now, now hold on, oh crabby one. Don't get all bent out of shape with your panties in a bag of ruffles. You're clearly a brave soul willing to risk—" The heron is interrupted by a loud ruckus coming from two squawking pelicans engaged in a jousting contest. "Would you two shut it up over there. Can't you see we're trying to have an intellectual conversation over here?"

He turns to Justin and continues. "Some birds will never learn. Anyways, where was I? Oh yes! You came out here looking for something, and I'm going to give it to you." The heron starts acting giddy, flapping his wings in excitement, which causes his feathery companions to wildly call out. "My gift to you is—drum roll, please—the gift of visualization!" He laughs aloud in pleasure letting out another *"Fraaank."*

Thinking for a moment about what he said, Justin responds in bewilderment. "I don't get it. What is that supposed to mean?"

The wading bird answers him in a slow, deliberate manner. "Virtually anything you can imagine is or can be possible." He can see Justin still doesn't understand and continues. "Oh, come on, you get it. Think, believe, dream, achieve."

"That sounds a bit cliché," replies Justin.

"Maybe. But some of life's most valuable possessions are the intangible ones, wouldn't you agree?"

"Such as?"

"Such as peace, love, happiness, freedom of speech, the right to choose, and Wi-Fi. Should I go on?"

"No need, I understand. You are saying that we must first visualize that which we seek."

"Exactamundo!" says the heron. "Visualize that which you seek, and you might be surprised to find it one day."

"What else?" replies Justin.

"What do you mean what else? That's it! What more did you expect to hear from a talking East Coast bird that migrated west? After all, I'm just a gray heron with a simple message." The western snowy plovers, brown pelicans, and vultures collectively cry out in support of their winged compadre. "Best of luck on that return paddle, hopeless romantic, and tell Yori something sweet the next time you see her. Ta-ta. Oh, by the way, you came to the wrong place this evening. Go back and follow through with plan B."

The heron swiftly flies off, calling out one last "*Fraaank*" and vanishes into the night. On cue, the other birds disperse back in the direction they appeared from and the grip loosens on Justin's feet.

"Sometimes life tests us in mysterious ways not meant to be understood, and I think that might have been one of those."

He sloshes down the muddy shoreline and pushes the rowboat back into the water.

Justin sets down the oars midway across the bay to rinse off each of his dirty shoes in the placid, bone-chilling saltwater. Faint morning light illumes a silhouette of Morro Rock as the mighty Sol awakens from another sleepless night to provide energetic warmth. He slips back on the soggy shoes, grabs ahold of the wooden oars, and resumes rowing to the sound of a high-pitched peal in staccato rhythm.

"Kleek ki-ki-ki-ki-ki ker."

After a brief moment of silence, the chirping whistles repeat, only this time with much more volume and intensity.

"Kleek ki-ki-ki-ki-ki ker."

Justin looks over his shoulder at Morro Rock and witnesses a dense layer of fog instantaneously form in an otherwise clear, nautical twilight sky. The thick gray cloud of sea smoke abruptly blankets the mountainous rock and barrels through Morro Bay affixed to the enormous wings of a giant eagle. The majestic bird glides through the entire estuary in a matter of seconds, rapidly soaring past Justin like a runaway locomotive. He looks up to catch a glimpse of the awe-inspiring creature as it roars past and knocks him down in the boat, leaving behind an impenetrable trail of murky coastal fog and one last call out.

"Kleek ki-ki-ki-ki-ki ker."

The inauspicious marine layer seems to have clouded his judgment, and Justin suddenly finds himself lost in a state of hopelessness. His eyes close in despair, but he hears the heron's voice murmur through one ear and out the other. "Visualize the safe passage you seek."

Still on his back, Justin begins picturing specifics about the harbor including a layout of the various moored boats, distinct flags flying at certain locations, and the precise sounds heard in and around the bay. He envisions returning safely to the small boat dock, tying off to the weathered horn cleats, and making it back to the hotel without incident.

When he pops up to have a look around, a furry-faced sea otter playfully surfaces twitching its long, highly sensitive whiskers. The marine mammal locks eyes with the land mammal, lets out a sound resembling that of a human chuckle and plunges back underwater. The otter quickly resurfaces and begins circling the boat on its back. It then releases another grunting chuckle and slowly glides away grooming itself, quickly disappearing in the heavy layer of fog.

"Did that sea otter laugh at me, say hello, or suggest I follow? Hmm."

Justin confidently re-grips the splintered oars and cautiously paddles after the sea otter through waves of unrelenting fogginess. He narrowly avoids crashing into a large sailboat, brushing past close enough to read the name painted across its side in an animated purple font that reads *Transparency*. He recalls a memory of seeing the positioned boat in the harbor and slowly inches onward, realizing the dock should be just up ahead. Without warning, the rowboat suddenly thwacks into the dock, sending several cooing pigeons into panic mode, and the birds take flight in a hazy flurry of feathers.

Justin scrambles onto the small boat dock and secures his borrowed vessel to the metal cleats with a hitch knot. He unleashes an elongated sigh of relief and hoofs up the shaky ramp to civilization. The exact moment he reaches down to unlock the boat dock gate, a supernatural feather floats down and hovers motionless directly in front of him. The ornate pattern and radical coloring of the elongated quill are unlike anything Justin has ever seen and definitely not from this world. Complex swirls of electric blue and psychedelic purple dusted in a coat of scintillating silver sparkles highlight the feather's appearance.

He cautiously plucks the magical levitating feather midair and in doing so, receives a revealing mind message from the giant eagle. "You have passed today's test with great fortitude, having earned this mighty treasure as your reward. The feather you now hold grants access to all land animal life and gives you a unique ability to interact with living creatures in ways you never thought imaginable. But, be forewarned of what lies ahead in your journey and remember what the knowledgeable old man once said: patience is a virtue; expect the unexpected."

Justin returns to the room and Kaito pops up on the couch whispering, "What were you thinking? I watched you jump on that rowboat and paddle away earlier."

Justin holds up a finger in front of his mouth. "Shhhh." He quietly retrieves a backpack from the closet and waves Kaito over to the bathroom. "Lock the door and flip on that exhaust fan to drown out the noise."

Kaito anxiously speaks. "Where did you go for the past two hours? I've been worried sick."

"Two hours? No way, more like thirty minutes!"

"No, I assure you it was two hours. I've been waiting on the couch for you this entire time. Damn, Justin! You really scared the crap out of me. I thought something happened to you."

Justin explains to Kaito what just happened out on the estuary and asks him to hold the magical quill. He unzips the backpack and removes the gifts for them to collectively inspect. An unusual sensation radiates through Kaito's fingertips, provoking a distinct feeling of intimidation, and he quickly hands the lively feather back over, deciding then and there to never touch it again. Justin goes on to demonstrate each of the three gifts acquired during the Hawaii encounters while Kaito quietly observes the artifacts, opting to see with his eyes and not his hands. When the presentation concludes, and the items are stored away, the interconnected cousins conjure up plan C and agree to depart Morro Bay later that morning.

14

PAOHA ISLAND

After completing the drive from Morro Bay, the group arrives at a charming two-story beach house in the laid-back Seabright neighborhood of Santa Cruz where Justin resides with a class-mate from UCSC named Lily and his childhood friend Brandon. Lily's wealthy aunt has owned the posh property for many years and graciously permits the three of them to rent the home for a modest monthly fee with a strict agreement of no partying allowed. The house is located three doors down from Seabright State Beach and only fifteen minutes away from the college campus.

Justin unlocks the French doors to let everyone inside where he proceeds to give them a quick tour of the property. "Kaito, you can sleep right here on the living room couch. The kitchen is over there obviously, that slider leads out back to a private little yard, garage, and a half bath. Follow me, and I will show you the rest."

They walk upstairs, and he continues. "That's Lily's room. She gets the master, which is totally fair considering her aunt owns the place. This one is Brandon's room. Here's a full bath-room if anyone wants to shower, and my bedroom is down at the end of the hall." They walk up a second flight of stairs where he opens the door of a tiny room containing nothing more than a twin bed. "Melia, you can sleep in here tonight. It used to be a storage closet at one point, but it has since been converted into a cozy sleeping area for guests. And last but not least, the gigantic ocean-view deck. My favorite spot in the house." Justin opens an old, rickety wooden door to reveal a glass-walled rooftop deck with patio lounge chairs and a post-card view of the Pacific.

They walk back downstairs to order some gourmet sand-wiches from an online delivery service and relax in the living room discussing tomorrow's excursion to Mono Lake. Justin searches for lodging, and he books them modest accommodations for two nights at a simple hotel in the area. The group agrees to an early departure time in order to get a jump start on the six-hour drive that will take them inland from the Central Coast of California to an unlikely world at the transition between the Great Basin Desert and the Sierra Nevada mountains.

Later that evening, the four companions join Brandon, Lily, and a half dozen others at nearby Seabright beach for a sunset bonfire and a session of roasting marshmallows. Justin and Yori set their chairs close to the concrete fire ring and alternate turns using a long metal skewer to cook the light, spongy, sugar-based confections. She takes the first go at it, holding the skewer several inches above the hot coals, slowly turning the stick until the marshmallow has browned evenly of all sides. "Perfectly gooey and delicious. Your turn!"

Justin begins roasting one up for himself while listening quietly to the circle of peers who game plan a visit to the Santa Cruz Beach Boardwalk, a seaside amusement park founded in 1907. Right when the marshmallow reaches an optimum golden-brown color, he becomes distracted by the cackling laughter of Brandon, and it suddenly catches on fire. Justin quickly pulls the skewer away from the hot coals, inhales a deep breath, and lets out a short burst of air to extinguish the flame. At the exact moment when the light goes out, he sees a convoluted landscape image emerge in the bonfire backdrop and undergoes another bout of vertigo. He tries to fight off the dizzy spell to focus on the image, but the abnormal jerking eye movements make it nearly impossible to see anything at all.

Yori recognizes something is bothering him and leans close to whisper. "Are you OK? What's wrong?"

"Oh, it's nothing. I'm feeling a bit light-headed and tired." Justin closes his eyes, visualizing the image from the bonfire in much greater detail. He sees a small island with abundant hot springs and fumaroles on its surface that is primarily made of clay, mud, scattered volcanic ash, and basalt. His eyes open up. "Paoha Island! We need to visit Paoha island."

Yori looks at him in dismay. "What are you talking about? Are you all right?"

The vertigo subsides, and he tries to regain his composure. "Yes, I'm fine. Forget about it."

The crew takes off for an evening of entertainment at the Beach Boardwalk amusement park, but Justin and Yori decide not to go. Brandon assumes responsibility to look after Melia and Kaito, assuring Justin they will be home at a reasonable time, especially considering the long day they have planned for tomorrow.

On their return walk to the house, Yori attempts to clear the air. "Can I talk to you really quick?"

"Yeah, sure anything. What's up?"

"I'm not exactly sure what's going on, but I know you three are up to something, and it has me a bit concerned. As long as you can tell me it's nothing illegal and you won't get in trouble, I will support you through whatever it is you are involved in."

"You don't have to worry, Yori. It's nothing like that at all. You just have to trust me."

"I do trust you, Justin, which is exactly why I haven't mentioned anything until now. Look, I just wanted you to know that I am aware, that's all. It's your business and, in all honesty, I would prefer to stay uninvolved if that's all right with you."

Justin is pleasantly surprised to hear those words come out of her mouth. It didn't sit well with him, knowing she has been completely left in the dark. "Yes, I support your decision one hundred percent and will let Melia and Kaito know to keep a lid on it. Thank you for the vote of confidence. I really appreciate your openness and trust."

They go on to discuss how Yori will still accompany them on the trip tomorrow morning, but she will remain back at the hotel when they decide to visit Mono Lake.

When they return to the house, Yori retrieves a few miscellaneous items from her suitcase and enters the upstairs bathroom for a steamy, soothing shower. She washes her long flowing hair in a lavender-scented shampoo, uses a loofah bath sponge to gently cleanse her body, and rinses away the soapy suds under a pulsating water jet massage. After toweling off and blow-drying her hair, she slips into some comfortable shorts, pulls the UCSC sweatshirt over her head, and walks down the hall.

Meanwhile, Justin cleans up in the master bathroom, changes into some flannel plaid pajama pants, and waits in his bedroom. He turns on a wave light projector to create a colorful watery ocean atmosphere on the ceiling and plugs his cell phone into the gadget to play music from the internal mini-speaker system. When his favorite top one hundred Billboard song comes on, Justin tries to calm his nerves by performing a spontaneous booty-shaking dance number by the window. He dances and sings along with the hip-hop jam.

Yori enters the bedroom unannounced to find Justin standing barefoot and shirtless with his back turned to her. She giggles at his cute butt rhythmically swirling to the music and clears her throat to get his attention after briefly watching the unexpected but noteworthy performance.

Justin spins around on his heel to find Yori standing three feet away. "Sorry, I didn't know you were there. I was just, ahh…"

She closes the distance between them and places her index finger over his mouth. "Shhhh."

Their eyes lock in a passionate stare down that ultimately leads to an exhilarating kiss. Justin places his hands on her petite waist and slowly glides them up her back. He pulls her warm body close to his for some skin-on-skin contact, and they embrace in a second heated kiss that electrifies the sensual mood.

When the music changes to a sexy pop song, Yori places her hands on his bare chest and gently pushes him away to perform a slow, seductive dance. For the first time, she truly feels alive in his presence and yearns to share this affection with her new lover. She sways her hips from side to side while conducting synchronized hand gestures followed by an exotic pirouette that culminates in a slight bow and a sultry look. The alluring routine ignites Justin's external flame, and he moves in close to her for another round of passionate kissing and caressing. Their intense feelings for each other come to fruition when he scoots her up against the wall, and they kiss each other's necks.

Justin reaches to close the bedroom door, ensuring their intimate moment continues privately and uninterrupted.

He retrieves a small bottle of coconut-scented massage oil he purchased in Morro Bay and proposes to give Yori a tension-relieving muscle rub. She willingly accepts his generous offer by lying facedown on the comfortable bed with her soft black hair draped off to one side and butterflies fluttering in her stomach. Justin lightly drizzles the moisturizing lubricant across her back and begins to rhythmically slide his hands up and down the silky curves of her firmly toned body. The romantic interlude continues well past midnight, further bonding an innermost connection of the heart.

The following day takes the four companions on a lengthy drive from Santa Cruz to the small town of Lee Vining in Mono County, California. They check into a chalet-style hotel located two miles from the southwest shore of Mono Lake and unwind in the room for a little rest and relaxation before dinner. Justin contacts a local outfitter to reserve a three-person canoe for tomorrow morning and then spends a bit of time researching the area online, which he shares with the others.

"It says here that Mono Lake is a large, saline soda lake that formed over seven hundred and fifty thousand years ago. It's thirteen miles long, one hundred and sixty feet deep, and located at over six thousand feet of elevation. Although the salty desert lake does not have any native fish, it boasts an unusually productive ecosystem based upon trillions of Mono Lake brine shrimp that feed on a high population of single-celled planktonic algae. In turn, the brine shrimp, and countless black flies that feed on the brine shrimp provide an endless supply of food for two million migrating birds that annually pass through the area. Mono Lake encompasses the three-and-a-half-square-mile Paoha Island, which gets its name from the Native American word describing the plethora of hot springs and fumaroles on its surface."

Morning comes all too quickly, and they diligently prepare for an adventurous day of paddling. Yori sticks with the original plan to stay behind at the hotel and intends to reunite with them this afternoon. "See you guys later. Be careful and have fun on the water! I can't wait to hear all about it." After giving Justin a hug goodbye, she settles onto the cozy couch with a fuzzy blanket and a good book.

The anxious companions scramble downstairs for a bracing cup of coffee in the lobby and make the leisurely drive over to Navy Beach on the south shore. An employee of the outfitting company checks them in and promptly escorts them to a sixteen-foot, three-person fiberglass canoe. He answers their questions, hands them a pamphlet on boating safety, and wishes them all the best. They paddle across the clear, turquoise-colored water to Paoha Island and beach their canoe on a rocky, sulfur-smelling shoreline in preparation for an exploratory trek.

Justin scoops up a handful of lake water for a taste. "Mono Lake is supposedly two and a half times as salty as the ocean."

Meanwhile, Kaito unloads their backpacks from the canoe in preparation for the hike. "So, what's the strategy for today?"

"Well, I was thinking we should first check out the heart-shaped crater lake on the northeastern side of the island. It's the highest peak on Paoha at an elevation of nearly two hundred feet and should provide us with a good vantage point to scope out the terrain. Then we can either visit the abandoned tuberculosis sanatorium or south tufa towers on our way back."

Melia is scavenging along the moonlike shoreline and comes across an interesting oval-shaped pumice stone that fits perfectly in her hand. She places the light porous volcanic rock in her bag with the intention of giving it to Yori as a gift. "The boating pamphlet mentioned high winds notoriously kick up on the lake in the afternoon. We had better get a move on."

They traverse a loose, dried mud dune and cut through a giant field of prickly, dense brush en route to the heart-shaped crater lake found atop the highest cinder cone on the island. During the mile-and-a-half trek they spot several blue belly lizards, three jack rabbits, a pair of ground squirrels, and some old, crusty deer droppings but no coyotes, as indicated on one of the nine stones. From atop the crater, Justin reaches into his backpack for some binoculars and scans the perimeter. He locates the remains of two concrete dome structures from the 1930s sanatorium and suggests they hike down for a closer look at the creepy ruins.

The first building they approach is half-collapsed, lacks a roof, and contains nothing more than a cast-iron stove. After a brief look inside, they proceed to the second building, which has two separate rooms that were once divided by a now missing interior wall. Each room within the dome structure contains a rusty bed frame, broken sink, and an individual shower.

While exploring the building's crumbling exterior, Kaito stumbles upon a rusty old tractor partially hidden in the thorny brush and unsuccessfully attempts to turn the antique crank handle. He pretends to be a used-car salesman and calls Justin over to kick the tires and take it for a spin. They alternate turns sitting behind the wheel on an imaginary test drive through sprawling agricultural fields of the midwestern corn belt. Melia secretly takes a picture of the mischievous cousins entertaining themselves and instantly texts the image to Yori along with a humorous photo caption: "A splendid day on Paoha Island with two knucklehead farmers."

Kaito is feeling somewhat fatigued from the lengthy morning of exploration and cordially engages Justin in a conversation about ending their day. "I understand that you saw a vision of Paoha Island but in all fairness, the stone etching reads Mono

Lake. What if you were mistaken and actually saw the smaller Negit Island or perhaps another location somewhere in the area? Maybe we should paddle back to Navy Beach before the winds kick up and game plan a new escapade for tomorrow?"

"That's nonsense! I know what I saw." Justin closes his eyes to recollect the landscape illusion he witnessed in the Santa Cruz bonfire and continues. "But, let's say for the sake of argument that your hypothesis is correct. A lot of the terrain around here looks identical and there is a possibility we are in the wrong location."

Melia yells out at the top of her lungs from a nearby boulder overlooking the lake below. "This place is gorgeous!" She stands with her arms spread out high above her head and snaps a side-image selfie.

Justin continues speaking with Kaito. "I'm not opposed to your idea of calling off today's adventure and spending the afternoon with Yori. We can always check out some other locations tomorrow and make another go at it."

Melia spots something moving down on the shoreline and interrupts their conversation. "Hey, Justin. Let me see those binoculars really quick." She peers through the tiny handheld telescopes and watches a curious wolflike dog climb into their canoe. "It's a coyote!"

Justin snatches the binoculars out of her hand for a quick look and passes them over to Kaito, so he can have a turn. "Game on. Here we go!"

They scramble downhill through patches of prickly sagebrush and hide behind a rocky outcrop on the shoreline to secretly observe the canine sniffing every inch of their canoe.

After watching the animal inspect their watercraft, Justin makes the bold decision to advance by initiating a stealthy approach toward the unknowing coyote. He takes several steps forward in a crouching stance to avoid being detected and blindly signals the others to follow by waving them onward. When Kaito accidentally kicks a loose pumice stone, the volcanic rock clatters across the beach and catches the coyote's attention. The twenty-five-pound female leaps out of the canoe to the opposite side from where they are advancing and stands her ground with a predatory look.

Melia removes an energy bar from her pocket and takes charge of the situation by cautiously approaching the canine with an extended arm offering.

Justin calmly tries to stop her as she walks past him. "Melia. What are you doing? That's a wild animal with sharp teeth and a powerful bite."

She bravely proceeds forward one step at a time. "Relax, Justin. It seems fairly tame and is probably just hungry."

As Melia comes around the canoe bow to within ten feet of the canine, the animal lets out a series of low-frequency whines and takes two cautious steps backward. Rather than press her luck, she breaks the granola bar in half and gently tosses a piece that lands between them. The guarded coyote gingerly approaches the energy bar with its yellowish-green eyes glued on Melia. The coyote takes a big whiff of the crunchy snack and gobbles it up in a single bite. Its body language instantaneously changes from defensively alert to inquisitively friendly, and it whimpers for more. Melia tosses the other piece over and the wolflike dog snatches up the tasty treat. The coyote then performs a playful bow, followed by side-to-side head movements and a sequence of spins.

When Justin and Kaito move in alongside Melia, the waggish coyote trots off down the beach and stops several yards away to look back at them. It then conducts another series of spins and dives while letting off a loud yelp that resembles a high-frequency bark.

"I think she wants us to follow her," says Melia.

The female coyote leads them far down the shoreline to a hauntingly beautiful section of hot springs and tufa towers. She gives them one last stare down, lets off a lone howl, and disappears into the brush.

Tufa is a variety of limestone that forms when underwater mineral springs rich in calcium mix with lake water rich in carbonates. The delicate white-and-pale-gray tufa towers of Mono Lake protrude from the water's surface to heights of fifteen feet, resembling stalagmite rock formations found in underground caves. This specific tufa column section of Paoha Island has developed within a shallow-water hot spring that releases a tremendous amount of heat produced through geothermal activity, resulting in pools of extremely warm water that constantly emit a flow of dense vapor.

Justin confidently announces his presence. "Hello. Can anyone hear me?"

Melia crinkles her nose and cringes in response to getting a whiff of something nasty.

"What's that awful smell?"

An unusual vapor wreath suddenly forms on the water's surface and begins to slowly rise in one-foot increments. During the ascent, a diminutive spirit with long, wavy gray hair develops within the suspended cloud of haze to answer her question. The mystical elflike being speaks to them in a quirky voice and then disappears as the misty ring dissipates ten feet off the ground. "The aroma you speak of is methane."

The three companions look at one another in bewilderment. After a brief moment of silence, Justin takes the initiative to speak up. "We traveled a great distance to be here today and most definitely could use some guidance. Can you help us?"

The same elfin spirit appears within another vapor wreath escaping from the hot spring. "That which you seek lies closer than you think." The mythical creature points across the tufa tower hot springs to a small glowing object fifty feet away. "You must cross over and retrieve that magical piece of obsidian." The misty ring dissipates along with the spirit, but another vapor wreath forms, and he continues. "All of Earth's elements, materials, and compounds are contained within the smoky-glass volcanic rock." The vapor wreath and spirit vanish once again.

Melia lowers her hand inches from the water's surface. "Don't do it, Justin. That water is scalding hot and will burn your skin if you fall in."

Justin looks over at the thumb-size piece of obsidian that has now stopped glowing and visualizes himself hopping from limestone to limestone to retrieve the object and return unharmed. "I can do it, Melia. Hold my backpack." He hands her the bag and mentally prepares to tackle the dangerous obstacle course.

Kaito bravely volunteers to go in his place, but Justin waves off his offer and takes the first leap from shore. He makes a wobbly landing on a dome-shaped rock but quickly regains his footing and continues with several consecutive strides from rock to rock to reach the midway point.

The diminutive spirit momentarily appears in another escaping vapor ring. "The consequences are catastrophic if you fall into the one-hundred-forty-degree water. Slow down and pace yourself, earthling."

Justin adheres to the spirit's advice by proceeding at a decel-erated pace toward the obsidian that rests on a basketball-size piece of limestone inches above the waterline. He eventually reaches the final tufa cluster and lies down on his stomach to stretch out for the smoky volcanic rock. Unfortunately, the object is just a bit too far away, and he can do nothing more than slightly nudge it with his fingertip. So, Justin repositions his body to make a second attempt at snatching it up, but things don't go quite as planned. He briefly latches on to the magical rock with two fingers, but the obsidian slips out of his grasp and falls into a shallow pool of steaming hot-springs water.

After quickly analyzing the predicament in front of him, Justin concludes that his best option is to simply reach in and grab the obsidian. Of course, that is easier said than done, considering the extreme danger of placing one's hand into hot water for any length of time. Without hesitation, he removes the shirt from his back to wrap his arm and thrusts his hand into the vapor-oozing hot spring. The intense heat from the impact takes his breath away but fortunately, he is somehow able to retrieve the object. A burning sensation shoots up his hand, instantly causing the old snakebite scar face to swell on his forearm.

By the time Justin hobbles back to shore, his hand has turned bright red, with several small blisters from the apparent second-degree burns. He places the obsidian in his backpack, slips on a dry shirt, and wraps up the wound with a roll of gauze from the first aid kit. They immediately return to the canoe and begin the long paddle back to Navy Beach. Melia rows up front while Justin recuperates in the center and Kaito paddles from the rear section.

"How's the hand holding up?" asks Melia.

Justin tries to make a fist, but the swelling and pain prevent him. "It's really sore, but I'll live." A thin layer of dry, crusted salt has formed all over his exposed body parts that came in contact with the salty vapors of tufa towers. "Did you know there are twenty-seven bones in the human hand?"

When they arrive back at Navy Beach, Justin grabs his backpack and walks straight to the car while Kaito and Melia handle returning the canoe. He settles into the back seat with his cache of supernatural items, closes his eyes, and lets out a giant sigh of relief. A few minutes later, a car door slamming interrupts his catnap and they take off along Test Station Road to the hotel. Justin buckles his seat belt and closes his eyes, listening to Kaito and Melia excitedly recap the day's events.

All of a sudden, Melia cries out from the passenger seat, "Kaito! Look out!"

He swerves the car to narrowly avoid hitting a golden retriever but overcompensates the turn, sending the vehicle screeching off the road on a slight decline. The car tires lose traction in some loose gravel, causing the vehicle to spin around twice and come to a crashing halt on the side of an embankment.

Justin wakes up in a hospital bed feeling groggy and confused. He lies motionless with his head turned to one side, watching a wall-mounted screen that monitors his heart rate and blood pressure, while listening to the steady beep pulsating from the machine. He inspects the gauze bandage on his left hand and reaches out for a glass of water.

A nurse in the recovery room notices he has finally woken up and moves in alongside him.

"How are you feeling, Justin?"

He takes a sip from the straw. "Thirsty and tired. Where am I?"

"You're at Mammoth Hospital recovering from a car accident. Can I get you anything?"

"I'm OK. Where are my sister and cousin? Are they all right?"

"They are both fine and waiting patiently in the lounge to see you. Let me go get the doctor so she can explain your condition." The nurse scurries out of the room.

A middle-aged woman enters in a traditional white doctor's lab coat. She inspects his charts and closes the door for privacy.

"Hello, Justin. My name is Dr. Singh, and I will be monitoring your progress during recovery. I'm glad to see you've woken up. How are you feeling today?"

"Stiff and sore from head to toe."

"Yes, well, that's understandable considering the automobile accident yesterday afternoon. You suffered multiple injuries, including a laceration above the eyebrow, second-degree burns on your hand, a slight rib fracture, and numerous bumps and bruises. Fortunately, none of the injuries are life-threatening, and you should make a full recovery."

"When can I go home?"

"We need to keep you here under observation for the remainder of today to ensure there aren't any further complications. If all goes well, we can release you from the hospital this evening. Do you have any questions for me at this time?"

"No, not really. I'm sure I will later. Right now I could use something to eat."

"Of course. I'll have the nurse bring you in some food."

The nurse returns with a tray of food and some apple juice. She checks his vital signs, helps him to the restroom, and mentions she will inform the others he has woken up. Several indistinguishable visions surrounding the accident swirl through Justin's mind, and he has a flashback in slow motion. He visualizes the eight mysterious gifts escaping from his backpack within the spinning vehicle followed by bright flashes of light as each one is absorbed into its stone.

Justin retrieves his backpack and a plastic bag of items he was wearing at the time of the accident. Fortunately, the pocket watch, folding knife, and all nine stones are intact but just as he visualized, the magical gifts have somehow vanished. He gives the ninth stone a good look, closely inspecting the octopus image on one side and Death Valley in kanji on the other. He attempts to access the mysterious powers through his breath-hold technique, but the endeavor fails miserably, and he stows the items away in frustration. He walks over to the window for a look outside and sees two colorfully intertwined dragonflies hover down from far above on impressive thirty-inch wing-spans. The insects' metallic rainbow coloring and large glowing eyes appear otherworldly, triggering Justin to realize the magic still exists within him as long as he believes. He watches the mating pair gracefully float off into the distance and begins to daydream. In a swirling moment of emotions, he vows to complete the ninth expedition in the desert and conquer this uncanny journey bestowed upon him once and for all.

15

THE DESERT

After laying low for two more days in Mono Lake to allow Justin some recovery time, the crew picks up a new rental car and departs for a desert excursion in hopes of completing the unsolved mystery. They arrive at the rustic, western-style Panamint Springs Resort in Darwin, California, near the Panamint Range, a rugged fault-block mountain range ten miles inside the western edge of Death Valley National Park. The area has been inhabited by indigenous Northern Paiute people of the Great Basin for over eleven thousand years and gets its name from the Paiute word *Panumunt*, meaning water people.

Early the following morning, they complete a thirty-three-mile drive east to the Mesquite Flat Dunes, an immense region of mountain-fringed sand dunes reaching one hundred feet high. There are no formal trails to follow, so they strike out on foot to the high point a half mile away and photograph two adventure seekers sandboarding down some star-shaped dunes. After scanning the area with binoculars, they double back to the car and drive a couple of miles down the highway to visit Panamint Valley Playa, an extremely flat, dry lake bed that periodically fills with water. They explore the cracked-clay surface of disappearing Lake Panamint and eventually plop down under a mesquite tree to rest.

At the conclusion of their exploratory day in the desert, Justin drops the others off at the hotel and game plans one additional stop before resuming the search tomorrow. He drives down an unmarked gravel road one mile from the resort and travels along a bumpy roadway at slow speed for two additional miles before turning right into the trailhead parking lot of Darwin Falls, an otherworldly oasis in the midst of one of the hottest, driest deserts on Earth.

He sets off on a brief hike at the mouth of a gravel-bottom canyon that is walled by dramatic plutonic rock formations. The isolated ravine narrows three-quarters of a mile in when the trail enters a lush sanctuary of cottonwoods and willows. The final stretch involves multiple creek crossings en route to a two-tiered waterfall that consists of a visible twenty-foot lower section and an additional sixty-foot upper section. Water flows down the rock face and splits into two channels, creating an inverted letter Y as it spills into a shallow swimming pool. Several small fern gullies surround the falls and provide refuge for local wildlife, including quail, lizards, dragonflies, frogs, and various songbirds.

Justin removes his hiking boots, rolls up his pant legs, and steps into the natural swimming pool for a refreshing break from the long day of desert exploration. He trudges along in ankle-deep water, kicking up sand and pebbles while listening to the soothing sound of birdsong that permeates the air. The once crystal-clear pond becomes cloudy from the disturbance, and he feels something unusual brush across his foot. The murky surface water starts to displace as a softball-size creature scurries toward the falls. The movement stops at the base of a boulder where the inverted Y spills into the swimming pool, and he witnesses several slender arms latch on to the rock as an octopus hoists itself up into plain sight. The morphing creature rapidly scales the twenty-foot section of the falls and disappears into a grotto that appears reachable from the snaking trail up.

Without hesitation, Justin slips on his boots and hikes up the slippery path to the grotto. He peers inside the dark, misty cavern and spots the amber-colored octopus frolicking in a tiny pond hardly deep enough to cover its own body. When the curious creature realizes he has stepped inside the grotto, it puffs up in defense, and its color changes into reddish-brown. The mysterious organism produces a series of infrared flashes that illuminate the room while it observes Justin's body language. His calm demeanor soothes her stress level, and tensions ease as it begins to croon a pleasant song in a peculiar tone. The inquisitive octopus slides underwater and completes three revolutions on its way over to Justin, who reaches out to the mysterious creature in a friendly gesture. The octopus accepts his invitation by wrapping a tentacle around his forearm and crawling up to his shoulder.

After a few moments of chummy interacting, the female octopus changes its pleasing tone and vocalizes a series of high-pitched tweets in rapid succession. The alarming call seems to be a code of sorts, unlocking a secret passageway in the rock. The mystic creature slithers down his leg, plunges back into the shallow pool, and propels herself into the dark cavernous opening. Justin stands motionless, unsure what to do next. Should he follow the octopus into the unknown or wait? His befriended octopus simplifies the decision when it reappears at the entrance and encourages him to follow by spritzing fluorescent-green ink that lights up the hidden chamber. Justin walks over to have a look inside and realizes that it's not just a hidden room but the beginning of a cave system that leads deep into the mountains.

He squeezes through the tight opening, hoists his new-found friend onto his shoulder, and cautiously proceeds down the sloping corridor guided by the occasional fluorescent spritz. A hundred paces in, Justin sees three mysterious figures conversing around a strange light source, and he ducks behind a large rock hoping to avoid detection. The skittish octopus hides behind his back and peeks over his shoulder while letting off a whistling uh-oh. "Shhhh. Keep it down, little buddy or they might hear us."

He peers around the corner to get a closer look at the water people who resemble the ancient Greeks. They are dressed in opaque-white fine-spun garments with matching woven sandals, radiant olive skin tone, and long brown hair held back in headbands. The nervous octopus covers her eyes with one of its eight arms and lets off another whistling uh-oh. Justin momentarily ducks down to regroup and silence his companion. When he stands back up to peer around the corner, he sees two of the water people staring in his direction, and suddenly feels something prick the side of his neck. Paralysis instantly sets in, and his limp body falls to the ground.

Justin is dragged over near the light source by one of the three water people as they discuss what to do with the foreigner. One of them appears feminine, another masculine, and a third one who doesn't speak demonstrates both traits and seems to be their leader. The masculine one fears for the safety of their people, preferring to eradicate the intruder before it's too late, while the feminine one pleads her case to let him live by mentioning the unprecedented octopus's interaction with a human being. After hearing both sides of the debate, their apparent leader signals for the octopus by producing a series of low-pitched tweets in rapid succession, followed by an encouraging hand gesture.

The intimidated octopus remains curled up and camouflaged at Justin's side. She maneuvers on top of his chest, morphs back into an amber color, and replies to the low-pitched tweets with several of her own. Their communication continues with a second exchange of varying-pitched vocalizations followed by the octopus injecting fluorescent-green ink into the illuminated sphere that hovers just above the ground. The water people watch a brief story of Justin's past eight encounters unfold in the colorful swirl of lights, giving the octopus a chance to slip away unnoticed. When the brilliant glow from the orb subsides, they huddle closely together, and the decision is made. Their leader concludes he will be set free in exchange for the nine stones as planned all along.

The masculine one speaks to him. "Our species first visited Earth long ago during an exploratory mission of the solar system. We were surprised to discover the planet's complex nature ranging from the magnificent flora and fauna to diverse landscapes and colorful human beings. Early into the campaign, our leader conjured up a method of capturing what this planet entails in order to take the information home and share it with our people. So, we planted memories into the mind of your great grandfather Saito during his coma, which included a path to locate the nine stones along with visions of the animals and locations leading to each of the encounters. Thanks to your help, the powerful gifts were then gathered up from the various entities, constituting a well-rounded collection of planet Earth's history, its habitants, and their beliefs. As a reward for your efforts, we offer you an opportunity to meet your ancestors in exchange for the nine stones. Are you ready for this once-in-a-lifetime journey into the unknown?"

Justin feels the paralysis momentarily lift as he contemplates whether to hand over the stones.

The feminine one addresses him next. "Keep in mind that whatever realm, world, or dimensions you will visit shall include a real possibility of never returning."

"What? I could get stuck?"

"Yes, there is that chance, so you must decide if the risk is worth the reward. Otherwise, you can turn around and walk out of here on your own terms. The choice is yours."

Justin closes his eyes and visualizes safe passage to a faraway land, meeting his ancestral line, and returning to Earth with an amazing story of his own. "I accept the offer."

"Your destiny awaits. Farewell, and may our paths cross again one day."

The nine stones magically escape from his backpack and levitate in front of him chest high, glowing in a pulsating buzz of energy. Justin becomes overwhelmed by another bout of vertigo and one by one, flashes take him through the previous eight encounters, transitioning into poignant moments with Yori that lead to premonitions of their future reunion. Then, the water people's leader reaches out with one hand and draws the stones into his possession.

The masculine one removes an unusual tubular weapon from his robe, aims the object directly at Justin, and zaps him to induce another bout of paralysis. His eyes grow heavy, and the weight of his body lightens until he floats inches off the ground as energy builds up around him. He begins to accelerate up toward the clouds and glances across the desert horizon to witness the pinnacle moment of a full solar eclipse. A streaking ball of light surrounds him as he gains momentum and bursts through the stratus cloud layer before passing out from the sheer velocity.

Later that afternoon, Kaito, Yori, and Melia become concerned when Justin doesn't return from the waterfall visit. He was supposed to be gone only a little while, and yet it has been several hours. After sending him unanswered text messages and leaving a concerned voicemail, they speak with the hotel manager who lends them an old pickup truck to look for him at Darwin Falls. "If you don't find him by sunset, we'll contact the local authorities to begin a search party."

Kaito jumps into the driver's seat of the single-cab pickup with the women sliding into the passenger side next to him. The truck tires screech and kick up dirt as they pull away from the hotel and barrel down the highway fearing the worst. They arrive at the trailhead where the rental car is parked but see no sign of Justin and set out on foot looking for him. Much to their surprise, they find him lying on his back outside the grotto entrance, alive but unconscious. Yori grabs his right hand, Melia his left, and Kaito delicately tries to wake him up. Thankfully Justin's eyes slowly open, and he begins to regain his composure. He looks up at Kaito, glances over at Melia, and then smiles at Yori. "Boy, am I glad to see you three. You will never guess where I just came from. I can't wait to tell you all about it."

www.ingramcontent.com/pod-product-compliance
Lightning Source LLC
Chambersburg PA
CBHW022006170626
46808CB00001B/308